Wait for Me

Trust in Me

SAMANTHA CHASE

Cover design by Dawn Adams
Cover image © LifeJourneys/Getty Images, Sean De Burca/Corbis

Published by Sourcebooks Casablanca, an imprint of Sourcebooks, Inc.
P.O. Box 4410, Naperville, Illinois 60567-4410
(630) 961-3900
Fax: (630) 961-2168
www.sourcebooks.com

Printed and bound in Canada.
MBP 10 9 8 7 6 5 4 3 2 1

About the Author

New York Times and *USA Today* bestselling author Samantha Chase released her debut novel, *Jordan's Return*, in November 2011. Although she waited until she was in her forties to publish for the first time, writing has been a lifelong passion. Teaching creative writing to students from elementary through high school and encouraging those students to follow their writing dreams motivated Samantha to take that step as well. When she's not working on a new story, Samantha spends her time reading contemporary romances, blogging, playing Scrabble on Facebook, and spending time with her husband of more than twenty years and their two sons in North Carolina.

Wait *for* Me

Prologue

William Montgomery did not get to be the financial success story he was by being unobservant. Sitting in his grand office suite, he made sure that his position allowed him to take notice of everything going on around him.

For instance, right now he had all three of his sons in the office; it was something that didn't happen particularly often. Sure, Mac and Jason worked with him daily, but Lucas? Well, it was like reeling in a reluctant fish to get him into the office. William usually had to put his foot down about once a month to get Lucas out of hiding and come in and take care of business. By the scowl on his son's face, William knew that he hated every minute he was forced out of his self-imposed exile.

Lucas was his youngest son and the only one who vowed to never join the corporate world that had earned the Montgomerys their fortune. Unfortunately, Lucas's career in the NFL was cut short by a knee injury. While his son could have continued to work in that industry, he decided to turn his back on it and become a recluse; his injury was more than just physical, it had clearly messed with him emotionally as well.

William's attention was momentarily diverted as his assistant walked into the room. Emma Taylor was like a ray of sunshine. When his long-time assistant had retired two years ago, William had worried about how he would function without her. But the young and eager junior assistant had stepped in to fill those shoes, and now they worked as if they had been together for decades.

Emma walked across the room and handed Mac his coffee with a smile; next, she headed over to Jason with the same serene look on her face. Both of his sons smiled absently in return and William had to stop himself from snickering in amusement. It would take a bomb to distract either of them from their work.

Now Emma approached Lucas. This part always had William sitting a little bit forward in his seat. She always saved Lucas for last. Her approach was slow, as if she was waiting for him to notice her. When he finally looked up, she gave him one of her most beaming smiles with a whispered, "Here's your coffee, Lucas. Black, two sugars, right?"

William chuckled softly. For almost two years she had been bringing Lucas his coffee—there was no need for a reminder on how he took it. This was all part of what had become the routine of their monthly conversation.

"Thank you, Emma," Lucas said quietly, a small smile crossing his normally stern face. William liked to see his son smile; it didn't happen often enough. Even when William got him to engage with the family, he was often quiet and sullen. Seeing this brief look of happiness was something that William looked forward to.

It wasn't good for Lucas to live the way he was—cut off from everyone and everything. He needed to move on from his disappointment over losing his career and work on rebuilding his life and his future. William looked at Emma again: the way she snuck one last glance at Lucas as she headed back to her desk, and how once her back was turned, Lucas looked up in her direction.

Interesting.

No, William Montgomery had not gotten to be the financial success story that he was by being unobservant. He knew the art of negotiation and was a genius in the boardroom. How much different could playing matchmaker be?

Chapter 1

If there was one thing that Emma Taylor craved, it was a vacation. She wasn't even overly picky about the destination; it was just an overwhelming need to get away for bit. Glancing at her calendar, she knew that she had time coming to her, it was just a matter of picking the time that would work best for her and Mr. Montgomery, Sr.

Sighing, she put the calendar away. It didn't matter how much she needed to get away, there always seemed to be something that came up around the office that for some reason, her boss felt only she could handle. Emma supposed she should be flattered that he held her in such high regard; however, her mental state was slowly getting the better of her. Something had to give and soon.

"Emma, my dear, I am heading out," William Montgomery bellowed as he exited his office with his wool coat draped over one arm and his briefcase in the other hand. "I'm taking Monica up to the mountains for a long weekend. Do we have everything under control here?"

"Yes, sir," she replied with a smile. He really was a wonderful man to work for, and Emma absolutely adored how he still made time to get away with his wife of nearly forty years. You didn't often still see a couple so in love after so many years; Emma's parents certainly hadn't been. She quickly stopped herself before she got too caught up in her own reverie and returned her attention to her boss. “Everything is fine here; you go and enjoy your weekend and tell Mrs. Montgomery that I said hello.”

“She loved those brownies you sent home with me last week. She asked if you might consider baking some extra batches for us around Christmas.”

“It would be my pleasure.” Baking was more than a hobby for Emma, it was a passion that she indulged in whenever she had the free time. She knew her friends and coworkers appreciated it and that just made her enjoy it even more. “Tell her to let me know when she wants them and I’ll be sure to get them to her.”

“You’re a treasure, Emma.” He smiled. “Someday you’re going to make some man very happy!”

“From your lips to God’s ears,” she said with a wink.

Clearing his throat, William looked around the office and then leaned in toward Emma slightly, his tone of voice dropping to a near whisper. “There’s a project I’m working on that I don’t really want to involve the boys in just yet,” he began. “A courier will be bringing by some paperwork either tonight or tomorrow, so please call me when it arrives.”

It was a bit of a struggle to keep the surprise off her face. Mr. Montgomery never did anything that didn’t involve his sons. Her curiosity was piqued, but she managed to keep it to herself. “Not a problem, sir. I’ll let you know as soon as it gets here.”

“That’s my girl,” he said as he straightened, and then looked as if he was carefully considering his next words. “You know, we really are caught up on everything around here so, if you’d like, once the courier comes by with those papers, why don’t you take off?”

Emma was stunned silent. How could he know that she had just been dreaming of a little time off? "Really? But what if he shows up this afternoon?"

"Then leave this afternoon," he said simply. "Rose is more than capable of covering for you and like I said, it's not like anything major is going on. It will be fine. You go and enjoy yourself. Do something fun. Maybe go out of town for the weekend!"

Oh, if only, she sighed inwardly and then smiled up at him. "I will certainly give that thought some consideration," she said and was rewarded with one of his infectious grins.

"Be sure that you do, Emma. Everyone needs a little time away once in a while."

She couldn't agree more. With a smile and a wave, Emma wished him a safe trip and promised to call as soon as the courier arrived with his papers. Once she was sure he was out of sight, she allowed herself to slump in her seat. An extended weekend. A quick glance at her watch showed it was barely eleven o'clock. It would be wonderful if the courier arrived within the next couple of hours so that she could be leave the office by two.

What to do? What to do? She thought to herself. For all of her desire to get away, Emma had never really taken the time to think of where she wanted to go. The first thing to pop into her mind was the mountains, because that's where Mr. Montgomery was going. She'd heard him describe his family's home there and if she were honest, she'd admit that it was someplace she'd want to see one day.

The thought of the Montgomery family had Emma sighing. They were so fortunate; not just because of their wealth and success, but because they had one another. As an only child of very self-absorbed, divorced parents, Emma had always longed for a big family. While she knew that she was essentially stuck with the family she had, she truly hoped someday she would marry into a big family.

And then the image of the ideal man came to mind.

Lucas.

Looking over her shoulder to make sure no one was watching, Emma allowed herself a moment just to lose herself in the thought of what it would be like to marry a man like Lucas Montgomery. He was strong and handsome and quiet and hardworking—in Emma's opinion he was the perfect man. His once-a-month visits to the office were the highlights of Emma's job.

And wasn't that just sad.

The man barely spoke to her whenever he was there but Emma was comforted by the fact that he barely spoke to anyone. Ever. Another small sigh escaped her lips. Everyone knew the story of Lucas's football career and the injury that ended it; it had been covered on every newscast and in every newspaper in the country. The part that nobody knew anything about was why it had forced him into such a state of seclusion.

Behind her, Emma heard Mac and Jason heading her way, deep in conversation. She quickly straightened in her seat and started shuffling papers, doing her best to look busy.

"Did Dad leave for the day?" Jason asked.

Emma looked up at him. He had a lot of the same features as Lucas, dark hair, green eyes, and chiseled jaw, but he didn't make her heart race in the least. "You missed him by maybe fifteen minutes. Sorry!"

The brothers looked at each other. "Thanks, Emma."

"Was there anything you needed?" she asked quickly, doing her best to be the efficient assistant that she always was, even though her mind was a million miles away, picturing their brother with his arms around her!

"Nothing that can't wait," Mac replied. "Did he mention what time he and Mom were getting on the road?"

She shook her head. "He didn't but he sure seemed anxious to leave."

They each gave a small laugh and a smile and wished her a good day as they turned to leave. Emma grimaced. It probably wasn't the smartest thing to be attracted to one of her boss's sons but why did it have to be the one son who was so unattainable? Why couldn't she crush on Mac or Jason? They were both nice enough. Why was it that surly Lucas of the little to no words was the one who made her weak in the knees when he gave her one of his small smiles?

"Because you are clearly a glutton for punishment," she mumbled softly as she shook her head. "This is why you need to get away for a little while. Meet some new people and maybe find someone who *isn't* Lucas Montgomery." Like a runaway train, her dialogue continued in her head. "Someone who would willingly talk to me, engage in conversation with me; maybe even someone who notices when I purposely wear my best clothes or fix my hair in a new style. That isn't too much to ask, is it?"

With Lucas, it probably was. Emma didn't date much, but she had to admit that she tended to be drawn to the kind of men who were slightly unattainable. Apparently, she had decided to up her game and go for the king of unattainable.

"I'm heading to lunch!" a voice called from behind her and Emma turned to see her assistant, Rose, heading toward her desk. "You want me to bring you back anything?"

"I'll take a salad if you don't mind," Emma answered as she reached for her purse.

Rose stopped in front of her desk and frowned. "It wouldn't kill you to eat a burger once in a while like the rest of us," she said sternly but once Emma raised her eyes to her, she smiled.

"Please," Emma protested. "If I allowed myself to indulge in a burger for lunch, I wouldn't stop at that. There would be fries and milk shakes and maybe even some cake."

"And what's wrong with that?" Rose teased.

Emma couldn't help but laugh. "The problem is that it wouldn't take long for me not to fit into any of my clothes, and I happen to like my current wardrobe."

"As do we all. But a real meal once in a while wouldn't kill you," Rose reminded as she accepted the cash Emma was holding out to her. "I'll be back in a bit."

"Thanks, Rose!" Emma called after her and sat back down. There was never a lack of things to do and the next hour flew by. Before she knew it, a salad appeared in front of her and Emma went into multitasking mode, eating and working.

"I've got an envelope here for a Mr. Montgomery," a male voice said, and Emma nearly jumped out of her skin. She never even heard him approach!

"I'll sign for that," Emma said with a smile. Her curiosity was making her anxious; she desperately wanted to know what it was that her boss was working on that didn't include his sons. Once she signed the electronic pad and the courier left, she eyed the package warily. She wanted desperately to tear it open but held herself in check and reached for the phone.

"Just wanted to let you know that the courier just left, Mr. Montgomery," she said cheerily when her boss answered the phone.

"Excellent!" he boomed. "Now, go get Rose situated and enjoy a nice long weekend!"

"Are you sure?"

"When have you ever known me not to be one hundred percent confident in what I'm saying?" he teased.

He had her there. The man never seemed to experience a moment of doubt. "Okay, okay. I'll just put this envelope on your desk and—"

"No!" he interrupted a bit too harshly and Emma gasped in surprise. "I mean, I really need those papers and if they're on my desk, the boys might get curious and open the envelope."

It was funny to hear him refer to his two grown sons as "boys." She tried to focus on what she needed to do with this secret envelope. "I can put it in the safe or just lock it in my desk, if that would work for you?"

He sighed with a hint of frustration. "Emma, I don't want you to stress out over this but I have a favor to ask."

"Sure. Anything you need."

"I really don't want to wait to go over those papers."

"I can fax them to you," she suggested.

"No. We promised to not have an office up at the house. It's our retreat."

"I can scan them and email them and then you can read it on your laptop."

"I didn't bring it."

Emma couldn't hide her frustration. "Okay, so if you knew these were coming and that you were going to need them, why didn't you just wait for them?" As soon as the words snapped out she regretted them. "I'm sorry; that was completely unprofessional of me."

"No need to apologize, Emma. I'm afraid I'm the one being difficult." He paused as if carefully considering his next words. "I have a proposition for you," he finally said.

Something in his tone had Emma feeling a bit uneasy. "O-kay," she said slowly.

"I know I said that you could leave now and to enjoy a long weekend," he began. "Have you given any thought as to what you were going to do or where you were going to go?"

"No, not really."

"Well, maybe, if it wouldn't be too much trouble, there is a fabulous spa up here not far from our house and I think you would really enjoy it. Monica can book you a room and arrange for a massage and—"

"Wait a minute," she interrupted. "You want me to drive up to the mountains and bring you the papers in person?"

"I know, I know, poor planning on my part, but I would be extremely grateful to you if you could help me out with this."

"I don't know, sir," she admitted honestly. "I've never driven up there and it's getting late—"

"Nonsense!" he boomed. "You're only two hours away! If you leave now and go home and throw some things in a bag, we'll take care of the rest. I'll send you the directions to your phone or you can just use your GPS, whichever is easier for you."

As much as Emma wanted to refuse, the thought of a night at a deluxe spa was quite tempting. "I guess I could do it, but don't feel like you have to book the spa for me," she said, trying to make it seem like she wasn't doing this simply for the perk of a massage.

"Are you kidding? You're doing me a huge favor! You can have two nights there if you'd like!"

Now that got her attention and before she could stop herself she squeaked, "Really?"

"Absolutely," he said, sounding more than a little thrilled. Emma could hear him telling his wife to make all of the arrangements before returning his attention to the phone. "Consider it taken care of. We'll give you all of the information when you get here."

"Thank you, sir," she said, relief and anticipation filling her voice. "I'll call when I'm on my way."

"Don't stick around the office too long. I'd feel better knowing that the majority of your drive was while the sun was up. These November days seem to be getting shorter and shorter."

They firmed up their plans and as soon as they hung up, Emma grabbed the envelope, placed it in her briefcase, and then walked over to Rose's desk to give her instructions for the remainder of the week.

Within fifteen minutes, Emma Taylor walked out of Montgomerys before six o'clock for the first time in two years, a wide grin on her face.

"It's going to be treacherous driving on your evening commute tonight. Snow is expected in the area early this evening and it's going to come down fast and furious."

"Damn weather," Lucas cursed under his breath as he pulled into his driveway. He was returning from his monthly trip into town to stock up on food and supplies. That was something new; he used to have everything delivered, but with a couple of days of stubble on his face and a ball cap pulled down low, no one bothered him.

Glad that he was fully stocked, it took a little time to get it all from his truck and into the house. Once it was all inside and put away, he looked at his supply of wood. While he had a generator and knew that if the storm got bad enough to lose power, he'd be fine, he liked to be well prepared. Looking at the clock and seeing that there were several hours of daylight left, Lucas headed out into the backyard and toward the stack of firewood waiting to be cut.

The physical exertion felt good; Lucas knew that it wasn't in his best interest just to sit around the house. Swinging the ax had him using more muscles than he did in the average day, and while at first his body protested a little, it didn't take long for him to get into the swing of things (literally) and feel good. Even in the cold, he worked up a sweat, and once all the cutting was done, it was another chore to move all of the wood to the shed that was built onto the back of his house.

By five o'clock, Lucas felt a satisfied sense of exhaustion as he stepped back into the house, prepared to settle in for the night. The first flakes were already falling and it didn't take long for the weather to change and turn into a full-blown blizzard. As he built a fire in the main fireplace, a chill ran through his body and a sense of unease filled him. It wasn't like Lucas to feel restless. He'd grown accustomed to his isolation and found that he'd made peace with being alone.

His knee ached and his muscles were sore from exertion. He walked around the house searching for something—for what, he couldn't be sure. All he knew was that everything felt suddenly out of sorts. After checking all the rooms and seeing that nothing was out of place, he found himself back in front of the fireplace. It was completely quiet in the house with the exception of the occasional popping coming from the fire. When his phone rang, he jumped higher than a grown man should.

"H'lo," he answered gruffly, not even bothering to check his caller ID.

"Lucas? Are you okay?" His father. There were few things that Lucas could count on anymore but one of them was that his father would call him at least once a day just to make sure that he was doing okay and had a conversation with another human being. While at times it annoyed the hell out of him, other times, like now, the calls were a comfort.

"Fine, Dad. How about you?"

"Oh, your mother and I are up here by you. She is positively giddy about the snow."

Lucas laughed. As much as he hated being cold, he loved the way the snow looked. He clearly had gotten that fascination came from his mother. "She always gets like that," he said with a laugh. "You just up here for the weekend or staying longer this time?"

"Depends on the storm," William said, his tone a little distracted.

"Dad? Are you okay?"

"What? Oh, um, yes, yes, just fine. How about you? Do you have everything you need in case we get snowed in?"

"Today was my day to stock up so I'm good for a while."

"This storm really came out of nowhere, didn't it?" William asked, worry now lacing his words.

"Not really," Lucas said. "It's been in the forecast but it's just a little more intense than they originally thought. Nothing new for this area. What's going on, Dad? Sounds like you've got something on your mind. You're not worried about this storm, are you? We've lived through ones like this dozens of times before."

"I know, I know, it's just that..." His voice trailed off.

"No, I don't know. Are you sure you're okay?"

"I'll be fine," William lied. "What about you? Are you there by yourself?"

Lucas laughed. "That's an odd question. Of course I'm here by myself. Who else would be here with me?"

Nervous laughter escaped before William could stop it. "What was I thinking?" he said, trying to sound lighter. "As long as you have everything you need. You'll call if you have a problem, right?"

Lucas pulled the phone away from his ear and looked at it like it was a foreign object. Call if he needed anything? What in the world? "I'll be fine, Dad," he reassured. "In case you've forgotten, I prefer a good storm; it keeps me inside where I like to be."

"Lucas," his father began, "it's not good for you to be by yourself all the time. You need to get out of the house more, maybe come back to work or..."

"I appreciate the concern," Lucas said with

frustration, "but I really don't feel like having this particular conversation right now. I just got done stocking the wood shed and I was just about to go and take a hot shower to ease some of the soreness out of my body."

"You know I only nag because I love you, Son, right?"

No words could have taken the wind out of his sails more than those. Pinching the bridge of his nose, Lucas closed his eyes and mentally counted to ten before answering. "I know you do, Dad. I honestly do. This is my decision, though, and I need everyone to back off, okay?"

His father made a sound like he was going to argue, but then changed course. "Fine. I promise to back off. Stay safe during this storm and we'll talk to you over the weekend, all right?"

"Thanks, Dad," Lucas replied as he hung up the phone. Shutting it down, he placed it on the counter, his shoulders feeling the tension from the conversation. Lucas couldn't understand why this was such a big deal for everyone. It wasn't as if he was asking all of them to stay shut in with him.

His knee was throbbing now. All he wanted was a hot shower, an even hotter dinner, and a chance to put a heating pad on his knee. It sounded like a good plan for the evening, so good that it sounded like what he did every evening. That thought made him frown as he walked into his bedroom. Sure it would be nice to get back into the land of the living again, but the life he wanted, the one that he'd worked so hard for, was long gone.

Some people would say he was lucky; he'd lived his dream for many years and he went out while he was still on top. The problem was that he hadn't wanted to leave: he'd been forced out. It was funny because when it had happened, promises were made to him left and right about how there would always be a place for him within the organization. Once his therapy proved that his injury was more severe than originally diagnosed and that he would be in treatment longer than anticipated, those offers came with less and less frequency, until the phone finally just stopped ringing. Lucas hated pity, and the fact that he was having a daily pity party for himself annoyed him even more.

Stripping down and stepping under the steaming shower spray, he let the hot water beat down on him as he sighed wearily. All of the tension eased from his body, and with it all thoughts of his previous life. An inner pep talk reminded Lucas that he enjoyed the life he had created since his football career ended. He finally had his privacy; reporters were no longer camping out, desperate for a picture or a quote from him. He could come and go as he pleased with little to no recognition. His time was his own.

In the last eighteen months, he'd agreed to work for the family organization, and while it was far from his dream job, at least he had the privilege of working from his own home, making his own hours while having something to keep him busy. When he wasn't taking care of Montgomerys business, Lucas had taken up photography, nature photography to be exact. The act of going out and walking around in the parks and the massive properties his family owned was therapeutic; at the same time, it allowed the creative side of him to come out. Both sides gave him a great sense of satisfaction that he hadn't felt in a long time.

Toweling dry and then dressing in a pair of faded, well-worn jeans and a sweatshirt, Lucas strolled into his kitchen and went about deciding what to make himself for dinner. That was the beauty of living alone: he could make whatever he felt like, whenever he felt like it, and then could eat in front of the television and have the remote to himself. It was some sweet bachelor living, and he was sure that the masses would be envious.

Reaching into the freezer, Lucas was about to pull out a steak to grill when the glare of headlights caught his attention. No one ever came out this way—he was set far back from the road—and in this snow at this time of day, clearly the person had to be lost. With a curse, he walked toward the window near the front door and watched in horror as the car skidded dangerously and then went off the narrow path of his driveway down into the ravine below.

"Dammit," he muttered, running to grab his boots, coat, and phone before heading out the door. Once outside he ran toward the spot where he saw the car go down. It was easily a ten foot drop and he could hear the sound of the horn blaring as if someone was lying on it.

With another curse, he carefully made his way down and did his best not to slide and end up injuring himself too. "What kind of idiot drives around in a snowstorm after dark?" he muttered as he reached the car door. The windows were fogged and the sound of the horn was near deafening. He yanked the car door open and found the driver slumped over the steering wheel. Doing his best not to jar them too much, he reached into his pocket for the small flashlight that he always carried and jumped back in horror at the sight of blood coming from the driver's head.

"Emma…"

Chapter 2

What the hell is she doing here? Lucas's mind raced as he checked Emma for a pulse and tried to assess where else she was injured. She wasn't moving and that was killing him. "Emma?" he said, trying to keep his voice soft and calm. When she didn't respond, he said it with a little more urgency and held his breath, hoping that she'd answer him.

She didn't.

"Dammit," he mumbled. The snow was coming down so hard and fast that it was a total whiteout. As much as he feared moving her, leaving Emma in the car and calling for an ambulance wasn't an option. Reaching into the car, he unbuckled her seat belt, softly whispering to her the whole time. As gently as he could, Lucas scooped her up into his arms and slammed the car door shut. He looked at the hill in front of him, wondering how he was going to get them both up the slick surface.

Cursing again, he said a silent prayer and slowly and carefully made his way back up. It wouldn't have been an easy task for someone in excellent physical condition; he was hampered not only by the snow but his aching knee. If it hadn't been hurting earlier, it was certainly going to after this little excursion.

It felt like hours but he finally got them back up to the house and once inside, he raced to lay Emma down on the sofa closest to the fireplace. She was pale, but the wound on her head was bleeding less. Lucas ran quickly to his bathroom and found his first-aid kit. When he returned to Emma's side, he tried calling her name again to see if she'd respond.

She didn't.

Having been an athlete his whole life, Lucas was familiar with how to treat some injuries. He cleaned the spot on her forehead and gently washed the blood away from the rest of her face. Feeling her hands, he could tell that she was beginning to warm up from being by the fire. Carefully he began to remove her coat and then went to take off her shoes. With each item, he checked to see if there were any other injuries that weren't as clearly visible as the one on her head.

Once her shoes were off, he gently rubbed her feet and then her ankles and nearly sobbed with relief when she made a slight sound of protest. He sent a silent prayer heavenward and then softly said her name again. "Emma?"

Emma felt as if she'd been hit in the head with a hammer. Clearly she must have died, because the last thing she remembered, her car was spinning wildly and then everything went black. The throbbing in her head increased and she mumbled, "Great. I would be the only person to go to Heaven and still have pain." The sound of male laughter nearly made her scream. She tried to sit up, but found that it hurt too much to move.

"Shh...easy," the voice said again. "Don't try to sit up, Emma. Tell me where you're hurt."

The voice sounded familiar and Emma started to wonder what was going on. If this was Heaven and God was talking to her, wouldn't He know where she was hurt? Why was He asking her? When He asked again,

Emma wanted to put her hands over her ears. "Why are you shouting?" she finally asked. "Everywhere. I hurt everywhere, okay?"

He chuckled. "That's my girl," he murmured.

"What?" she whispered as she struggled to open her eyes and see who was talking to her. It felt like a hot poker was flaming behind her right eye, and it took all of her strength to sit up partway. "*Lucas?*" Emma looked around, confusion written on her face. "What are you doing here?"

"I was going to ask you the same thing," he replied softly.

"Where are your parents?"

"They're at their place. Why would you ask?"

"Their place?" she asked.

"Yes, their place."

"So your father isn't here?"

"No."

"And your mother?"

"With Dad." A look of amusement began to cross Lucas's face.

Emma put a hand to her head and lay back down. "I'm so confused," she mumbled.

Rising from his spot beside her, Lucas walked into the kitchen to grab some ice to help Emma's head. Why was she here? Why would she think this was his folks' place? And really, why was she even going to his parents' place? In all the years Emma had worked for Montgomerys, she'd never come to one of the family homes. What the hell was going on?

He put the ice in a bag and wrapped it in a towel before heading back over to where Emma lay resting on the sofa. She looked very small and fragile lying on his big oversized sofa. Her eyes were still closed and the grimace on her face told him she was definitely still in pain. As much as he wanted to find out the extent of her injuries, there was no way to get them safely to the hospital to have her checked. Lucas had no doubt that it wouldn't take long for them to skid into another ditch.

Back at Emma's side, he gently placed the ice on her head and she winced. The thought of causing her any more pain nearly killed him, but he knew the best thing they could do was try to ice the lump that had formed on her temple.

"So," he began softly, "what made you come up here in a snowstorm?"

Pushing Lucas's hand aside, Emma held the ice pack in place. "I didn't know there was going to be a storm," she began, her voice trembling slightly. "Your father needed some papers and we were all caught up at the office so he suggested that I take a long weekend."

"A long weekend?"

Emma nodded. "He told me that to thank me, your mother made reservations for me to spend a couple of nights at a spa up here."

"A spa?"

"Yes, Lucas, a spa. Are you sure you didn't hit your head, too?"

"What? Why?" he asked, confusion etched on his face.

"You keep repeating everything I say."

"I don't mean to do that but the whole thing seems a bit...bizarre. I mean, why couldn't you just fax the papers?"

"Your father said he didn't have a fax at the house," she said simply.

"He does—"

Emma cut him off. "Then I said I'd email them but he said he didn't bring his laptop. I guess your mom likes him to relax and step away from work while they're up here."

Lucas was glad Emma's eyes were closed because the frown on his face would have told her he didn't believe one word she was saying. None of it made any sense! His father had an office at their mountain home that rivaled the one at Montgomerys. Why would he deliberately lie to Emma?

"Anyway, he was concerned that I don't take a whole lot of time for myself and so when he offered the extended weekend and then sweetened the deal with the spa, well, how could I say no?"

"What kind of spa?" he asked, even though he couldn't really care less. He was trying to keep her talking; the more she talked, the more he could tell if she had any kind of serious repercussions from banging her head.

"Oh, you know, the usual. Deluxe, tranquil rooms, manicures, pedicures, massages…total pampering."

"And that appeals to you?" he asked, somewhat surprised, because Emma seemed very practical and low maintenance, the type of woman who wouldn't be interested in wasting time and money at a spa.

"Appeal to me?" she repeated. "Right now, the way my whole body hurts, I'd kill for a massage."

"Not a good idea."

She pried open one eye and glared at him. "How could that *not* be a good idea? I was just in a car accident and my whole body is in pain. Massages relieve pain, right?"

"On the surface, sure, you're right, but the reality is that the body needs to heal a little first, otherwise massage can escalate the injury."

As much as she wanted to argue the point, it made sense. And if anyone would know about what would escalate an injury, it was Lucas. She knew he'd been through months of intense rehab and had tried everything known to man to get his knee back in shape so he could return to the football field. Unfortunately, nothing had worked. "Okay, fine; no massage right now, but as soon as this snow stops, I'm heading over to the spa."

"That won't be happening any time soon," he said with resignation.

"What? Why? How long is this snow supposed to last?"

"Well, considering that it was coming down at the rate of several inches an hour and it's been snowing for well over an hour..."

"Please don't make me do the math, Lucas. My head hurts enough already."

That made him laugh. Emma had the ability to do that when no one else could. "Okay, no math. The last I heard it's supposed to snow well into tomorrow afternoon and they're predicting up to two feet."

"That is totally not helping my headache," she murmured and slowly sat up and made herself comfortable. She stared at the fire roaring in the fireplace and then at Lucas, who was watching her warily. "Relax, it's just a headache."

"We don't know that, Emma. You probably have a concussion."

"You really are a little ray of sunshine, aren't you?"

His expression was near comical. "Look, I know a thing or two about concussions, Emma. You hit your head pretty hard. You were bleeding. We can't get to a hospital to confirm or deny, but for right now I'm going with the likelihood that you do have one."

"But I might not."

"But you might."

"Lucas," she whined.

"Don't argue with someone who has had their share of bumps on the head," Lucas said as he rose from the sofa. "Let me get you some Advil or something to help with the pain. Do you want something hot to drink? Coffee? Tea?"

"Do you have cocoa?"

"Cocoa?"

Emma sighed. "Yes, cocoa. You know, the hot chocolate beverage. It sometimes comes with tiny marshmallows in it. Any of this ringing a bell?"

His smile made Emma feel as if everything was going to be all right. "Now that you mention it, it sounds vaguely familiar. Unfortunately, I'm fresh out."

"Fresh out?" she asked sarcastically as a small smile of her own crept across her face.

"Okay, I confess; I don't normally keep a stash of cocoa in my house."

"Not a manly drink, huh?"

"For someone with a concussion, you're awfully snarky," he said and for the first time since she'd met him, Emma thought he almost sounded…playful. Lucas graced her with a smile as he searched the kitchen for the needed supplies.

"Water will be just fine," Emma said as she watched

him combing the cabinets for other drink options for her. Within minutes she had taken the offered pain reliever with a full glass of water that Lucas had brought over to the sofa for her. "You don't have to wait on me," she said as she placed her glass down on the coffee table. "I'm fine, really." She only wished she believed her own words.

While her awe at being in his home had proven to be a nice distraction, now that reality was setting in, so were some aches and pains that Emma hadn't noticed a little while ago. The ice was helping her head, as was the ibuprofen, but every time she moved, something else seemed to bother her.

Deciding that sitting idle was probably not the best option, she went to rise from the sofa and cried out in pain. Lucas was immediately at her side. "What is it? What's wrong?" Carefully he wrapped an arm around her waist and helped Emma sit back down. "Where does it hurt?" he asked as he scanned her body for any obvious signs of injuries.

"My ankle," she said through clenched teeth.

Lucas cursed. "Okay, let's get your sock off and take a look at it." His tone was soothing and although Emma appreciated his kindness, she was beyond frustrated with the situation.

The swelling of her ankle was obvious. Without a word, Lucas rose and went to the kitchen for another ice pack. "For crying out loud," Emma mumbled under her breath. "Can I seriously not get a break here?" She flopped back onto the sofa and threw an arm over her eyes. *This is what you get for taking some time for yourself.* Maybe this was the universe's way of telling her that she didn't deserve to take a vacation.

She sensed Lucas more than she heard him and nearly jumped when the ice pack was gently placed on her ankle. What a sight she must be: large bump on her head, enormous ankle, looking like a drowned rat, no doubt, after coming in from a blizzard. Nope, no chance of this forced time together leading to any kind of seduction. Of that Emma was certain.

Where had that thought even come from?

"I was planning on making some dinner when I first saw your car pulling in. Are you hungry?" he asked.

The truth was that Emma was starving. Of course, eating as if she'd been fasting for a month was a surefire way to kill any hope of Lucas finding her attractive. Just the image of eating a steak with her bare hands almost made her giggle. "Um…sure. I could eat."

Wasn't that the understatement of the year? She could eat? Luckily she hadn't added phrases like "a whole cow" or "everything in sight!" If she was going to fail, might as well fail epically, right?

She could hear Lucas moving around in the kitchen and forced herself to sit upright again. Thankfully he seemed focused on his task and didn't try to keep up the small talk. Emma allowed herself finally to look around at Lucas's home. It was sleek yet rustic. The walls were made of solid logs, the floors were natural hardwood, and the fireplace was massive and made of stone. It was an open floor plan; the living room, dining room, and kitchen were one giant space. There looked to be a small hallway off the kitchen but she couldn't see what was down there. A doorway next to the fireplace piqued her curiosity.

Part of that curiosity was fed by the fact that she really had to use the bathroom. "Um, Lucas?" she finally asked.

When he simply stopped what he was doing and looked at her expectantly, she cringed at having to ask. "Could you point me in the direction of the bathroom?" Her face was probably twenty-seven shades of red. Ugh…

Rather than telling her, Lucas walked over and helped Emma to her feet. Wrapping an arm around her waist again, he murmured, "Lean into me. Try not to put too much weight on that foot."

Emma was more than willing to lean into Lucas; hell, that had been a long-running fantasy for years! Doing exactly as he instructed, they slowly made their way through the doorway next to the fireplace and Emma gasped at the sight.

Lucas's bedroom.

It was magnificently done in earth tones and the fireplace was open to this room as well. His king-size bed took up one wall, and next to it he had an overstuffed chair with a matching ottoman. The windows ran floor to ceiling, separated by French doors leading out to what looked to be an enormous deck.

"You okay?" he asked.

"What? Oh, yes," she stammered. "I just stepped the wrong way." *Liar, liar, liar!* There was no way she was going to tell him how much his bedroom suited him or that she was now imagining him sprawled out in that massive bed.

If Lucas had suspected anything else, he kept it to himself and continued moving Emma toward the master bath. This time Emma forced herself not to react. The bathroom was a wonder of stone tile and marble, with many spa-like features. The shower could easily fit four people and the sunken jetted tub was like a small swimming pool. When she didn't move from his arms, Lucas cleared his throat.

"Oh, thank you. I think I can manage from here," she said and didn't dare look at Lucas. Emma wanted to smack herself in the head. *Manage from here?* It wouldn't matter if the floor was covered in broken glass, there was no way she was asking Lucas to help her! As soon as he removed his arm from around her waist, she missed the support of his strength. Taking a small step forward, she was thankful when she heard the door close. Immediately she sank against the double vanity.

And almost let out a scream.

Whatever she was picturing in her mind about her appearance had been far too generous. The bump on her head was a hideous shade of purple and all her makeup was gone. Her skin was pale and her normally sleek and styled hair was now completely out of control. The curls that she took painful care to straighten were a riotous mess around her face.

Fabulous.

Just abso-freakin-lutely fabulous.

"I am never taking a vacation again," she chanted as she hopped across the bathroom to take care of business. By the time she was back in front of the vanity, Emma wished she had her overnight bag with her. At least then she would have been able to fix her face and put her hair up in a ponytail or something.

"Well, it's not like he ever found you attractive before," she reminded herself. Doing her best to stay off of her foot, Emma carefully hopped out of the bathroom and was almost back in the living room when Lucas spotted her.

"What the hell?" he said as he stormed toward her. "Why didn't you call me?"

"It wasn't necessary."

"Really?" he asked sarcastically.

"Yes, really," she said defiantly as she put her sore foot firmly on the ground and bit back a curse at the pain that shot up her leg. "I told you before I don't need you waiting on me. I'll be fine."

Lucas's face was a portrait of barely concealed rage. He towered over her five-foot-four frame and glared down into her now wide blue eyes. "I am not going to keep having this same argument with you tonight, Emma," he said in a tone so low that it was nearly a growl. "You cannot possibly be this stubborn."

"Really? You want to lecture me on being stubborn?" she snapped back. "Because let me tell you something, Lucas, you wrote the book on being stubborn!"

He wanted to argue, he really did, but he was too taken aback at her words. Honestly, Lucas couldn't remember the last time anyone had talked back to him or dared to challenge him. Since his injury, people took pity on him or tried to be upbeat and encouraging; this was the first time anyone told him to his face that he had a problem.

He kind of liked it.

"Well, it's a good thing we're not talking about me then, isn't it?"

Now it was Emma's turn to growl. "Look, I don't know how it is that I ended up here at your place rather than your folks' but I am certainly not an invalid." Lucas arched one dark eyebrow at her and then pointedly looked at her head, then her foot. "I'm not intimidated by you, Lucas. I know that right now it all looks bad and I'm not going to lie to you, I feel like I ran into a brick wall."

"You basically did."

"But," she interrupted, "I am a grown woman and can take care of myself. I don't need you to carry me around or treat me like I'm going to break."

"Your ankle could be broken," he reminded her.

"Still bringing that sunshine, huh?" she asked, and Lucas finally smiled again. "I don't think it's broken. It hurts but I can put some weight on it." They were silent for a moment and then Emma looked around or rather, toward the door.

"What's the matter?"

"Is the snow still coming down?"

"'Fraid so. Why?"

Emma chewed on her bottom lip for a moment before answering. "Well, it's just that, after I got a look at myself in the bathroom mirror, I was just sort of wishing for my overnight bag. My clothes are dry but a little stiff and I would love to be able to change."

"I hate to disappoint you, but right now there is no way I would venture out there and down that hill to your car again. That will have to wait until morning." Lucas knew he was one hundred percent justified in what he was saying, but hated the look of utter dejection on Emma's face. Without another word he walked into the bedroom, coming back out in less than a minute.

"I don't have anything in your size, obviously," he began, "but I put out some stuff you can change into and if you want, you can take a shower while I finish making dinner. How does that sound?"

"Heavenly," she replied with a sigh. "Thank you."

Lucas stood back and let Emma hop back toward the master suite. It killed him to do it, but he wanted her to feel comfortable and to trust in him. If she wanted his help, he would gladly provide it, but as of right now, he was smart enough to realize that she was trying very hard to remain independent. Lucas was a reasonable man. He just wasn't sure how long he could let her keep this up. As soon as he heard the bathroom door close, he reached for his phone and called his father.

"Lucas! This is a surprise. Twice in one day!" his father's voice boomed over the phone.

"Well," Lucas began, "I had a bit of a surprise myself."

"Really? What's that?"

"Don't even try to play innocent here, Dad. I think you know perfectly well what surprise I had."

William stayed silent. Clearly he was waiting for Lucas to take the lead.

"What is the matter with you?" Lucas snapped, stepping into the office off of the kitchen just in case Emma came out and heard him. "How could you make Emma drive up here in a storm?"

"We didn't know there was going to be a storm, Son," William began calmly.

"Oh, really? Because thanks to your inconsiderateness, Emma got hurt!"

"What? What happened? Is she okay?"

"No, she's not okay," Lucas snapped. "She has a damn concussion, I think, and a sprained ankle and her car is in a damn ditch! What is wrong with you? How could you do that to her? What was so damn important that you had to risk her safety?"

"I have no excuse, Lucas. I forgot some paperwork that I wanted to look over and I thought I was helping Emma."

"How was inconveniencing her helping her, Dad?"

"She never takes any time off. I thought if I could at least get her away from the office, I could make sure that she actually did something for herself."

"Did it ever occur to you that she doesn't take any time for herself because you don't let her?"

"Excuse me?" William said, his tone indignant. "What the hell is that supposed to mean?"

"It means that you work her too hard. You don't let her delegate and you treat her as if she is the only one you can trust to do anything."

"You don't know what you're talking about! You come in what, once a month? And you think that gives you the right to judge?"

"I call it as I see it," Lucas said simply.

"You're crazy."

"I don't think so. And all of that is completely not the point. I want to know why it is that she showed up here at my place rather than yours. We don't live so close to one another that she could have made a wrong turn and miraculously showed up here. Now what gives?"

"I don't often give out the address to our house; I'm used to sending stuff to you. I guess I just answered automatically with your address when she asked."

It was a plausible excuse, Lucas knew, but right now the whole situation still seemed bizarre. He was about to say that again when his father interrupted.

"Is she okay? Where's Emma right now?"

"She's taking a shower."

"She must not be too hurt then if she's off by herself in the shower." Lucas could practically hear his father grinning.

"I can't get to her stuff because her car's down in a ditch and believe me, it wasn't easy getting both of us up out of the damn ditch with her unconscious. She just needed to freshen up."

William hummed his approval. "It's too dangerous to try and get her to a hospital."

"I know that, Dad," Lucas said wearily. "I'll keep an eye on her overnight. It's not good to let someone with a concussion sleep too much. Believe me. I know that part well enough." And right then and there they were both thinking of all of the times Lucas had taken a hard hit while playing football. Lucas had to force himself not to go down that road. "I'll take care of her, Dad, but this discussion is not over."

"I don't know what you're talking about, Lucas. There's nothing to discuss. I made an honest mistake. I gave her the wrong address. I was completely at fault for not checking the weather, but that's it."

"Uh-huh. We'll see."

"Go check on her and I'll call you in the morning to see how she's doing, okay?" Lucas readily agreed, hung up the phone, and headed back into the kitchen to finish their dinner.

How had this day gone so wrong? As much as there were times when he appreciated being isolated and alone, being isolated and alone with Emma was going to be a struggle. When he'd had his arms around her earlier it had felt good—too good. For almost two years Lucas hadn't allowed himself even to think about how it would feel to touch Emma and now that he had, it was going to be hard to forget.

He put the phone down on the kitchen counter, walking toward the back of the house and looking out at the property. It was pitch-black out now, and the snow was still coming down heavily. There was no doubt in Lucas's mind that they were going to be stuck inside for the entire weekend.

He'd been alone for too long. How the hell was he supposed to survive this?

Chapter 3

Thirty minutes later, Emma emerged from the bedroom feeling ten times better. The hot shower had certainly helped and the ibuprofen had finally kicked in, easing more of her aches. Her ankle was still sore, but she found that she was maneuvering around a little bit easier.

Dressed in one of Lucas's T-shirts, which was more like a dress on her, and wrapped in his robe, Emma slowly made her way toward the kitchen and the delicious aroma that was coming from it. Lucas's back was to her, but she saw him stiffen slightly before turning around.

"I hope you don't mind that I borrowed your robe," she said as she sat down on one of the stools at the breakfast nook.

Lucas was speechless. The Emma Taylor he saw once a month at his father's office was always beautiful, but this woman sitting across from him simply took his breath away. Her auburn hair was damp and curling wildly around her face. She had on no makeup and her deep blue eyes were staring at him right now with curiosity.

Oh, right. She had asked him a question.

"No, it's fine. Like I said, I don't have much here that you would be able to wear. I'm glad you can use it."

"Your shirt was plenty big but I was still a bit chilled."

He nearly groaned. Turning his attention back to the meal preparation, all he could picture in his mind was Emma wearing his T-shirt, most likely with nothing underneath. That image stayed there and he cursed when he burned his hand taking the steaks out from under the broiler.

"You all right?" she asked.

"Fine," he lied, hating how hoarse his own voice sounded. "I wasn't sure how you liked your steak."

"Rare, preferably, but however you made it will be fine. Is there anything I can do to help?"

You can take off that oversized robe and let me see if the reality is as good as my imagination. Lucas shook his head to clear his thoughts. Now was totally not the time to be thinking this way. They were more than likely stuck together for the weekend, and it was going to be long enough without him indulging in naughty thoughts of Emma in various states of undress.

Emma continued to look at him expectantly and finally Lucas cleared his mind enough to respond. "No, no…everything's ready. We'll just eat here at the island so that you don't have to move." He quickly plated their steaks and added the potatoes that he'd baked. "I'd offer you some wine but I don't think it's a good idea with your head injury."

Emma rolled her eyes at him. She wasn't much of a wine drinker anyway, but the fact that he was still being so dramatic over the bump on her head was getting on her nerves. "That's fine. I'll stick with water."

After setting down the plates, Lucas poured her another glass and took a seat opposite her. Right now he thought it was in his best interest to have three feet of granite between the two of them. He wasn't feeling too confident in his restraint at the moment. Utensils in hand, Lucas was about to cut into his steak but waited to see how Emma was enjoying hers.

Her smile said it all. "It's rare," she said and looked up at him.

"It's how I make mine, and I just naturally assume everyone eats theirs that way. Plus, if you didn't, I could always have put it back under the broiler. I can't un-cook it if it's too well done but I can certainly tighten one up if it's too rare."

"It's perfect, Lucas. Thank you." Her voice melted over him and Lucas felt his body tightening. His throat felt dry and if he didn't know better, he'd swear he was starting to sweat. How could she have this much of an effect on him? He'd spent many hours in her company and never felt like this.

Forcing himself to take a bite of his dinner, he stopped cold as Emma purred with pleasure. Lucas had to wonder if she even realized she'd done it. He took a large forkful of steak and focused on saying the alphabet backward in his head, chewing until his jaw hurt, all the while looking only at his plate. When he finally allowed himself to look up, Emma was smiling at him. "What?" he asked.

"Nothing," she replied with a chuckle. "It's just that I think you need to work on your social skills a little. You've been on your own for too long."

"What's that supposed to mean?"

"It means that it wouldn't kill you to try a little small talk while we eat."

"Small talk?" he repeated. "We were talking just fine a few minutes ago. I figured you'd prefer a little silence rather than me talking with my mouth full."

Emma let out a hearty laugh and Lucas couldn't help

but join her. “You’re right. The silence is preferable to that. Sorry. Maybe it’s me who needs to work on my social skills.”

“Your social skills are perfect,” he said before he even realized the words had slipped out.

Emma took another delicate bite of her steak, clearly deciding to ignore his odd compliment. “Everything is delicious, Lucas. I appreciate you cooking for me.”

“I couldn’t let you starve, could I?” he said, his tone more harsh than he intended and once again, he regretted his words. The look of devastation on Emma’s face nearly brought him to his knees. Thinking quickly he simply added, “Then we’d really have a problem with my social skills.”

The words were said lightly and had the desired effect; soon Emma was smiling and they returned to the comfortable silence while finishing their meal. When they were done, Lucas cleaned up and noticed how sleepy Emma was looking. Looking at the clock, he saw that it was only nine o’clock, but for all he knew, she was someone who went to bed early.

“Listen, why don’t you head on in and take the bed. I’ll sleep on the couch.”

“Oh, I couldn’t do that, Lucas. You’ve done so much already and really, the couch is perfectly fine for me.”

Lucas sighed wearily and hung his head. “Emma, I would really appreciate it if you didn’t argue with me on everything. You are a guest in my home, an injured guest. Please take the bed. I normally fall asleep out here anyway.”

Looking over her shoulder toward the bedroom, she sighed. “I hate kicking you out of your own bed.” That had all kinds of images coming to mind and she kept her face diverted so that Lucas couldn't see the blush creeping up her cheeks.

He was suddenly at her side, guiding her into the bedroom. They stopped next to the bed and Lucas went about folding the comforter and sheets back, arranging pillows, and generally fussing with just about everything in sight. Emma bit back a smile.

"I'll keep the fire going through the night and close the blinds here if you'd like," he said gruffly, not willing to meet her eyes either.

"Lucas," Emma said softly, waiting for him to stop moving around and look at her. When he finally did, she spoke again. "You can stop fussing with everything. I'm not happy about making you sleep on the couch, but I appreciate your hospitality."

"You're not making me do anything, Emma. You're injured and I want you to rest comfortably while you can."

Something in that statement struck her as odd, and her face must have conveyed that point because Lucas stepped forward and explained. "A head injury is a funny thing; you can feel fine one minute and then the next everything could be wrong. I'll be waking you up every couple of hours to make sure you're okay."

Emma gaped at him. "Make sure I'm okay?" she parroted. "How?"

"Simple stuff; I'll just ask you a couple of questions to make sure your thinking is clear."

"My thinking is never clear when I'm asleep, Lucas. Wouldn't it just be better to let me get a full night's sleep?"

He shook his head. "Afraid not. I've been through this enough times to know the drill."

"So when will you get to sleep? And how will you know when to wake me up?"

"I'll set the alarm on my phone for every couple of hours and I'll probably get the same amount of sleep as you."

Emma made a face. Hell, if she was going to be forced to be woken up all night by her ideal man, couldn't it be for pleasure rather than for practicality? Her life really did suck. "I don't suppose I have any say in the matter?"

Lucas shook his head. "You do not."

Cursing under her breath, she glared at him and said, "Fine," before she began to untie the robe sash from around her waist. Not caring that Lucas was standing there watching her every move, she let the garment drop from her shoulders and flung it on the foot of the bed before crawling awkwardly between the sheets. It wasn't until she was sitting back against the pillows and ready to reach for the bedside lamp that she looked his way. "Anything else I need to know?" she asked defiantly.

Lucas looked like he wanted to say something, but then thought the better of it. "Get some sleep, Emma," was all he said before storming out of the room.

Reaching for the lamp, Emma turned it off. If only it was as easy to turn off her feelings for a man who clearly couldn't get away from her fast enough.

One hour and fifty-five minutes later Lucas was sitting on his couch staring at his cell phone like it was a time bomb. In five minutes he was going to have to go in and wake Emma up and check on her to make sure she was okay. The thought of seeing her in his bed, looking tousled and sleepy, was wreaking havoc on him. Clearly he must have done something wrong in this life, because he was surely being punished.

Most nights it didn't bother him to fall asleep on the sofa, but tonight he couldn't seem to make himself comfortable enough to sleep. Maybe it was the worry he felt over Emma, or maybe it was the knowledge that she was in the other room in his bed that was keeping him awake. Either way, he was going to have to get some sleep eventually.

The phone let off a little warning bell that told him to go and check on his guest. With a sigh of resignation, Lucas stood and walked like a condemned man going to the electric chair. He pushed the bedroom door open. The room was softly lit by firelight. His gaze immediately went to where Emma was curled up in the bed. Her hair fanned out on the pillow and her beautiful face was completely relaxed in sleep. Lucas could have watched her all night.

Unfortunately, he had a task to accomplish. He quietly walked over to the bed and whispered her name. When she didn't move or respond, he said it again a little louder. Still nothing. With no other choice, Lucas reached out and gently shook her shoulder. "Emma," he said with a little more force and watched as her eyes fluttered open.

It took a moment for Emma to remember where she was and when she was able to focus and saw Lucas staring down at her, her still-sleepy brain wanted to reach out and tug him down beside her. Bad sleepy brain!

"What time is it?" she whispered as she pulled herself up to a near sitting position.

"It's a little after eleven. How's your head?"

Emma had to think for a minute. "It actually hurts a little."

"You're due for more ibuprofen. I'll get that for

you." Lucas went into the bathroom and rifled through the medicine cabinet before returning to the bedroom. Carefully he handed her the tablets and then the glass of water. Emma placed the glass on the bedside table and then looked at him expectantly.

"Did I pass?" she asked.

"Pass?"

"The concussion test," she said and then yawned widely. "Can I go back to sleep now?"

Lucas chuckled. "Not yet. Tell me your full name." She did. "Tell me where you work." She did. "Tell me what day it is." And she did.

"Anything else I can tell you?" Emma asked again as she slowly slid back down under the blankets.

Yes, that you don't want to go back to sleep. That you want me to crawl in the bed with you. "No," he said softly, pulling the blankets back up over her shoulder. "Get some sleep."

Emma hummed a response and Lucas walked over to the fire to add another log from the bedroom side, watching as the flames roared to life again. A quick glance at the lounge beside the fire had him rethinking his plan for the evening. His knee had a dull ache and really, he'd pushed himself too hard today. As much as Emma needed his attention, he needed to spend a little less time walking around as well.

She was already back to sleep and Lucas walked out to the living room, grabbed his phone, and shut out the lights. Back in the bedroom, he grabbed a T-shirt and a pair of flannel pajama pants and went into the bathroom to change. Once he was done, he got comfortable on the lounge, set the alarm again, and finally let himself sleep.

Chapter 4

THEY REPEATED THAT ROUTINE THREE MORE TIMES before Emma had realized that Lucas was sleeping on the lounge by the fire not five feet from her. Good thing she hadn't noticed earlier, otherwise she would never have gone back to sleep.

From her spot on the bed, she watched him settle back in on the lounge. "Have you been sleeping there all night?" she finally asked.

"Pretty much," he said wearily.

"Why? I mean, you said you were going to sleep on the couch."

Lucas growled lowly and sat up and faced Emma. "This was just easier, Emma. I'm not used to having to get up every two hours, so I thought I'd make it easier on myself and sleep here." His tone was sharp and he didn't care. There was no way he was going to admit to Emma or to anyone that the real reason was because his knee wasn't strong enough to get him from one room to the next.

"Oh," she said and quietly lay back down, turning her back on him.

That one act caused a mountain of guilt. Lucas sighed and scrubbed a hand across his face before gently calling out to Emma. When she rolled over and looked at him, her eyes sad and wary, he felt even worse. "I didn't mean to snap at you," he began. "I guess you were right last night about my social graces or whatever. I'm not a morning person and just a little out of sorts." He offered her a small smile and was rewarded when she returned it with one of her own.

"I'm sorry I've disrupted your life so much, Lucas. Believe me, this is a far cry from where I thought I'd be this weekend."

"It's not your fault." He knew who was responsible, but stopped himself from telling her. "It's still dark out, why don't you go back to sleep."

"What about you?"

"I plan on going back to sleep. Like I said, it's still dark out."

Emma sighed but didn't move.

"What's the matter? Is your head bothering you? Do you need something for it?"

"No, it's just that—"

"Are you thirsty?"

"No, I'm just—"

"Is your ankle bothering you?"

"No, no, that feels fine, I think—"

"Are you cold? Because I can put another log on the fire."

"Lucas!" she cried out with exasperation.

"What?"

"Stop asking so many damn questions for crying out loud and let me answer one!" Emma sat up and took a deep breath before facing him. "I'm a little weirded out by the situation."

"Weirded out? What the hell does that even mean?"

"It means that I can't go back to sleep now, knowing that you're over there watching me sleep."

Lucas rolled his eyes. "I wasn't watching you sleep, Emma," he lied. "I just didn't want to keep going back and forth throughout the night. This was easier."

She looked at him with disbelief. "It's fine, it's not like I thought you were being creepy or anything…"

"Creepy?" he chuckled.

"Yes, creepy."

"How would taking care of you and making sure that you didn't have a serious head injury be creepy?" This he had to hear.

Emma couldn't help but chuckle with him at the ridiculous conversation. "Well, I mean it's not like you were watching me through the window or something, but it's just a little…awkward, shall we say…to know that a stranger is sleeping in the room with you when you weren't aware of it."

Lucas looked at her in disbelief. "Stranger? I'm hardly a stranger, Emma. We've known each other for years."

"You know what I mean!" she said and flopped back down on the pillows and then winced at the pain it caused in her head. When Lucas immediately jumped up to see if she was all right, she held out a hand to stop him. "I'm fine, Lucas, relax."

"You don't look fine, Em; you look like you're in pain."

She wanted to correct him, but got tangled up in his calling her Em. They'd always been rather formal with one another, and the fact that he used her nickname stopped her in her tracks. She could only stare at him.

"Now you're scaring me," he said and came to sit next to her on the bed. "Talk to me; tell me the months of the year."

"Oh, for crying out loud," she mumbled, sitting back up, and found that they were nearly nose to nose. "I'm not in pain, not really. I just fell back too hard and it hurt for a moment."

"You mean on the fluffy pillows? That hurt your head?"

Emma burst out laughing, she couldn't help it. "You know something, Lucas? You can be quite funny sometimes." She leaned forward in her fit of laughter and touched his arm. Suddenly she looked up and met Lucas's intense green eyes, and her breath caught.

There was something there that stopped her in her tracks: heat and raw, naked desire. Had she ever seen that before from Lucas? No, and she'd never seen it so starkly in any other man either. Emma couldn't look away; she matched his heated gaze with her own and licked her lips in silent invitation. Leaning in ever so slightly, Emma secretly hoped that Lucas would close the distance between them and finally she would know what it felt like to be kissed by him.

Lucas watched the movement of Emma's tongue across the lips that he'd dreamed about all night, and knew that all he had to do was move that last little bit and he'd be able to taste her for himself. Her eyes were locked on him and he felt his entire body tighten in anticipation. It would be so easy to take what he wanted.

But he couldn't.

It was one thing to have a one-night stand with someone who meant nothing to him merely to satisfy an urge. Emma meant too much to him to treat her with the same disregard. The problem was that he wasn't looking for a relationship. No, Lucas was at a point in his life where he needed to work through his own demons, and sleeping with Emma, while satisfying on many levels he was sure, would not be good for either of them in the end.

So he pulled back.

Lucas saw the question in Emma's widening eyes, and rather than address what had almost happened, he chose to go another route. "You go back to sleep, Emma," he said as he stood. "I'm awake now. I'll check on the weather and see what we can do about your car." He never looked at her; he simply turned and walked out of the room, gently closing the door behind him.

How was she supposed to just go back to sleep now?

Carefully lying back down with more calmness than she actually felt, Emma had to wonder at what just happened. One minute Lucas had been looking at her as if he could eat her alive and the next he was walking out the door as if nothing had happened.

Well, to be fair, nothing actually had happened, but it could have. Emma wasn't a world-class dater but she certainly knew when a man was attracted to a woman, and there was no doubt in her mind that Lucas was attracted to her. What had she done to turn him off?

The image of herself the night before came to mind and she groaned with disgust. Of course. She probably looked like a disaster: no makeup, morning breath, and her hair its usual mass of untamed curls.

It was amazing there weren't skid marks from his departure.

It was good to know that the makeup industry wasn't lying to her. Clearly she did need all of that crap. Rolling onto her side, Emma looked at the clock. It wasn't even six. How often had she wished for a day just to lie in bed? Though part of her wanted to get out of the bed and yell at Lucas that, while she may not be the most beautiful woman in the world first thing in the morning, he wasn't looking so hot either.

Which would just be a big fat lie, and she prided herself on not being a liar.

The man looked good enough to make her forget her own name and every other ridiculous question he'd asked her throughout the night. Unfortunately, she was in a no-win situation. With nothing left to do, Emma decided to do the only thing she could.

Pull the blankets up over her head and pray for the day to just end.

~

Of course the day didn't end, and Emma only managed another three hours of sleep before she forced herself out of the bed. She carefully tested her ankle and was relieved that it actually felt better. There was still no doubt in her mind that she was going to have to baby it a little, but at least she knew she would be able to get around easier today.

Walking over to the full wall of windows, she opened the blinds and saw nothing but white in front of her. Everything was coated heavily in snow. She sighed. There was no way she was leaving Lucas's house today, that was for sure. Thoughts of her car came to mind and she willed them away. There was no use making herself crazy over it; the car was a wreck and she'd have to get a tow truck here to get her out and then rent a car.

With her inner pep talk complete, she went into the master bathroom and decided to indulge a little. Last night was all about freshening up; today Emma needed to relax. A sad thought at only nine thirty in the morning, but with the way her day started, she needed all the help she could get.

Grinning at the oversized tub, she turned on the faucet and began filling it. Her body ached in general from the crash yesterday and submerging herself in the jetted tub was too good an opportunity to miss. For a minute she thought about checking with Lucas first, and then decided against it. She was going to put off being in the same room as him for as long as humanly possible.

There was nothing around that suggested Lucas even used the tub. There were no bath salts or anything out on the vanity. So, deciding to be a little inventive, Emma reached into the shower and grabbed a bottle of shampoo and dumped some into the water to give her a mock-bubble bath. She smiled as the bubbles grew and when the water was at a decent level, she stripped off Lucas's T-shirt and climbed in.

And made the most unladylike groan at the pleasure the hot water and the jets were giving her.

"Emma? Are you okay?" Lucas's frantic tone came from the other side of the door and Emma couldn't find her voice. "Emma?" He knocked and then stormed in.

And froze.

"Lucas!" Emma screeched. "What the hell?"

"I heard you moan and thought you hurt yourself," he stammered, but his eyes never looked away.

"I wasn't moaning in pain," she said, feeling rather embarrassed. "The water and the jets felt good. I didn't realize I was that loud." She wanted to dunk herself under the bubbles and hide until he left.

Lucas looked like he had been punched in the gut. He didn't move, but he didn't say anything either.

"Um, Lucas?" Emma said, breaking the silence. He finally seemed to snap out of his reverie and looked at her face. When she nodded to the bubbles and then looked back at him, he got the picture.

"Oh, right. Sorry," he said and backed out of the bathroom, closing the door behind him.

Emma sagged with relief once the door was closed. What in the world? For a minute there she thought Lucas was going to strip and join her. Wouldn't that have been nice! But no, clearly she still was looking too much like a troll to tempt him.

Well, she wasn't going to let it bother her. She sat back and let the jets do their magic on her body. It really seemed to work, and twenty minutes later she had to force herself from the tub. Drying herself off with a towel from the heated towel bar, Emma couldn't help but wish once again for her overnight bag. Besides wanting her toothbrush, she'd kill for some moisturizer right about now.

Wrapping the towel around her, Emma realized that she hadn't brought Lucas's robe in with her. Opening the door, she stepped into the bedroom to grab it and ran directly into Lucas.

"Oh!" she cried as his arms came around her to steady her. Dammit, why here? Why now? Why couldn't she have just stayed in bed all day and avoided all of this? If she'd listened to her original instincts, she wouldn't have to fight the urge to snuggle closer into Lucas's arms and beg him to finally kiss her.

A muscle ticked in Lucas's jaw as he stared down at

the damp and barely covered Emma. He had knocked, dammit, and when she hadn't answered he'd felt that he could come into the bedroom and grab an extra sweat-shirt without seeing her.

This was way more of Emma than he could handle seeing.

He stared down at her and swallowed hard. "I was able to find a towing company to come out and get your car," he said, his voice sounding like gravel. "They should be here within the hour."

"Oh." Slowly she raised her eyes to his and released her breath, bringing her body into closer contact with his.

"Emma," he sighed, so ready to say to hell with his doubts and just take what he so desperately needed from her. "I…"

"Yes, Lucas," she whispered, and he swore she became more beautiful right before his eyes.

"I…" He hesitated and studied Emma's face. He saw desire there for sure, but he saw something else: trust. She trusted him. He silently cursed because he knew he didn't deserve her trust. Emma did not strike him as the kind of woman who would be okay with a one-time encounter and he was in the awkward position of being somewhat of an employer to her. As much as it pained him, again, Lucas knew that he could never betray her trust. "I just needed to grab another sweatshirt. The snow has stopped but it's still below freezing outside."

He released her immediately and Emma nearly wept at the loss of his warmth. Frantically she reached for the robe and turned her back to Lucas as she put it on, all the while cursing him for sending her such mixed signals. Before she could turn back around and speak her mind on the subject, she heard the door close and knew he was gone.

The urge to scream was nearly overwhelming. Dropping the towel to the floor, Emma kicked it into a corner and then stomped back into the bathroom. She ransacked the bathroom in search of a spare toothbrush and was rewarded when she found a new one in the back of one of the drawers. She scrubbed her teeth and then took her hair down from its messy twist and shook it free.

"Damn him, damn him, damn him!" she said, slamming a cabinet door shut after being unable to find a suitable comb for her hair. Storming from the bathroom, Emma went to the bedroom and went about the task of setting everything back to its original appearance. She wanted to wipe away all traces of her having been there. With any luck, she could get a ride with the tow truck driver into town and get a rental car and get home. There was no way she could spend another night here with Lucas playing whatever game this was.

Yanking open the bedroom door, she stomped over to where Lucas stood in the kitchen, his coffee mug suspended midway to his mouth.

"When the tow truck gets here, I want him to get me into town so I can get a rental and get home," she stated bluntly and then crossed her arms across her chest in defiance.

"No." Lucas finally took a drink of his coffee, putting the mug down with a little too much force on the countertop and wincing when the hot liquid splashed on him.

"No? What do you mean no?" Emma's tone got louder and she took a step toward him.

Lucas was just as fired up as she was, possibly even more so. She'd had him tied in knots since she got here.

Who was he kidding? Emma had him tied in knots for well over a year. "I mean," he said menacingly, closing the distance between them, "no. The tow truck driver has more important things to do than chauffeur you around looking for a rental car. Did you think you were the only car trapped in this storm?"

"It's not your decision to make, Lucas. I may not be able to drive my own car right now but I can damn well leave if I want to!" If her voice hadn't trembled on the last word, she would almost have believed her own bravado.

Lucas almost had too.

"Emma," he began patiently, "no one is saying you can't leave, but the towing company has to battle enough things right now without adding driving you around to their list. All of the roads aren't even cleared yet and you'll probably be hard pressed to find a rental place open. Be reasonable."

Right now Emma didn't want to be reasonable. She wanted to kick, scream, and pout. None of this was fair. All she'd wanted was to get away for a few days, dazzled with the possibility of an all-expense paid weekend at a spa. Look where it had gotten her. She took Lucas's patience as condescension and she simply snapped.

"Reasonable? I'm supposed to be reasonable? I drive up here into the unknown in the middle of a damn snow storm and nearly get myself killed! My car is probably totaled, and has your father even bothered to see what's happened to me? No! I mean, I risked my damn life to get some stupid papers to him and he hasn't even called me to see if I'm okay? Who does that?"

Lucas was ready to defend his father but Emma had merely stopped to take a breath.

"I have worked my tail off for Montgomerys, and this is what I get? I'm snowed in and stuck here with a man who treats me like I've got the damn plague!" Her chest was heaving by the time she was done and the lack of response from Lucas was the final straw for her. Emma didn't care if she had to walk all the way back into town herself, she was getting out of here. She spun on her heel to get away from Lucas when he grabbed her by the arm and hauled her back.

"What the hell are you talking about?" he snarled. "I have never treated you like you have the plague!"

"Oh, really?" she asked snidely. "You have spent the better part of my time here going between looking at me like you want me to walking away like I disgust you! And you know what, Lucas? It's pretty damn insulting."

They were pressed together from chest to thigh and Emma almost purred with delight at the feel of him, and then remembered that every time she gave in to that feeling, Lucas seemed to pull back. Doing her best, she gave him a look of disgust. "Let go of me," she said through clenched teeth.

"Not a chance," he said just before he lowered his head and claimed her lips with his. Everything in Lucas's head told him not to do this, that it was a mistake. But the sight of Emma so riled up had him needing to give in to all he'd been denying himself.

The kiss started out punishing; he had to make Emma feel all of the anger and frustration he'd been feeling, but as soon as she caught up to him and clenched the front of his shirt in her fists to pull him closer, Lucas was lost. One hand came up to cup the back of Emma's head and he heard her whimper.

There was no turning back. One taste was never going to be enough. Lucas changed the angle of his head and swept his tongue into Emma's mouth to mate with hers and everything in Emma seemed to soften. She melted against him and Lucas found himself gentling the kiss, stroking instead of taking. Emma's hands let go of his shirt to work their way up around his neck. The feel of her hands on his skin, raking up into his hair, was driving him wild. He wanted to feel her hands on other parts of him and not while they were standing in his kitchen.

Lucas reluctantly left her mouth and worked a trail of kisses along her cheek to her throat, nudging the collar of his robe aside to taste more of her skin. Emma's head fell back to give him better access as she sighed his name.

He could get very used to hearing her say it like that.

His hands began their own journey, first skimming down her back, then cupping her rear before trailing up her sides to the swell of her breasts. Lucas was certain that he was going to go mad if he didn't have her soon. In his mad dash to claim her as his, one hand slid to the sash of the robe. He was about to pull it free when there was a very loud knock at the front door.

"What the…?" he asked as he raised his head. Emma's face was flushed, her breathing ragged, and he had never seen a sexier sight.

"I think it's the tow truck," she said quietly.

Lucas stepped back from her and watched as she righted the robe and tried to fix her hair. If it weren't so important to try and get Emma's car free from the ditch, he would gladly have ignored the door. "Dammit, Emma, I've got to go out there." He skimmed a hand along her cheek and ran a thumb along her now-swollen lower lip.

"I know."

Reluctantly, Lucas went to the door and looked back at Emma once again. He wanted to say something, anything, but what was there to say? If he hadn't made the call, there was no doubt he'd be deep inside her right this minute. But maybe this was for the best; after all, wasn't he the one who knew better? That their sleeping together would be something Emma would come to regret?

The distance between them right now would help them to both see that. Without another word, Lucas stepped outside and closed the door behind him.

Emma stood speechless in the kitchen. Well, how could she possibly doubt his feelings for her now? It was obvious that he wanted her and surely he could tell that she felt the same way. But where did this leave them?

Who knew how long he'd be outside with the tow truck? And when he came back inside, then what? Was she supposed to be waiting for him? Waiting to pick up where they'd left off? Was she supposed to just forget what had almost happened? Right, like that was going to happen. Ever.

The sound of a cell phone ringing in the distance had Emma searching for its whereabouts. She walked over to the living room and found Lucas's phone on the sofa. The display showed it to be his father, so she decided to answer it.

"Hello?"

"Emma! My goodness, girl, how are you? Lucas told me about the accident, but you were in the shower so I told him I'd wait until today to call and check on you! Are you all right? What can I do to make this up to you?"

His tone was near frantic and Emma had to suppress

a smile. Not twenty minutes ago she would have said she was furious with her boss, but hearing the sincerity in his voice right now had Emma reconsidering. "I'm better today, thank you, sir."

"Oh, stop being so formal," he chided. "Lucas said you had a concussion."

"That was his opinion, but I don't think it was all that bad. He woke me up every two hours last night and had me reciting state capitals and the months of the year and I passed with flying colors."

"Ah… I remember the days when we had to do that for him. It's never a good feeling to watch someone you care about and not know the extent of their injuries."

"Well, I'm down to just a mild headache—that is completely manageable—and my ankle is feeling better too. Lucas was able to call a tow truck and he's outside with the driver right now in hopes of getting my car out of the ditch."

"I am so sorry, Emma. I had no idea that a storm was brewing. I tend to think that the weather where we live is exactly as it's going to be up here. I never seem to be able to accept that there can be such a difference in a two-hour drive."

"It's okay, Mr. Montgomery. I'm fine, really, and my car? Well…"

"Don't you worry about a thing. We'll take care of all of the repair costs and the rental car for you. This was completely my fault and I just feel sick at the thought of what could have happened if you'd gotten hurt anywhere but on Lucas's property."

"Yes, thank heavens for small miracles," Emma murmured. "Are you and Mrs. Montgomery okay? Did you have any trouble with the storm?"

"Us? No! We're used to this sort of thing even when it sneaks up on us. Luckily Lucas takes after us. He said he had stocked up on supplies yesterday so the two of you should be fine for the duration."

"Um... I'm not sure about the duration. I'm hoping to bum a ride with the tow truck driver into town to try and find a rental car place so that I can get home."

"No, you can't!" he replied too quickly. "Emma, the roads are a mess. You shouldn't be out driving just yet. Plus, everything up here is closed down because a lot of the roads haven't been plowed yet. I can't bear the thought of you possibly getting hurt again."

She smiled at his concern. "I appreciate that, but I think it would be best if I tried to get home."

"Why? Has Lucas done something to upset you?"

"Oh, no, nothing like that," she lied. "It's just that he really lives a very solitary life up here and I'm just frazzled from the wreck. I think it would be best if we each had our own space. I don't understand how I ended up here rather than your place though..."

"I'm afraid I had a senior moment," he admitted sheepishly. "I'm just so used to rattling off Lucas's address to people and having things sent to him that when you asked, I automatically gave his address. I'm embarrassed to have to admit it. You know that's not like me at all."

No, it wasn't like him at all, and she knew her boss well enough to know that he wasn't being one hundred percent honest with her, but she couldn't quite put her finger on why he would do such a thing.

"I'm just relieved to know that you're all right. Promise me that you won't get on the road until they're cleared better."

She wanted to argue with him just as she had with Lucas earlier, but she supposed they both had a point. "I promise. I'm not happy about it, but I promise to wait until it's safer to drive."

"Excellent! Maybe wait until Sunday and let Lucas just drive you home and we'll get a rental car for you Monday morning. This way we can kill two birds with one stone: I know you'll get home safely and I have an excuse to get Lucas into the office for a second time in a month."

Emma smiled at his words. She knew how much it pained her boss that Lucas spent so much time away from his family and the rest of the world. She only wished that he wasn't pinning his hopes on Lucas falling in line with those plans. "We'll see. I can't force Lucas to let me stay here for another two days and then drive me all the way home. That's not my fight to have with him."

William had to give her credit for her compassion for his son. Some people in her position might be more than willing to do his bidding to win his favor, but not Emma. No, she understood Lucas, maybe better than he did, and didn't want to do anything that would cause more strife. "You're a sweet girl, Emma. I wouldn't expect you to fight this battle with Lucas for me. All I ask is that you consider it."

"I will, sir," she assured him. "I have no idea how long he'll be outside with the tow truck." As she said the words, she walked to the window by the front door and looked out to see what kind of progress was being made. The driveway had been cleared. When had that happened? But for all she could see, her car had yet to make an appearance. "Would you like me to have him call you when he comes back inside?"

"That would be wonderful," he replied. "Oh, and Emma?"

"Yes?"

"Make sure he doesn't overdo it out there. I know he doesn't think that we can tell, but…he's still not doing well with his knee. I don't think he wants any of us to know or to ask, but since you're the only person who's been with him for any amount of time in his house, please make sure he's okay."

There was sadness in his voice and Emma's heart broke a little for the parent and for the child. Though they were both grown men, it didn't seem to matter; to William Montgomery, his concern for his youngest son would never end. "I'll make sure he takes it easy," she promised before hanging up.

If only she knew how…

Chapter 5

THE KITCHEN WAS REALLY A DREAM, EMMA THOUGHT, as she went about making lunch for her and Lucas. She had no idea how much longer he was going to be outside with the tow truck driver, but she needed something to do, and messing around in the kitchen seemed like the perfect way to kill some time. As his father had told her earlier on the phone, Lucas had just stocked up and there was a wide variety of foods to choose from.

Knowing that he would most likely appreciate something hot after being outside in the cold, she first opted for some soup. There wasn't enough time to make any from scratch, but she found two cans of chicken corn chowder that she doctored up. Then came the sandwiches, some nice grilled cheese with bacon. Oh, if only her assistant could see her now! There wasn't a salad in sight and Emma was perfectly okay with it. With the soup simmering and the sandwiches being warmed in the oven, all Emma had to do was wait for Lucas to come back inside.

She didn't have to wait long.

Fifteen minutes later Lucas came through the door and Emma jumped. She had been staring out the back windows at what seemed to be miles of snow-covered land. She turned when she heard him and almost gasped at what she saw. He was covered in snow, his skin red, and at his feet were all of her bags and belongings from her car. He nearly slumped to the ground once the door was closed.

"Oh, my gosh, Lucas! What in the world?" She nearly ran over to him and it didn't take long for her to realize that he was in pain. Without a word, she took the hat from his head and began to help him remove his coat.

"Emma," he said by way of warning her but she ignored him.

"Hush," she said quietly and went back to helping him get as much of the snow covered clothing off as possible. With his coat, hat, and gloves on the floor, Emma watched as he slowly removed his boots. It was hard to miss the hiss of pain when he bent forward.

"Go put on dry clothes," she told him. "I've got lunch ready."

Lucas stood straight up and looked at Emma as if he'd never seen her before. He opened his mouth to argue, but all she said was "Go" and he slowly lumbered back toward his bedroom, where he slammed the door.

Emma made a tsking sound and went about picking up his belongings and taking them into the mudroom near the back of the house to dry. After that, she headed into the kitchen to serve up their food. Before she was finished, Lucas stepped from the bedroom, walked over to the living room, and sat down wearily on the sofa, his head falling back against the cushions.

It was a no-brainer at that point; making up a tray, Emma carried it to Lucas and placed it over his lap. He looked up at her in surprise and what she saw in his eyes took her breath away. Gratitude, plain and simple. How long had this man been taking care of himself? How long since anyone had done something as simple as preparing a meal for him? How long since he'd even let anyone?

She gave him a weak smile and turned to walk away. "Are you going to join me?" Lucas asked, his eyes warm on hers.

"I was just going to make myself a tray," she reassured him. Within minutes she was sitting on the sofa beside him, making herself comfortable and trying not to spill her soup. "I wasn't sure what you wanted to eat but I figured this was your house and if it was here, you'd pretty much enjoy it."

He gave a small laugh. "Can't argue with that logic. But seriously, Emma, thank you. You didn't need to do this."

"Are you kidding me? It was nice to have something to do. I felt so helpless sitting in here where it was warm and dry while you were stuck out there. I hate that you had to do that for me."

"We're not going to go through that again, are we?" he asked. "None of this was your fault and you need to let it go."

"How did you get the driveway cleared away so fast?"

"I have a plow blade attachment for my truck. I simply pulled out of the garage and went to work."

"Oh, thank goodness. I thought you had shoveled that whole thing yourself!"

"Not anymore," he mumbled to himself. "It didn't take too long and I wanted to have it done before I called the tow truck. It would have been pointless to have them drive all the way out here if they couldn't get onto the property."

Emma nodded. "How bad did it look?"

"The road?"

"No, my car. Was it bad?"

Lucas took a hearty bite of his sandwich and seemed to chew slowly. Emma did not take that as a good sign. "It was about what I expected," he said finally.

"Meaning what exactly?"

"It looks like you ran it into a tree. The front end is pretty banged up, but luckily you weren't going very fast so it could have been much worse. I had Bill take it to his shop. He's a friend of mine and I trust him and his work. He'll get a good look at it probably tomorrow and have an estimate to us by Monday."

"Us?"

"Emma, Montgomerys is going to take care of this. It wasn't your fault and you were on company time. We'll take care of the repairs and your car rental for however long it takes to get your car fixed." In that moment, he sounded very much like a boss and Lucas saw something cross across Emma's face. Confusion? Disappointment?

"That's very generous, Lucas. Your father called while you were outside with the tow truck and he told me the same thing. I don't expect the company to take care of this expense, but I appreciate the help."

"Well, it was Dad's fault," Lucas stated firmly, still angry at what could have happened to Emma because of his father's inconsiderate behavior.

"I could have told him no, Lucas. He didn't hold a gun to my head and force me to drive up here."

"No, but he certainly did all that he could to sweeten the deal for you." Emma frowned at that statement. "What? What's the matter?"

She looked over at him and gave a sad smile. "I was actually really looking forward to it—the spa, the pampering, all of it. I never indulge in things like that because it always seemed so frivolous, but once it was offered to me? I found that I really wanted to do it."

"Well, maybe you'll get another chance."

"I'm not driving up here again until the summer-time!" she joked and Lucas laughed with her.

"How about someplace local? I'm sure we can arrange something like that for you when you get back." Again, he came across sounding like her employer, and even though that was exactly what he was, he still hated sounding like that to her. "It's the least we can do."

Emma seemed to sober instantly. "That's a very generous offer, but I don't expect the company to pay for a day at a spa for me. It's really not necessary." Her tone was formal, as if she were talking to someone in the office.

They ate the remainder of their lunch in silence and Emma rose to take both of their trays into the kitchen. "I don't expect you to wait on me, Emma," Lucas said, his eyes watching her as she moved around the room.

"Well, you fussed over me yesterday when I was hurt and now it's my turn to fuss over you."

"Why would you say that?" he demanded, sitting up straighter on the couch. "I'm not hurt."

Emma stared at him point blank, eyebrows arched. "Really?" she asked sarcastically.

"Yes, really," he replied defiantly.

"Okay, stand up."

"What?"

"You heard me. Stand up." She crossed her arms over her chest and waited.

"And what will that prove?"

"Stand up and walk around the sofa without limping or scowling."

Lucas did *not* like the challenge in her tone. "And if I don't?"

"Then you'll just be proving me right. I'm not a fool, Lucas. Your knee is hurting and there's no shame in that. You probably messed it up yesterday carrying me up from my car, and then again today helping the driver get my car out of the ditch. Why is that so hard to admit?"

"Because you don't know what the hell you're talking about," he snapped. "There's nothing wrong with my knee, and I resent you saying that there is."

"Then prove it."

Rage built in Lucas faster than he thought possible. In the two years since his injury, no one had provoked him like this. People left him alone; even the physical therapists stopped pushing him when he refused to be challenged. How dare Emma come here and make these ridiculous demands on him!

Sure his knee hurt; anyone would feel some sense of pain after the way he had exerted himself in the last twenty-four hours. But it wasn't like he couldn't handle it. Lucas knew he could get up right now and do a damn jig and never let on that he was feeling any kind of pain. He glared at Emma and saw that she hadn't budged.

Fine. He'd prove her wrong and then they could move on with their day. Placing both hands firmly on the sofa Lucas braced himself and pushed to a standing position and went to take a step.

And crumpled back down to the sofa with a growl of disgust. Emma was at his side immediately and he heard her soft curse. "I cannot believe that you are so stubborn that you would rather risk aggravating an injury than admitting that you have one."

His first instinct was to argue, but she had hit the nail on the head.

"What do you need? Heat or ice?"

What he needed right now was to have his solitary life back and to be left alone in his misery. One of the reasons he'd quit going to rehab was because he hated having anyone help him; it reminded him that he wasn't the man he used to be.

"Lucas?" she said, snapping him out of his reverie.

"Ice," he mumbled and sat back on the sofa, lifting his leg up onto the coffee table. In no time at all, Emma was beside him and rolling up the leg of the flannel pajama pants he had thrown on earlier. All Lucas wanted to do was push her away but he just didn't have the strength to.

He flinched when she placed the ice pack on his scarred and swollen knee, refusing to look at her. Lucas didn't want to see the pity in her eyes. There was the sound of Emma's feet walking across the room and he heard her moving around in the kitchen before coming back offering him water and ibuprofen.

"Do you have anything stronger?" He shook his head. "Okay, then. What do you usually do when this happens?"

"Who said this ever happened before?" Lucas knew he was sounding like a belligerent child, but couldn't summon the energy to care.

"I'm trying to help you," she said wearily. "This is all my fault, and I'm trying to do what I can to help you. Can you please just cooperate?"

"Really? Like you cooperated last night?"

"Did you not wake me up every two hours? And didn't I answer all of your stupid questions each time?"

"Stupid ques… Look, I know how to handle a concussion, Emma; you don't know the first thing about a knee injury!"

"So teach me! For crying out loud, Lucas, we've got nothing else to do here! You refused to let me even speak to the tow truck driver about leaving, so you're stuck with me for the weekend. Now either let me help you or deal with the fact that I'm going to sit here and nag you all afternoon." She sounded pretty smug and she knew that she had left him no choice.

"Fine," he sneered. "Normally when this happens I take the OTC stuff and ice it for a while. I do my best to stay off it and by the next day I'm usually better. Satisfied?"

"Hardly. What does your physical therapist have to say about this? Why is this still happening? I thought you had the surgeries to repair the injury?"

"That's none of your damn business." Lucas so did not want to have this discussion. He'd avoided talking to anyone about this and he certainly didn't want to talk to Emma about it. How did he explain that he'd elected out of the last two surgeries because even though the problem would have been repaired, he still wasn't going to play football ever again? Rather than continue to go under the knife, Lucas had simply given up and decided to live with the limp and the pain as a reminder that he couldn't go back.

"It doesn't matter what the therapist thinks or says; sometimes injuries just don't heal."

Emma looked at him suspiciously. "I would think

that you would have gone for a second or maybe third, fourth, and fifth opinion to get yourself better."

"Who says I didn't?"

"Did you?" she challenged.

"Christ, Emma, what do you want from me?"

"I want to understand why you choose to live such an isolated life! I want to know why with all of your money and connections that your knee isn't healed and that you don't seem to care! I want to know why you seem to have just given up on life!" Her tirade ended on a near shout. She opened her mouth to speak only to have Lucas cut her off.

"You want to know why, Emma? Is that it? Well, let me tell you, sweetheart, it isn't pretty."

"Lucas, I…"

"No, you wanted to know, well, here it is. When I hurt my knee I was having my best season ever. I had endorsement deals and was making more money than I'd ever dreamed of. I thought life couldn't get any better, and then I messed up my knee. I had the first surgery and the doctors were optimistic and my coaches and agents were optimistic. It didn't take long for them to realize that I wasn't healing properly. So they called in some specialists.

"More tests were run and more doctors looked at me and saw a secondary injury, and so they did a second surgery. Everyone was cautiously optimistic at this point. I was still promised the sun, the moon, and the stars by everyone around me. I was promised that I'd be back to full strength by the following season and all of my endorsement deals were still in play." Lucas took a steadying breath and adjusted the ice pack on his knee.

"After the second surgery and another round of physical therapy, they let me go to a couple of practices to see how my endurance was, and my knee gave out before I even hit the field. A trip back to the hospital showed that I would probably need at least another two surgeries, but even with that, I'd never play football again."

"Oh, Lucas, I'm so sorry."

And that was what he had wanted to avoid: her pity. Now that he had started, however, he had to finish. "I had a team of doctors encouraging me, but my agents and coaches had pretty much moved on and all of the endorsement deals closed. I realized I had no reason to have the surgeries. They weren't going to give me what I wanted most: my career back. Why should I subject myself to more pain and therapy and recovery for nothing?"

"But it wouldn't have been for nothing; you wouldn't have this pain! You wouldn't have to worry about watching what you do." Emma stopped and thought for a moment. "Oh, gosh, Lucas. Is that why you removed yourself from everything and everyone? So that no one would know that you weren't fully recovered?"

His eyes bore into hers. "I didn't want anyone's pity, just like I don't want yours."

"It's not pity that I'm feeling, Lucas, it's…"

"What? What is it, Emma? Are you telling me that right now you're not sitting there thinking *poor Lucas*? That you don't wish things could be different for me?"

Emma's gaze hardened. "Actually, no. I'm thinking what an egotistical jackass you are. You had the opportunity to live the kind of life that most people dream of, and because you couldn't keep having that one, you threw another one away. Some people don't have the means to recover from a catastrophic accident and have no choice but to go through their lives with their impairments. You chose to keep yours and hide away. So no, Lucas, I don't pity you; I think you're a coward."

Lucas made to try and stand up and then thought better of it. "That's right," she mocked, "you can't get up. You have an injury of your own making. Sit there and wallow in the sheltered world you created." Turning from him, she stalked to the doorway where her bags were. "I'm going to get dressed," she stated. "I may not be able to leave here, but I don't have to sit here with you and your bad temper."

"You wanted to know all the gory details, Emma," he reminded her.

"You're right; I did. I guess I just didn't expect such a disappointing tale. My mistake. From now on I'll keep my curiosity to myself." Lifting her bags, she headed toward the bedroom and shut the door behind her.

~

Lucas's first instinct was to go after Emma and defend himself, tell her how wrong she was, but what was the point? She was right. Lucas created a world where he was by himself in a misery of his own choosing. No, he hadn't chosen to get injured, but he had chosen to stay that way.

He sighed heavily. In less than twenty-four hours Emma had learned his deepest secret, the one he hadn't shared with anyone. Now what was he supposed to do? His knee throbbed, and all Lucas wanted to do was howl and rage at the unfairness of it all. He'd been a professional football player, dammit! He'd made more money than he'd known what to do with, and had his pick of women any night of the week. Now look at him: he was sitting in a secluded house in the mountains unable to walk across the room and face a tiny slip of a woman.

Thoughts of their earlier kiss came to his mind and Lucas gave a mirthless laugh. He'd known that Emma was attracted to him well before this weekend. He'd seen it in the way she would watch him or smile at him whenever he went into the office. But when he'd touched her, especially this morning, he'd discovered just how much he wanted her. He wanted Emma with a fierceness that had nothing to do with the way he'd been denying his body for way too long and everything to do with the woman before him.

What was he supposed to do now? If things had been different, if there'd been no tow truck to disturb them, Lucas had no doubt he'd have taken Emma to bed and not let her up until it was time to take her home after the roads had cleared. In the span of a few short hours, however, everything had changed. Her opinion of him certainly had, and Lucas was in too much pain, mentally and physically, to deal with seduction.

Turning his head, he glanced at the bedroom door and wondered when she was going to come back out.

On the other side of the door, Emma lay curled up on Lucas's bed. What had possessed her to go on such a rant? She was normally way more even-tempered. She certainly never pushed someone when they were down, and Lucas was most certainly down. He didn't deserve her cruelty, he deserved compassion. Had she given him any? No. That was a bitter pill for her to swallow.

While her job was certainly not a factor in what had

just transpired, Emma couldn't help but wonder what was going to happen come Monday morning when she was back in the office and Mr. Montgomery found out how hideously she'd treated his son. She groaned and curled up even tighter on the bed.

The clock read that it was barely one in the afternoon, and between the disturbed sleep the previous night and the emotional toll of their argument, Emma decided that with nothing else better to do, she'd give in to the urge to nap. Maybe everything would look better after she'd slept and cleared her head a little.

It wasn't the coward's way out, she reminded herself, it was simply a matter of doing what was necessary to not make this bad situation even worse.

Chapter 6

THE SUN HAD NEARLY SET BY THE TIME EMMA opened her eyes. She sat up slowly and glanced at the clock, surprised to see it was nearing five. When was the last time she'd indulged in an afternoon nap? Too long ago to remember.

Standing and stretching, she walked to the wall of windows and blinked hard. Surely it couldn't be snowing again? It was too dark and shadowed for her to tell for sure, so Emma walked over to her bags, pulled out some clothes to change into, and went into the bathroom to freshen up. Maybe some cold water on her face and clean clothes would wake her up from what was turning into a nightmare.

How much longer was she going to be stranded here with Lucas?

When she stepped out into the living room, Lucas was exactly where she'd left him earlier; the only difference was that now he was watching the large plasma TV that was mounted on the fireplace mantle. There was a football game on—she had no idea if it was actually football season or if he was watching old footage of his own career.

She hoped it was football season.

Lucas turned his head when he heard the bedroom door open. He didn't know what he was supposed to do or say, so he chose to wait and let Emma take the lead.

"Is that snow I'm seeing coming down again?" she asked.

"'Fraid so," he said cautiously, not sure what would set her off at this point.

"Fabulous," she grumbled and headed for the kitchen. "How's your knee?"

"A little bit better. This ice pack is pretty much melted away now, but I think I can manage to get up and make some dinner."

Emma froze and stared at him. "You're kidding, right?"

Lucas arched an eyebrow at her. "Excuse me?"

She sighed dramatically. "Could you please just sit and relax? There is no reason for you to get up. I am perfectly capable of handling putting dinner together."

"You're a guest in my house..."

"Yeah, yeah, yeah," she said as she rummaged through the cabinets in search of what to make. "I'm a guest in your house. That's just great. That doesn't mean that you have to jump up and wait on me. I can certainly put dinner together. I managed just fine with lunch, didn't I?"

Now it was his turn to sigh with frustration. "Yes, you did. Geez, Emma, all I'm saying is that I don't expect you to do all the work."

"I don't consider it work. I enjoy cooking. And although I think it's a little late to take something out to thaw, I think I could whip up some omelets for dinner if that's okay with you."

He nodded. "That's fine. Thank you."

Emma went about gathering ingredients from the refrigerator and was impressed with what she found. When she hummed with approval, Lucas wanted to know what she was doing. "Well, it's just that you seem to be a step above the average bachelor."

"What exactly does that mean?"

"It means that you have real food here. Your freezer isn't stocked up with frozen entrees and your refrigerator is not just housing condiments. You have fresh fruit and vegetables and all kinds of goodies."

"Goodies?" He laughed.

"Yes, goodies." Emma shut the fridge door and put her armload of ingredients down on the counter. "You don't have what I would need to make any desserts from scratch, but you've got plenty here to make a gourmet meal." She looked down at what she had to work with. "Just not tonight." She smiled at him and was relieved when he smiled back.

Twisting around she found the pans that she would need and the paring knives to cut the vegetables. Out of the corner of her eye saw Lucas stand. And wince. She slammed the frying pan down on the stovetop burner.

"What?" he snapped.

"I've got everything under control, Lucas! I don't need you to get up and help. I am more than capable of doing this!"

His head dropped forward and it was a tense several seconds before he spoke. "I wasn't getting up to help you, Emma. I was thinking I'd grab a quick shower while you cooked. I should have done that earlier when I came back inside but I was too uncomfortable." His tone was harsh. Would they be able to have one civil conversation this weekend or were they doomed to fight over everything?

"Sorry," he said sincerely. "I'm going to grab a quick

shower. I shouldn't be too long but don't hold dinner if it's ready before I'm out, okay?"

Emma nodded and watched as he walked away and shut the bedroom door. A smile crept across her face. Without an audience, she was free to play in the kitchen again.

Twenty minutes later, Lucas was practically salivating from the aroma coming through the bedroom door. She was simply making eggs, how could they smell so good? He opened the bedroom door and stepped out into the living room and saw Emma fluttering around the kitchen. "It smells great in here. What are we having?"

Emma looked up and smiled at him; her whole face lit up and Lucas felt like he'd been kicked in the gut. What would it be like to come home and have her look at him like that every day? He shook his head instantly at the thought; that was never going to happen because someone like Emma deserved a man who could take care of her, not one who could barely take care of himself.

"Well," she said, interrupting his thoughts, "I made us some western omelets, home fries, and you had a loaf of Italian bread that I toasted to go along with it. And," she said, her voice trailing off as she walked toward the front door, "the best part of the whole thing?" Emma reached into one of the bags she'd left by the door and pulled out some sort of food storage container and held it up like a trophy. "Dessert!"

That piqued his interest for sure. "You were bringing dessert to the spa?" he asked with a barely contained laugh.

"No," she said with only a hint of defensiveness. "I was actually bringing this to your mom. She loves my homemade brownies, so I had a batch in my freezer that I was going to surprise her with. Since I'm not going to see her, there's no point in letting them go to waste, right?"

Lucas had heard stories of Emma's baking skills. Both his parents had been singing her praises on that front for what seemed like forever. Knowing she had put a lot of work into their dinner, he didn't want to seem overly enthusiastic about finally trying her famous dessert. "That sounds great," he said. "But let's eat this dinner before it gets cold."

There was a small dining table in the kitchen and Emma had it set and ready for them. The fire was roaring in the fireplace and the television had been shut off. Lucas stopped for a moment and realized there was music coming from someplace.

"You have a great music collection," Emma said as if reading his mind. "I hope you don't mind that I put something on. I always have music playing at home when I cook."

"No, that's fine; it's kind of nice actually." He waited until Emma took her seat and then took the chair opposite her. The table looked perfect, the food looked and smelled amazing and this was all very…cozy. He was treading into dangerous territory and didn't think there was anything left he could do to stop it.

So he decided to embrace it.

"So, if you weren't stuck here with me right now, what would you be doing?" Lucas asked as he cut into his omelet. He had to bite back a groan because it was so good. The last thing he needed to do right now was sit here making sounds of pleasure while trying to engage in a normal conversation.

"Well, I'd like to think that I'd be getting a full body massage right about now."

"What?" he asked, nearly choking on his food.

"The spa? Remember? If I wasn't here right now, I would have been indulging in all kinds of pampering. I've never gone for a massage before. I'd like to think that it would be amazing. Or maybe I'd be enjoying a cocktail while I got a pedicure."

"I highly doubt that a health spa would serve cocktails."

"Maybe," Emma replied with a shrug, "but in my mind I'd be in a fluffy white robe with an exotic drink in one hand while my feet were getting pampered."

There was no way he wanted to continue this particular conversation, because now all he could imagine was Emma in a fluffy white robe with nothing on underneath and him giving her a foot massage. He cleared his throat and took a long drink of the juice she'd put out for them before speaking again.

"So what are these papers that were so important that my father couldn't wait until he got back to see?"

Emma froze. She knew William hadn't wanted his sons to know what he was working on, but in all fairness, she still had no idea what it was either. So technically, she wouldn't be betraying a confidence because she honestly didn't know what they were, and that was exactly what she told Lucas.

"That seems a little odd; he tells you everything," he commented. "He didn't mention anything before he left yesterday?"

"It was really kind of weird," she replied honestly. "I mean, he was getting ready to leave, it was before lunch, and all of a sudden he threw it out there that he was expecting some papers. When they arrived, he made it seem as if they were urgent. Thus my trip up here to the wrong house." Emma laughed at the words but Lucas knew she was only trying to make light of their situation.

"That's another topic altogether. My father is sharp as a tack. I find it hard to believe he simply forgot his own address and accidentally gave you mine."

"What would be the point? Why would he want me to go to the wrong house?"

"Who knows? I know it bothers him that I live up here alone and I don't invite anyone over. Not him, not my mother or brothers, no one."

"So you think he wanted me to come here first just to check on you? That seems a bit excessive." She made a face at the thought and it really angered her a bit that her boss would deceive her this way.

"At this point, it's anyone's guess. I hate that he sent you on a wild-goose chase and you ended up getting hurt." He stopped speaking and looked over at Emma intensely. "Which reminds me, how are you feeling? You haven't said anything all day about your head or your ankle."

"My head is down to a dull ache and my ankle is a little tender but fine." She toyed with her hair to cover the lump on her forehead and Lucas reached out to tug her hand away. "Lucas…"

He studied her for a long moment. "It looks much better. You were lucky; it could have been much worse."

She simply nodded. "I know. Thank you for taking care of me."

"Well, it seems as if you got the opportunity to return the favor today," he said and Emma laughed. "What? What's so funny?"

"We have got to be two of the worse patients ever! I mean, here we are, two people who clearly have injuries and all we did was fight about them!"

"In my defense, I'm a guy," he said simply. "And guys do not like to admit to any weakness."

Emma had to agree with that summation. "Okay, noted. In my defense, well"—she hesitated—"I don't have one. I simply don't like people fussing over me." With that she saw that they had both finished their meals. "Was your dinner okay?"

"Fishing for compliments?" he teased.

"Always," she said with a saucy smile as she stood and began clearing the dishes. "How's the knee doing? Do you want to put the heating pad on it now?"

"That would be great," he replied. "I mean, thank you for thinking of that."

Emma knew it bothered Lucas to ask for help, and so she decided to put him to work on something minor just so he'd feel useful. "How about you find something for us to watch on the TV while I finish cleaning up in here and then I'll go and get the heating pad from your bedroom?"

"How did you know I used one?"

"When I was hunting for a toothbrush earlier, I found it in the linen closet." When she realized she had just admitted to snooping, she blushed. "Sorry."

"No need to apologize. A proper host would have thought of getting that stuff for you."

"You've been very proper, Lucas," she said lightly as she wiped down the table and Lucas's eyes went dark. He had been trying to be proper; he'd been kicking himself after every time he touched her. The last thing he wanted was her gratitude for his "properness" dammit. But as she finished her task, completely oblivious to the dialogue going on in his head, Lucas knew the best thing to do was to put distance between them.

Within minutes, they were seated on the sofa; Lucas at one end with the heating pad on his knee and Emma at the other, her legs stretched out on the sofa between them, a plate of warmed brownies within reach. "What kind of stuff do you like to watch?" he asked cautiously, certain that she was going to request a soap opera or some sort of Jane Austen movie.

Reaching over, she took the remote from his hands and scanned the channels until she found a James Bond marathon. Lucas looked at her as if she were crazy. "What? What's wrong with 007?"

He shook his head. "Nothing. Nothing at all. I just never met a woman who willingly wanted to watch a James Bond movie, let alone a marathon."

"Now I have to admit, I'm a sucker for Sean Connery, but I certainly have no problem with Daniel Craig either."

There was no way he was going to debate why she chose one over the other and decided to just let himself relax and enjoy an action-packed movie with the beautiful girl.

It was a sensation he hadn't experienced in far too long.

Chapter 7

THEY WERE WELL INTO THE THIRD MOVIE WHEN LUCAS noticed Emma's eyes were starting to close. She had reclined further on the sofa and somehow her feet were now in his lap and he was gently massaging them. When did that happen? She looked so relaxed and so comfortable that he hated to do anything to disturb her. Considering his options, he decided to just pretend that he hadn't noticed that she was nearly asleep and put his focus back on the movie.

Emma, on the other hand, was doing her best to stay awake and wanted to purr with delight at the touch of Lucas's hands on her. She was trying not to react, but his hands were truly magic. She snuggled down lower on the sofa and almost smiled when Lucas automatically shifted to accommodate her while never taking his hands from her feet. Sighing silently, Emma decided to give in to the urge to close her eyes and just enjoy the sensation.

She felt as if she had just closed her eyes when Lucas softly called her name. She wanted to open her eyes, she truly did, but she was so comfortable and her eyes just felt so heavy that all she could do was murmur his name quietly back to him.

His name on her lips washed over Lucas like silk and he bit back a groan. It was well after midnight and his legs were starting to cramp from sitting in the same position for so long. He had long since taken off the heating pad, but what he really needed to do right now was get up and move around. When Emma didn't wake up, he carefully lifted her feet from his lap and shifted so that he could stand, then placed them gently back on the sofa. She sighed and curled onto her side and Lucas smiled. The woman slept like the dead. Waking her the night before to check for a concussion had been no small task.

He stood and watched her for a few moments and smiled as she hummed in her sleep. He tested his knee by taking a few hesitant steps, then lifted it to his chest several times for good measure. Yup, the ice and heat always did the trick. If only he could get to a point where it wouldn't be necessary to use them at all. Ever.

Have the surgery.

That nagging little voice in his head told him daily to have the surgery, but Lucas always chose to ignore it. He knew what he was doing. What was the point of opening himself up to more invasive procedures when he'd never get back all that he lost? What could he possibly gain from putting himself through all of that again?

The freedom not to have to sit for hours on end alternating heat and ice while you're in pain.

"Shut up," he mumbled as he headed to the kitchen to get himself something to drink. It was too late for a beer, so he opted for some water, leaning against the countertop while he looked in the direction of the sofa.

Emma.

What was he supposed to do now? He hated to wake her but he'd feel like crap if he just covered her and left her on the couch while he took the bed.

It's your bed...

"I know, I know," he said softly out loud. Still the thought bothered him. He may live on his own and be a little rough around the edges, but he was still a gentleman. Flexing his leg again to be sure that he was okay, Lucas put his glass in the sink and headed back over to the couch and stared down at Emma.

"It's not like I haven't done this before," he said with a sigh and reached down to scoop her up into his arms. She curled into him and Lucas felt her warm breath on his neck and groaned. He was a glutton for punishment.

It was one thing to carry Emma when she was unconscious and hurt, it was another to carry her to bed while she was all warm and sleepy and know that he wasn't joining her in the bed. He thought of their kiss earlier and had to force his mind instantly into another direction. He had wanted her desperately right then and there, and if he were honest, he'd admit that he wanted her the same way right now.

But she was asleep.

"Lucas," Emma whispered sleepily against his neck. She slowly lifted her head from his shoulder and looked at him through slumberous eyes. "What are you doing?"

Looking down at her sleepy face, Lucas couldn't help but smile. "You fell asleep on the couch and I wanted you to be comfortable."

"Why didn't you wake me?"

"I tried," he replied softly. "You're not an easy woman to wake."

Emma yawned and placed her head back on Lucas's shoulder. "I would have been fine on the couch."

"It's not very comfortable."

"You sleep there," she reminded him.

"I'm used to it. I promised you the bed, so I'm just helping you get there." No sooner were the words out of his mouth than he was standing next to the bed and lowering Emma on to it. She looked up at him with her big blue eyes and Lucas's mouth went dry.

She cleared her throat and blinked. "Is the marathon over?"

Lucas chuckled. "I think it goes on well into tomorrow. You'll have time to watch more of it then."

"Are you going back out there to watch TV?"

He leaned forward and pulled the comforter over her, doing his best to hide the temptation. In yoga pants and a T-shirt, Emma shouldn't have been so appealing, but she was. "Go to sleep, Emma. You can watch those movies anytime."

"It's not about the movies, Lucas," she said. "I guess I'm asking if you're going to go back to the living room or if you're going to stay in here with me." He could practically hear her heart beating nervously.

Lucas could only stare. There was no way he could answer her at the moment; not with the blood pounding in his ears. She was offering him exactly what he wanted, but there was a war waging within himself. The primitive male in him wanted to strip them both down and finish what they'd started earlier in the day. But the practical man in him, that annoying little voice, reminded him that she was his employee and that engaging in any type of physical relationship with her would not be wise.

He heard Emma sigh. "Aren't you going to say anything?" she asked.

"Emma, there is nothing that I want more than to climb in that bed beside you," he said honestly, and felt weak at the relieved smile on her face. "But I don't think it's a good idea."

Emma's heart sank. She had been certain that Lucas was going to want to sleep with her. That's what had made her able to ask him so boldly to join her. "Why not?"

"For starters, you're injured." Emma was about to tell him that was a lame excuse, but he cut her off before she could get the words out. "Secondly, you work for me."

"I don't work for you, Lucas. I work for your father. There's a difference."

"Not to me there isn't," he said firmly. "You're an employee of Montgomerys and I'm one of the owners of Montgomerys. You may be my father's assistant, but you still work for the company that I own."

Emma pushed off the bed and stood toe-to-toe with him. "That's rich, Lucas," she spat. "You're going to hide behind the company right now? Most of the time it practically takes a stick of dynamite to get you out of your cave here to remind you of the company, and now you're using it as an excuse not to sleep with me? If you don't want me, Lucas, then just say so. You don't have to make up ridiculous excuses. That's the coward's way out."

Lucas inhaled sharply at her words. "That's the second time today you've called me that," he warned in a low growl. "I don't appreciate it."

"Then don't act like one. At least be man enough to be honest with me." Her breathing was ragged. Emma knew she was provoking him and didn't care. He'd been nothing but frustrating her for months and even more so since she'd arrived here yesterday. There was only so much she was willing to take.

"Dammit, Emma, I am being honest with you!" he yelled. "I'm trying to be the good guy here and you're turning it into something it's not!"

She heard his words; they just weren't the ones she wanted to hear. "That doesn't change my opinion," she said as she crossed her arms and stood staring defiantly at him. "I wasn't asking for some sort of long-term commitment—I wouldn't dare. I was simply asking you for tonight. I thought it was the logical conclusion after the kiss we shared earlier."

Lucas was dumbfounded. He wasn't sure what exactly about her declaration ticked him off the most—the fact that she wouldn't dare ask him for a commitment or the fact that she was being so flippant about the whole thing. He leaned toward her until they were nose to nose; his eyes bore into hers.

"There is not one thing logical about this whole situation, Emma," he growled. "I wouldn't think you to be the kind of woman who'd want a one-night stand with her boss." He'd hoped to anger her, possibly discourage her. He certainly didn't expect to encourage her.

"Then I guess you don't know me very well," was all Emma said as she reached out and wrapped her hand around the back of Lucas's neck and pulled him toward her. As soon as her lips touched his she knew she'd won.

Lucas wrapped both arms around her and literally swept her off of her feet. "Be sure, Emma," he said breathlessly between kisses. "Be very sure about this."

With her mouth traveling ravenously down his jaw and throat, Emma managed to say, "Believe me, Lucas, I'm one hundred percent sure."

It was all the encouragement he needed. Carefully lowering them both to the bed, Lucas was content just to keep kissing Emma. Her mouth was soft and wet and she tasted like heaven. The purring sounds she made as his hands began to wander were like hitting the launch button.

In an instant everything changed, as somehow Emma managed to reverse their positions and was on top of him. She lifted her head and smiled down at him, a slow, soft, sexy smile, and Lucas felt everything in him go hard. Without breaking eye contact, she lifted her T-shirt over her head. She smiled triumphantly at him as she sat there in a white lace bra and her yoga pants.

She was unleashing the beast in him, the one he hadn't allowed to come out since before his injury. If he wasn't careful, Lucas knew he could be too rough. He took a calming breath and waited to see what she was going to do next.

Lazily, Emma let her hands trail down Lucas's chest to the hem of his T-shirt. Her hands found their way underneath the fabric, and as they traveled up, Lucas accommodated her by simply pulling it over his head. Bending forward, she trailed kisses from his belly back up to his throat until she made her way back to his mouth and settled in for a while.

When she finally lifted her head, her eyes were glazed and Lucas's gaze was eating her up. He reached out and cupped her face in one of his large hands, running his thumb over her swollen lower lip. "I could lie here all night kissing you, Emma," he said gruffly, "but I'd be lying if I said that was all I wanted to do."

She smiled with womanly satisfaction. "What is it that you want to do, Lucas?" she whispered, and then let out a squeal of delight as he switched their positions again so she was on her back underneath him.

"I'm not really good with words, Emma," he said with a wicked smile. "I'm more of a man of action."

Emma found that she could easily live with that.

Chapter 8

THERE WAS NOTHING LIKE A GOOD FULL-BODY STRETCH when waking up. Emma always found that a great way to start her day. The feel of a very warm, hard male pressed up against her back as she stretched, she decided, was an added perk.

Peeking over her shoulder, she met Lucas's slumberous eyes. "Good morning," she said softly, and when he chose to say nothing Emma felt the first pangs of panic. She had essentially said last night would be a one-time thing—well, not one time, but one night. No, they had gone beyond one time multiple times over. Was he regretting their night? Was he angry at her for provoking him until he couldn't say no?

Even now, Emma could not believe how brazen she'd been. Never in her life had she been so turned on and so determined to have exactly what she wanted. From the way Lucas was staring at her right now, she was beginning to regret being so bold.

She turned her gaze away from him and glanced at the clock. It was after ten. No surprise there, they had finally fallen asleep some time right before dawn. Giving up on Lucas having something to say, Emma made to move from the bed.

Lucas's arm banded around her waist and pulled her back against him.

Emma turned her face slightly toward her pillow and

smiled. So he wasn't as unaffected by their night as he was trying to make her believe. The feel of him pressed up against her back had that boldness coming to the surface again. "Something I can do for you, Lucas?" she asked sweetly and she heard him chuckle.

It was well after noon before he breathlessly turned to her and said, "Any chance you'd be willing to throw together some more of those grilled cheese sandwiches?"

Emma laughed out loud.

Later in the afternoon, Emma was sitting on the sofa reading a magazine she'd brought with her when Lucas came in from outside. She looked at him expectantly. "Well, how goes the big thaw?"

"I can't speak for everywhere but it looks as if the plows have come through around here. It's still below freezing out so I'm sure that if anything thaws, it's going to freeze up again quickly. Have you watched any of the weather reports on the TV?"

She shook her head. "Sorry, I got caught up in my reading."

Lucas stepped forward and before she realized his intent, he'd grabbed the magazine from her hands. *"Ten positions to make him crazy in bed?"* He looked at her incredulously, reading the rest of the headlines on the cover of *Cosmo.* With a chuckle, he handed it back to her, then leaned down and placed a searing kiss on her lips. "Trust me, Emma, there's nothing that article can teach you." Without another word, he headed into the mudroom to hang up his coat.

Emma merely sat there and fanned herself with the

magazine. "Well," she said quietly to herself, "I guess that answers that." Tossing the magazine aside, she reached for the remote and turned on the TV to try and find the local weather. Lucas came and sat beside her and together they listened as the forecaster predicted nothing but warming temperatures.

Inwardly, Emma knew this was good news. She could go home safely and get back to her everyday routine. Unfortunately, doing so meant leaving all of this behind. She wasn't stupid enough to think that what she and Lucas had shared was going to carry over into their lives once she got home. No, they'd go back to the same awkward, quiet relationship they'd always had when he came to the office, kicking and screaming, once a month. That thought made her sad and a sigh escaped before she could stop it.

"What's the matter?" Lucas asked, concern lacing his voice.

"What? Oh, nothing," she stammered. "I was just thinking about all that's waiting for me. I have to call my insurance company and then talk to the repair shop about my car and deal with the rental..."

"I already told you that we're handling all of that."

"I know, I know, but eventually, I am going to have to handle it. It's still my car and I'll have to get back up here to get it and I hate driving a rental and..."

"You're rambling, Emma. What's really going on?" His tone was quiet, serious, and when Emma looked at him, her heart stopped.

"I'm not ready to go home yet," she said honestly.

A small smile tugged at Lucas's lips. "I don't recall kicking you out."

She relaxed a bit and chuckled. "There's no reason for me to stay. It's already Saturday, the roads are clear…it's time to go home."

Lucas leaned forward and skimmed a hand down the side of her face. "You can't leave if you don't have a ride."

Her eyes met his. "You said you'd drive me home when the roads were clear," she reminded him.

"That's true. I did say that. But I'm not comfortable driving in these road conditions," he said lightly as he slowly began to lean toward her.

Emma thought that she could really get used to this playful side of him. This must have been what he was like before he got hurt. "There is the possibility of ice," she said with a dramatic sigh. "I would hate myself if something were to happen to your truck."

"Exactly," he said as he lowered his head to her throat and began taking light nips of her skin. "I appreciate your understanding. I would be really upset if something happened to…my truck."

"I'm a considerate person," she purred as she let her head fall back to give him better access.

"Very," he agreed before lifting his mouth to hers and claiming it. He couldn't get enough. Lucas had been sure that after last night he'd be just fine with packing Emma up and taking her home today. The roads were fine, the temps were climbing, and at this time of day, it was the perfect time to drive without it being hazardous.

Selfishly, however, he wasn't ready to let her go. Once they left his home, it was over. There would be no repeat performance, no continuing with an affair; once he had her home safely, there was no going back.

So he had to keep her here with him for one more night. Tomorrow. Tomorrow he'd be fine with walking away.

As Emma slid her body beneath his on the couch and wrapped herself around him, Lucas let all thoughts of tomorrow fade away so that he could fully embrace and enjoy the present.

~

By Sunday afternoon, they were on the road. Neither felt much like talking, so most of the drive was spent in silence. Emma knew that this time was going to come; there had been no way to avoid it, and yet she wanted very much to. How was she supposed to see him at the office and pretend this weekend had never happened?

True, he only came in once a month, and if she had enough advance warning, she could keep herself busy to the point of not having to really be around him. Chancing a quick look at Lucas from the corner of her eye, Emma gave herself a mental kick. Who was she kidding? When Lucas came to the office, she was going to do as she'd always done: she would smile and bring him his coffee just in hopes of him giving her one of those slow, soft smiles that she loved.

She was pathetic. If Lucas wasn't sitting right beside her, she'd be berating herself profusely out loud. Instead, she turned her attention to the passing scenery and just hoped that when they got to her home, she wouldn't do something completely foolish like beg him to stay.

Lucas wished he could figure out what was going on inside Emma's head. She'd been sitting there like a damn statue since they'd pulled out of his driveway and she was making him crazy. He expected some sort of scene, expected her to try and reason with him on all of the ways they could continue their relationship once she was back at home. But she hadn't said a damn word.

He thought maybe she'd have regrets and want to tell him how he should have had more self-control. But she never said a word.

Dammit, the woman had been a chatterbox all weekend and now that he really wanted her to talk, to tell him what was going on in her mind, she had clammed up! Women! Gripping the steering wheel until his knuckles were white, he drove on. The faster he got her home, the better. They'd had their time, their fun, and now it was over. She didn't want to talk about it? Fine.

No, he was lying to himself. It was anything but fine. Lucas thought back to just this morning when he'd found her in the kitchen dressed in one of his T-shirts and making pancakes. She'd looked so damn perfect standing there in his home and after he'd caused her to burn the first batch, he'd helped her make the second.

That batch had gone cold before they even got to it.

By the third batch, Emma had wielded the spatula like a weapon to keep him away. He smiled at that picture. They'd finally sat down to eat and then had showered together, but once he'd left her alone so she could pack it was as if a switch had been flipped. There had been no more silly bantering; they both had gone somber. He'd loaded her stuff into his truck and silently climbed in. Emma had programmed her address into his GPS so they didn't even have to talk about where to go.

For a man who had thrived on silence for almost two years, it was killing him now.

To break up the monotony, Lucas switched on the

radio. It didn't take long to realize that every song had a message of loving and losing, and it irritated the crap out of him. He slapped the system off. His action must have shocked Emma out of her own reverie because she gasped and turned toward him.

It was the first sound she'd made in almost an hour.

"Why'd you turn the music off?" she asked quietly.

"Nothing on that I wanted to hear."

"Oh."

And then the silence was back. How was it that they had talked all weekend and now there was nothing to say? How was he supposed to just drop her off at her place without having spoken a word to her?

He suppressed a groan. This was why he shouldn't have gotten involved. This whole thing had him looking like some sort of stereotypical player: he'd had his fun with her, his dirty weekend, and then he was done with her. Was that how she was going to remember him? No, he had to do something, say something to clear his conscience.

"So," he began awkwardly, "those papers that Dad had wanted, did he mention anything about them when you talked to him on Friday?"

Work. A safe topic. He felt dumb asking, as they had already had this conversation, but he couldn't think of anything else. "Actually, no. We talked more about how I was feeling and he apologized for all of the confusion with the directions. I know he said it was a simple mistake, but that was still kind of odd for him, wasn't it?"

Lucas agreed but didn't share his thoughts on his father's motives. "Yeah. He's not usually that careless. And it's still bizarre to me that he never mentioned needing them before leaving to come up here."

Emma nodded. "I thought so, too. Your father is very organized and meticulous in his planning; to just sort of throw something like that out there was a little weird."

"Well, clearly he was able to do without whatever it was, since he didn't call back and ask you to go over it on the phone with him."

"I don't think it was something he wanted to discuss."

"Why would you say that?"

Emma could have bitten off her own tongue. William had specifically said that he didn't want his sons to know about this, but how could she possibly say that to Lucas? "Oh, um, you know, he was feeling bad about my accident so he probably didn't want to bother me with work stuff."

Lucan made a noncommittal sound and put his full attention back on the road. "I guess we'll find out soon enough."

"I guess."

"Will you be at the office tomorrow?" he asked suddenly.

"Of course. Why wouldn't I?"

"I just thought maybe you would want to go to a doctor and get checked out to make sure that your head and ankle are healing okay."

"Oh," she sighed, secretly hoping that he had been leading up to asking her to lunch or something. "My ankle is just fine and other than an ugly bruise, my head is fine too. My hair hides it so no one has to see it."

Lucas had seen it plenty all weekend and it broke his heart a little every time. He thought of the many times her hair and been fanned out on his pillows and he'd wanted to kiss the injury away.

"I still think you should see your doctor," he murmured.

"Please don't start with that again, Lucas," she replied wearily. "We've been over this like a hundred times and I am fine. Please just leave it alone."

Lucas felt confident that this was the better way for them to leave things, with Emma being angry and irritated with him for nagging her. He could live with that. He shot one last glance at her, but Emma's attention was back to the passing scenery and so he let it be.

He'd lived with the silence for two years. What was another thirty minutes?

Monday morning, Emma woke up and went about her usual routine. She had spoken to Mr. Montgomery the night before and he promised her that a car would be there for her this morning to get her to work. She had showered and dressed and was pouring herself a glass of juice when she heard car doors slamming in her driveway. A quick peek out the window had her heart pounding.

There in her driveway were Lucas and Jason. They had dropped off a car for her to use and were getting back into Lucas's truck. She hadn't expected the Montgomerys to lend her one of the company cars; she thought a rental car company would meet her here this morning to drop something off. She'd have to talk to Mr. Montgomery when she got in, because she didn't feel right about driving one of their luxury cars.

Before she could open up her front door to say thank you, the men were gone. What had she expected? Lucas had barely said two words to her when he'd dropped her off last night. He'd helped her bring her things into her house and then said a very quiet good-bye before simply walking out and closing the door behind him.

She wanted to strangle him.

If she were honest, Emma had thought that Lucas would simply turn around last night and go back to his place. Knowing that he was here and he had Jason in the car with him, she figured she'd have to face him at the office this morning.

Not something she was looking forward to at all.

Walking back to her kitchen, she dumped her untouched juice down the drain and placed the glass in the sink. The thought of eating or drinking anything right now only made Emma nauseous. She walked back toward her bedroom to finish getting ready, and when she couldn't put it off any longer, she walked out the door, toward a car she didn't want to drive, to a place she didn't want to be, to see a man she wanted to avoid.

Happy Monday.

Chapter 9

Something wasn't right. William Montgomery looked around his office and knew without a doubt that something most certainly was wrong. It was only ten a.m. and the tension in the office was enough to make him scream. His plan had been perfect; there was no way for anything to go wrong! One look at Emma, however, had told him that something was off and Lucas had pretty much scared anyone who had tried to talk to him.

He was just about to go in search of his son when Emma knocked on his door. "Emma! Come in!" he beamed, hoping to get one of her famous smiles out of her. She came to stand in front of him but her expression was fairly strained. "I take it you got the car this morning. No problems, right?"

"Oh, no, sir. The car was waiting for me right on time. But, um, I was a little concerned that you sent me one of the company cars. I had thought that you would just get one from one of the rental companies in town."

"Why would I do that?"

"Well, you tend to only use the company cars for family. It's far too luxurious for me. I would have been more than happy with one of the economy cars from the rental agency."

"Emma, it's not a big deal. We have the cars and you needed one. There was no need to go through an agency."

She sighed. "I just…well, I'm not comfortable driving such an expensive car, that's all."

William laughed. "I don't think you'll have a problem. In all the years you've worked for us, you've never been in an accident until I sent you out in dangerous conditions." His tone became serious. "I cannot apologize enough. I never meant to put you in harm's way."

"I didn't think that you did it on purpose, sir," she replied kindly. "It was an accident, no one's fault. But about the car…"

William waved her off. "It's one of the safest cars on the market. Please, I'd feel better knowing that at least for a short time, I'm protecting you while you drive."

Her expression remained wary and she was standing ramrod straight in front of his desk. William noticed the large white envelope in her hand. When Emma saw where his attention was at she spoke. "Oh, I forgot to give this to you earlier. It's the paperwork I was trying to get to you."

"Oh, right, right," he said distractedly as he took the envelope from her hands. William sat back and studied her. "Are you sure you're all right, Emma? Have you gone to a doctor to make sure that you're okay?"

She smiled sadly at him. "No, I don't think that it's necessary. I feel fine."

"I know you'll think I'm just being crazy, but I would really feel better if you went and had a checkup. A head injury is nothing to take lightly."

"I'll see if I can get an appointment after work…"

"I'd feel much better if you went now. Rose can handle whatever we have going on. It's my fault that you're hurt and it would ease my conscience a little if I knew from the doctor that you were truly all right."

How could she possibly argue with that? "I hate to miss out on any more work; I have some stuff piling up..."

"I'll have Rose take care of it; it's more important that we take care of you. Paperwork can wait."

"I hate to inconvenience anyone," she said, clearly searching for a way to convince her boss that she really didn't need to go and see anyone.

"Emma, it's not often that I have to use a stern voice with you or demand that you do something, but I'm doing it now. This is nonnegotiable. I need you to go and see a doctor and get a clean bill of health before I allow you to come back to work."

Emma's mouth gaped. In the years she'd worked for William Montgomery he had never spoken to her like this, and in her fragile, emotional state, it almost brought her to tears. She mumbled a quick and quiet "yes, sir" and quickly left his office.

William felt as if he'd just kicked a puppy, but he really needed to know that Emma was okay. She was definitely out of sorts, and while it could have something to do with the accident, he had a gut feeling that it had something to do with Lucas. Once he was certain that Emma was gone, he called Rose into his office to go over his schedule for the day and then summoned his sons to his office.

By the end of the day, William Montgomery was going to figure out just what happened over the weekend and where his plan had gone wrong.

Lucas hated being summoned to his father's office.

Sure, it made working easier when they were in the middle of a big project like the one they were on now, but right now he didn't want to have to walk through the outer office and see Emma. He'd done a fine job of avoiding her all morning and if he had any hope of holding on to his sanity, he'd have to keep from seeing her.

He grabbed the required paperwork, and like a man facing execution, headed toward his father's suite. Keeping his head down and pretending to read something, he quickly walked by Emma's desk and noticed that she wasn't there. He breathed a sigh of relief, and then his mind started churning with thoughts of where she could be. Would she be in the office with his father? Was he going to have to work with her?

Lucas stormed through the door leading to his father's office with more force than necessary. All eyes turned to him—his brothers' and his father's. He mumbled an apology and set up at the conference table and sat down.

"Everything all right, Lucas?" his father asked.

"Fine."

William was about to speak when Rose walked in carrying a tray with a carafe of coffee and several cups. "Thank you, Rose," he said. "And when Emma calls, please put her through to me immediately."

"Yes, sir," she said as she walked out of the office, closing the door behind her.

Lucas was pretending to read over his paperwork. "Everything okay with Emma?" Jason asked, concern lacing his voice.

"I sent her home and told her that until I got clearance from her doctor stating that she was all right, she couldn't work."

"Was she not feeling well?" Mac asked.

"She said she was fine, but she seemed a little pale to me, and head injuries can be tricky. I hated to be firm with her, but it was for the best."

"Is she okay to drive herself to the doctor?" Jason asked. "Maybe you should call her and I can meet her downtown and—"

Lucas slammed his hand down on the conference table, and everyone turned to stare at him again. He had told Emma to go to the doctor and she had refused, but his father said it and she goes. True, he had forced her hand a little bit, which was what Lucas should have done.

"Is there a problem?" Jason asked, his lips twitching with amusement at his brother's obvious displeasure.

"Don't we have work to do?" he snapped. "I mean, I was told that I needed to be here because of this project and all we've talked about is driving Emma around. Seems to me if she needed help she would've asked for it. Now can we please get started?"

His brothers exchanged smirks while they took their seats at the conference table, and William soon joined them.

A new plan began to form in his mind and William did his best to keep his expression neutral, giving nothing away. If he played his cards right he'd get things back on track in no time.

"Ready to begin, boys?" he boomed and pulled up his chair at the head of the table. It was shaping up to be a great day!

Emma closed her front door and dropped her purse before heading into her living room to crash on the couch. A mild concussion. Unbelievable. If she and Lucas were on normal speaking terms, Emma knew she'd never hear the end of it. The doctor had cleared her to go back to work, but for today, she was staying put. Knowing that Lucas was in the office, she figured she'd take the day to recuperate and by tomorrow, he'd be gone.

Kicking her shoes off, she reached for her phone and dialed the office. Rose put her through to Mr. Montgomery immediately.

"Well?" William said expectantly. "What did the doctor have to say?" His tone was soft and it was almost as if he was trying not to be heard by the people around him.

"I'm sorry, but is this a bad time? I could have just given the update to Rose."

"No, no, it's fine. Are you okay? What's the prognosis?"

"Mild concussion," she said wearily, "but the doctor said that I'm fine to work. If it's okay with you, however, I'd like to take today to just rest and then I'll be in tomorrow."

"That sounds good. Did they have to do a lot of tests? Do you need me to drive you home?"

Where had that come from, she wondered? "No, that isn't necessary. I'm home already and don't plan on going out."

"It's probably for the best, Emma," he said gravely

and Emma had to wonder if he was really paying attention to what she was telling him. From her end of the conversation she was fine, but he was acting as if she'd given him bad news.

"I don't think you're following me, sir," she began. "I'm fine; there's no need to be so concerned."

"I'm very concerned, Emma," he replied. "I need to know that you're going to be okay. Is there anything you need? Anything I can bring you?"

It was as if he wasn't listening to a word she'd said! "I'm fine, Mr. Montgomery, really," she repeated with more emphasis. "The doctor even said I could come back to work right now. I'm just asking for the day for personal reasons."

William could hardly contain a laugh. Lucas was nearly falling out of his chair straining to hear the conversation that William had deliberately taken on the other side of the room and Emma must think he'd lost his mind. "Well, I'm sure the doctor knows best," he said with a sigh. "Take all the time that you need. Your health is what matters most here."

Unable to take any more of the crazy conversation, Emma told him that she'd see him in the morning and hung up. "That was bizarre," she said as she stood and went in search of something to eat.

Back in the office, Lucas waited for his father to fill everyone in on his conversation with Emma.

But he didn't.

He waited for one of his brothers to inquire about how Emma was.

But they didn't.

Lucas was beyond frustrated and he sighed angrily

and finally gave in to the need to ask for himself. "What did the damn doctor say?" he snapped.

William arched an eyebrow at his son. "I don't see what you're so upset about, Lucas. Emma's the one with the injury."

"Yeah, well, I was the one who pulled her from the damn car when she was unconscious, if you remember correctly. And I was the one who looked after her all weekend, so I think I have a right to know what the doctor said!" His tone was more demanding than it needed to be and his father's expression was a combination of shock and amusement.

"I didn't say that you couldn't know, Lucas, I merely pointed out that there was no need for you to be upset."

"You know what? I don't need this," Lucas griped as he stood and collected his paperwork. It was only three o'clock in the afternoon, and if he played his cards right, he'd be back in his own home before dark. "I'll fax you my portion of the numbers tomorrow," he said as he stormed out the door.

There was silence in the room for about ten seconds before Jason turned and asked, "What the hell's gotten into him?"

William held up his hand and went to close the door so no one would be privy to the conversation he was about to have with his sons. "Boys, I think I've stirred up a bit of trouble," he began and then went on to tell them about the weekend.

"So wait a minute," Mac interrupted, "you mean to tell me that you purposely sent Emma up there in a blizzard? Dad, she could have gotten killed!"

"In my defense, I didn't know there was going to

be a blizzard. I thought it was just going to snow a bit and then Lucas wouldn't let her drive in it. I'm just sick inside with the thought of what happened to her but in the end, she's okay."

"Is she?" Jason asked. "What did the doctor say, and why wouldn't you just tell Lucas?"

He laughed. "What fun would that have been? I've seen more emotion in your brother in the last couple of hours than I have in the last couple of years! Emma's fine; she has a mild concussion and the doctor told her she was fine to work."

"Then why were you being so secretive? From where we were sitting you made it sound like she was giving you bad news over the phone," Mac said.

"I was poking the bear," William replied simply. "Did you see the way he was acting while I was on the phone? That boy was desperate to know how Emma was and it was damn near killing him to sit back and wait. Those are not the actions of a man who has no interest in a woman."

"I don't get it. You think that Lucas has feelings for Emma? That's what all this is about?"

"Hell yes! I've been noticing it more and more over the last couple of months, but I knew that Lucas would never act on it so I put a plan in motion to make him do something about it."

"How can you be sure it did?"

William shook his head in disbelief. "Were the two of you not in the same room here with me? Was that normal behavior for Lucas? And earlier today, you both interacted with Emma. Did she seem like her normal self to you?" Both men shook their heads. "I don't know exactly what happened this weekend, but something sure did, and I'm guessing that it scared the hell out of Lucas."

"So what are you going to do now? He's heading back home," Jason pointed out.

"We'll see," William said cryptically and sat back down at the table. "Now, where were we?"

By the time Lucas reached the parking garage, he was calling himself every rotten name in the book. *Way to draw attention to yourself*, he mocked silently. He never should have touched her, never should have given himself the opportunity to have the best sex of his damn life, which left him craving more. He cursed and made his way over to his truck.

"Lucas?"

He dropped his head down and cursed again. There was no way to escape now.

"Where are you off to? It's a little late for lunch."

"Hey, Mom," he said dejectedly. "What are you doing here?"

She was a tiny little woman, maybe five feet two, and Lucas towered over her. In her hands was a beautiful bouquet of flowers and a balloon that read "Get Well." "I came as soon as I could. I wanted to give these to Emma. She's such a sweet girl and she keeps me spoiled with those brownies that she makes."

Lucas's mind wandered to the brownies they'd shared while watching movies at the cabin and his stomach growled at the recollection. "Yeah, they're good."

She smacked his arm. "That is the understatement of

the year!" She looked around and then focused on her son again. "Anyway, I was out and about and wanted to give these to her."

"She's not here. Dad sent her to the doctor."

His mother gasped. "Oh, no! Is she all right? What did the doctor say?"

Lucas pinched the bridge of his nose and reminded himself that he loved his mother. "You'll have to ask Dad. He spoke to her."

"Oh, well…okay. But that brings us back to you. Where are you off to?"

"I'm heading home."

"No you're not," she said firmly.

"Excuse me?"

For a tiny woman, Monica Montgomery seemed to expand before his eyes. "I said no, you're not." With one hand on her hip she looked up into her son's defiant face. "I have had just about enough of this one-day-a-month nonsense. When you came to the house last night, you promised to have dinner with me tonight and I am holding you to it!"

"I didn't promise—"

"Are you going to argue with me, Lucas? Seriously?"

He shook his head and remembered his manners. "No, ma'am, I'm not arguing. I just don't remember saying…"

"I'm making your favorite meal: pot roast, mashed potatoes, carrots, biscuits… I've been looking forward to it all day. You're not going to let me down, are you?"

He shook his head again. "No, ma'am."

She reached out, hugged him, and then tugged his face down so she could kiss his cheek. "Good. Now walk me back inside so I can at least put these flowers on Emma's desk." She made a tsking sound. "Poor girl. I hope she has someone to take care of her." Taking Lucas's big hand in her own, she gently tugged him back toward the building.

"I took care of her," he said under his breath, hating the fact that his mother was dragging his six foot self back to where he didn't want to go. There was no doubt that his brothers would give him shit for caving and coming back. Lucas knew he had no choice, and it was times like this that reinforced why he tended to stay as far away from the family and business as possible.

When their elevator brought them back up to Montgomerys' floor, Lucas promised his mother he'd see her at dinner and then made a beeline for his office where he quietly shut his door and collapsed behind his desk. He had been so close to escaping this hell, and now he was stuck for at least another day. He knew that dinner would lead to spending the night, and tomorrow his father would ask him to come to the office, and before Lucas knew what hit him, it would be too late to head home.

"Dammit." Lucas raked his hands through his hair and growled with the unfairness of it all. Hadn't he suffered enough? He'd lost his career, his identity, and after one weekend with Emma, Lucas felt as if he'd lost his privacy.

And the girl.

"Just another twenty-four hours," he reminded himself, "and I can go back to my own damn life." It seemed like a simple enough goal.

Emma was working late on Friday night. Everyone had gone home but there were still some things that she wanted to get caught up on from her time off. There wasn't much to do, but it was all tedious and time-consuming. Her stomach growled and she cursed herself for not ordering dinner earlier. There was always take-out on the way home, she thought.

By eight o'clock, she could barely see straight. Her filing was done, her computer files backed up, and the spreadsheets that Mr. Montgomery was going to need for a trip the following week were all prepared, copied, and collated. All in all, it had been a successful night. Emma stood and stretched and nearly screamed the place down.

"Lucas! You scared me half to death! What are you still doing here?" She placed a hand over her heart, hoping to slow down its frantic rhythm in her chest.

He stood dumbfounded at the sight of her. "Sorry," he said gruffly, "I thought everyone was gone."

"So did I," she snapped. He had stayed the week. In all of the years she'd worked for Montgomerys, Lucas had never stayed a full week. Why did he have to choose to start now?

"Why are you working so late, Emma?" he asked, stepping closer to her desk, closer than he'd allowed himself to get to her all week. "It's not safe for you to be here all by yourself."

Emma wanted to laugh at his words. She'd worked late countless times before; the only thing that made this situation unsafe was the fact that she was alone with Lucas and didn't trust herself. "I'm fine, Lucas," she said softly. "I just finished up and was getting ready to leave."

"Oh," he said and then seemed to stop to consider something. "Just give me five minutes and I'll walk you to your car."

"That's not necessary, really. Like I said, I do this all the time and there are security guards down by the garage. Go and finish what you have to do." She was talking faster than usual and gathering her belongings as she spoke. There was no doubt that Lucas would be able to tell that she was nervous, but if she could just make a quick exit, Emma knew she'd be okay.

"It's not negotiable, Emma. I know my brothers would do the same thing when you're all working late."

There was no arguing with that, but she wanted to. With an agitated sigh she said, "Fine. I'll wait while you finish up." Watching Lucas turn and walk away, she counted to ten and then quietly moved about the office gathering the rest of her things. His office was at the end of the hall and one of the farthest from the elevators. Emma knew she was acting childish but she didn't like having Lucas dictate to her what to do and when. Just because he'd slept with her didn't give him that right.

Tiptoeing, she made her way quickly toward the bank of elevators and pressed the down button and prayed that the ding wasn't as loud as she thought it was. "C'mon," she whispered, bouncing on the balls of her feet, anxious to get in the elevator and away from Lucas.

"Going somewhere?" This time she not only screamed but she must have jumped a good foot in the air. He was directly behind her and he spoke softly right into her ear.

"Dammit, Lucas! Why would you *do* that?" Emma rounded on him, her eyes full of fury.

"You told me that you'd wait and as soon as I walked away, you were sneaking out!" he lashed back.

"And I told you that I didn't need you to walk me out! Amazingly enough, Lucas, I have managed to get myself down to the parking garage, alone, for quite some time without you!"

Something in him snapped. Reaching out he grabbed her by the upper arm and pulled her closer. "I am so sick and tired of you fighting everything I say and do, Emma, you know that? Did it ever occur to you that I'm concerned? Did it ever cross your mind that maybe, just maybe, some of the things I say are for your own benefit?" Without waiting for answer, he pulled her toward his office.

"Wait! What are you doing? The elevator just got here!" Emma's words fell on deaf ears. Lucas pulled her into his office and gently pushed her into one of the chairs facing his desk. "This is just ridiculous," she said angrily. "You can't just shove me around, Lucas! You may be my boss but you have no right to treat me this way."

She was right. Lucas knew she was right and yet ever since their weekend together, wherever Emma was concerned, logic and reason ceased to exist for him. When she made to stand up, Lucas simply relaxed more into his own chair. "If you walk out that door I'll simply bring you back."

Emma was seething with rage at this point. "So what's the plan here? I just sit here in submission until you're ready to leave? That's kind of sick even for you, Lucas."

She was baiting him but he refused to be baited. He had no idea why he'd dragged her to his office. What he should have done was follow her into the elevator when it arrived and walk her to her car and then come back up here to finish his work. Scrubbing a hand over his weary face, he let out an equally weary sigh.

"Why are you still here, Lucas?" she finally asked.

"Working late, just like you."

"That's not what I mean. Why are you still here, a week after you dropped me off? You've never stayed for a full week. What's going on?"

Standing, Lucas came around the desk and stood in front of her. He'd been miserable all week. He'd thought of her. All week. He'd tried to leave a dozen different times, but always found some feeble excuse to stay. He was tired and frustrated and frustrated with being tired.

"I can't leave," he finally admitted and felt his entire body sag with relief.

Emma stared up at him, confusion written all over her face. "I don't understand why. Is it because of the project you've been working on?"

Lucas snorted with disbelief. "I can do that project in my sleep, so no, it has nothing to do with the project." Reaching down, he took hold of one of Emma's hands and tugged her gently to her feet.

"Then what is it?" she whispered, her eyes lingering on his lips.

"It's you," he said simply as he lowered his head to hers and claimed her lips as he'd ached to do all week long.

Emma was on board immediately, and he heard her drop her purse to the floor right before her arms tangled around his neck. She sighed his name and pressed closer to him.

"I can't sleep for wanting you; I can't concentrate for wanting you." He was trailing his lips down the slender column of her throat and lingered at the sweet spot right below her ear that he knew drove her wild. "I tried to stay away, I honestly did, but I couldn't do it anymore."

"I'm glad you didn't," she admitted right before letting out a sexy growl at what he was doing. "I didn't want you to stay away."

What followed was madness. Lucas pushed her wool coat from her body and let it fall to the floor. His hands roamed up and down her back and then lingered on her firm bottom, pulling her flush against him so that she could feel his arousal. "I want you, Emma," he said fiercely. "Let me have you."

No words had ever sounded sweeter, and in that moment, Emma would have given him anything. She frantically looked around for a place for them. "The sofa," she panted and then pulled him with her while he continued to nibble and taste her skin.

Emma couldn't believe this was happening. She was going to make love to Lucas right here in his office. It was something that she'd secretly fantasized about probably one hundred times, but doing this, right here, right now, was better than anything she'd ever imagined.

His hands ignited a million fires within her and all she wanted was to growl with frustration at how long he was taking. "Lucas, please." Emma kicked her shoes off but her movements were limited by the long skirt she wore.

By now they were reclined on the sofa with Lucas's big body pinning hers to the cushions. He lifted his head and looked at her. "You are so beautiful," he said reverently and then paused. “I don’t want to do this,” he admitted, but instantly corrected himself. “I mean, I want to do this, but I want us to be someplace private where there’s a bed. I don’t want to just take you on the office couch. I have more self-control than that.”

A wicked smile crossed Emma’s face. “Self-control is highly overrated.”

Emma woke the following morning alone and cursed. Sometime after midnight they’d arrived at her place, and after eating some drive-through burgers and fries, they’d picked up where they’d left off. Emma sighed with frustration.

“Bastard,” she muttered as she kicked the blankets from her body and went to snatch her robe from her closet. “I cannot believe that he would just slink off without even saying good-bye.” She was good and mad now, and nearly yanked the bedroom door off its hinges in her haste to escape.

And stopped cold.

There, in her kitchen, bare-chested and more handsome than any man had a right to be, stood Lucas. He looked at Emma over his shoulder and gave her one of his most sincere and sexiest smiles.

“What are you doing?” she asked, puzzled by the sight of him in her kitchen.

“I was hoping to surprise you with breakfast,” he said lightly. “I thought for sure you’d sleep in a little longer.”

Emma blushed. They had barely slept more than a couple of hours the entire night, so often had they reached for each other. She knew that she was exhausted and figured Lucas must be feeling the same. “What are you making?” she asked hesitantly as she slowly made her way toward him.

“French toast. I hope you don’t mind.” He went back to the task at hand and smiled when Emma came to stand behind him and kissed his shoulder.

“How could I possibly mind? What can be more perfect than waking up to someone making me breakfast?”

“I was hoping it would be breakfast in bed, but you woke up too soon.”

“Hey, I can easily go back to bed and just wait,” she said saucily and turned to go back toward the bedroom when Lucas grabbed her around the waist and hauled her against him.

Kissing her thoroughly, he reluctantly released her. “Give me less than five minutes and we’ll bring it in there together.” True to his word, he was soon placing their plates on a makeshift tray while Emma grabbed their coffee.

Lucas walked ahead of her and Emma noticed that something was wrong. “Lucas?” she queried. “Are you okay?”

He kept walking and didn’t answer her until they were both in the bedroom getting situated. “It’s been a long time since I’ve had sex standing up like we did last night”—he gave her a sexy grin—“multiple times. My knee is just a little sore today.” His tone was light, but Emma was beginning to know Lucas better and wasn’t entirely sure he was telling her the truth.

Emma climbed onto the bed and Lucas handed her the tray and then walked around to the other side to join her. She handed him his plate and they began to eat in silence. Lucas was no fool; he knew that Emma was concerned and wanted nothing more than to distract her from obsessing about his knee. He knew he was doing his best not to think about it.

"So," he began, "what do you have planned for today?"

She finished chewing the buttery piece of French toast and said, "Actually, I was planning on hitting IKEA today. I need a bookshelf for the guest room and that's a major excursion. I had planned on spending the afternoon there."

"For a bookshelf?" he asked incredulously.

"Have you ever been to an IKEA?" Lucas shook his head. "It's like a furniture and gadget mega store. I've been known to get lost in there."

Lucas chuckled. "Sounds like you may need some help to get around."

Emma beamed at him. "Are you offering to make sure I don't get lost?"

"Well, I hate to think of store security having to go searching for you." He winked.

"That's very generous of you," she teased back. "But are you sure? You don't seem like a shopping kind of guy."

Lucas shrugged. "I've got nothing else planned for today, and I thought maybe after we went on a bookshelf expedition, we could maybe go out to eat."

"You mean like a date?"

He nodded and suddenly felt a little vulnerable. Was he really going to keep this relationship—for lack of a better word—going? If there was no future for them, why was he prolonging the inevitable? "If you would rather not…"

"Oh, no, it's not that, it's just..." She nodded toward his attire.

"I am most definitely going to need a change of clothes today," he said with a small laugh. "Probably before we even go shopping."

Emma took another bite of her breakfast and let her eyes drift closed. "I do believe that I may have to keep you around for a while if for nothing else than to make this for me for breakfast every day."

Lucas watched silently as she finished her breakfast and then removed her tray. Emma looked at him quizzically as he settled back in beside her and merely stared at her. "What? Is there syrup on my face?'

"Darlin', if all you need me around for is to make French toast, then I've got to step up my game." Reaching for her, he smiled when she met him halfway. Lucas wrapped his arms around her and lowered them back down onto the mattress before kissing her.

"I don't know," Emma said between kisses. "It's going to be tough to top that French toast."

Lucas gave a wicked laugh. "I believe I am more than up for the challenge."

Chapter 10

TOGETHER THEY CARRIED THE BOXED-UP BOOKCASE into Emma's house and placed it on the floor of her living room. "I need a minute," Emma panted. "I'm not used to moving furniture."

"No problem," Lucas said as he sat down on the couch. "Are you okay?"

Emma sat down beside him. "Fine. Like I said, I'm just not used to moving furniture."

"That was more than moving furniture, that was moving furniture after doing a marathon."

She gave his arm a playful nudge. "It wasn't that bad."

"That store just never seemed to end," he said in dazed amusement. "It just went on and on and on and on. I didn't think we were ever going to get out of there."

"I told you, I have been known to get lost in there."

"And I'm sorry I didn't believe you," he teased, leaning over to place a gentle kiss on her forehead. "Where do you want this set up?"

"Just leave it for now. I'm not ready to deal with it." Emma stretched and yawned before settling in more comfortably beside Lucas. "Where were you thinking about going for dinner?"

Truth be known, earlier in the day Lucas has been looking forward to taking Emma out, but after their big shopping excursion, he was a little less than thrilled with the prospect. "Someplace quiet," he began cautiously. "Someplace intimate and private."

Emma pulled back and looked at him. "Are you afraid to be seen with me or something?" Her words were said lightly but Lucas sensed a small amount of panic in her voice.

"No, of course not. Geez, where'd that come from?"

She stopped for a moment. "This is because of what happened earlier."

"I don't know what you're talking about," he lied.

Emma made a face at him. "So you got noticed while we were out. Everyone was super nice and thrilled to get your autograph and some pictures with you. What's the big deal?"

Standing, Lucas walked to the kitchen and got himself a drink and then asked Emma if she wanted one. It was hard to disguise the limp. "It wasn't that it was a big deal, Emma, it's just that it was the first time in a really long time that I've gone out and had that happen. It's not something I enjoy."

"But everyone was so nice. What's wrong with that?"

Lucas sighed. "It just reminds me of…"

"What you lost," she finished for him and watched as he simply nodded. "Oh, Lucas, no one plays football forever. You just finished sooner than you wanted. You made that kid's day by taking your picture with him. Don't let it upset you; think about what a great memory you gave him. Make it about the boy and not about you."

Lucas knew she was right. He handed her the drink and sat back down. "It still doesn't change the fact that I want to take you somewhere intimate and have a quiet dinner with you."

Emma gave him a sexy grin. "I know just the place." She went to the kitchen and Lucas watched as she opened a drawer and turned back to him with a folder in her hands. She flung it at him.

"What's this?" he asked, confusion written all over his face.

"Take-out menus."

"I don't understand."

"You wanted intimate?" she reminded. "Well, how about dinner in bed?"

Lucas smiled. "Is it anything like breakfast in bed?"

"It's way better," she promised.

"Well, I'm all for new experiences."

Emma woke up early Sunday morning with Lucas beside her and smiled. They had shared Chinese food in bed in between lovemaking, and then had indulged in a hot fudge sundae. That had led to some steamy shower sex. Between the sex and the chocolate, Emma was a very satisfied woman.

"I don't suppose you'd want to make French toast again," she asked as she snuggled more tightly against him.

"I think you're getting spoiled," he replied sleepily.

As if, Emma thought to herself. It was the end of the weekend, and although she felt that they had made some progress in their relationship, she still had no idea what was going to happen from here. Would Lucas stay in town? Was he heading back up to the mountains? Was he going to want to keep seeing her? Sleeping with her? It was all too much to think about.

"You're awfully quiet over there," Lucas observed.

"Just thinking of how I could possibly top yesterday's breakfast."

Lucas chuckled. "You think about food way too much, Em."

"That's because you constantly have me working up an appetite." Rising up to look at him, she smiled. "Not that I'm complaining."

"Same here," he said. "If you really want that French toast…"

Emma placed a hand on his chest. "No, you stay put today. I will whip us up something. You just relax. I'll even bring you the paper."

"I don't want you to go out," he said, sitting up in the bed.

"I'm not. I get the Sunday paper delivered, so all I have to do is open the front door and there it is." Grabbing her robe, Emma strode from the room and went to get their coffee started. Then she headed to the door and reached out for the paper. Making up trays as Lucas had done the day before, she set a mug on one along with the paper and then went in search of what she was going to make them for breakfast.

Frowning at the contents of her refrigerator, she decided to do some scrambled eggs and home fries. Pleased with her decision, Emma glanced over and saw that the coffee was ready. She made Lucas's cup first and carried his tray in, smiling when she saw him sitting up in bed waiting for her.

"To hold you over until breakfast is ready," she said as she placed the mug on the nightstand and handed him the paper. Then, before she could stop herself, she leaned in and kissed him.

He hummed his approval and wrapped an arm around her to bring her closer. "I think I can wait on breakfast," he growled, and tried to coax her back into bed.

"Oh, no," she said, wiggling out of his grip. "I've got everything all set up and I would like to eat breakfast on the first try this time," she said laughingly as she quickly sauntered from the room.

Lucas watched her go with a look of pure male appreciation on his face. She was something else. He had no idea what he was doing here or where any of this was going, and if he were completely honest with himself, he'd admit that it scared him to death. He'd been careful not to get involved with anyone since his injury and yet for some reason he'd let himself get involved with Emma.

Involved. That didn't even come close to what he was feeling. One look at her and he ached. Being in the office with her all week and not talking to her, seeing her, touching her? He'd nearly gone mad. How the hell did he move forward from here? This wasn't part of his plan. Lucas knew that he could never be what Emma needed because he refused to be a part of the world that she lived in. He liked his solitude; he liked his privacy.

But his need for Emma? That was something that went way beyond like.

Off in the distance, Lucas heard her making their breakfast and smiled. There was no need to come up with an answer right now anyway. Right now he was a man who had a beautiful woman waiting to join him in bed again. He'd find the answers to where they were going soon enough.

Unless they found him first.

As was his habit, Lucas always went for the sports

section of the paper first and there, on the front page was his own image staring back at him. *Lucas Montgomery finally out of hiding?* the headline read. Lucas found his grip tightening as he continued to read.

> *In the almost two years since all-star quarterback Lucas Montgomery's career-ending injury, no one has seen him. Was he in rehab? Was he in hiding? Nobody knew and no one in Montgomery's camp was talking. Lucky for us, he emerged today seemingly from nowhere to meet and greet with some lucky fans...*

Lucas looked at the photo of himself and a couple of the teenage boys he'd posed with and felt sick. Hell, was nothing sacred anymore? He'd stopped and signed their papers and smiled for the camera and what did he get in return? Sold out to the local paper. Dammit.

> *With a fairly obvious limp, it seems that Montgomery still suffers from his injury. Though he was mum on whether or not he'd be returning to the NFL in any capacity, he'd certainly made these fans' day.*

A string of curses was coming from his mouth as he stood and reached for his clothes. Suddenly the room was too small; he was suffocating. This was what he'd wanted to avoid. He didn't want to be in the spotlight in any capacity. He didn't want anyone's pity or speculation on why he wasn't the man that he used to be.

Lucas was pulling his shirt on when Emma walked

in. "What's going on?" she asked, clearly confused as to why Lucas was turning her room upside down in his haste to get dressed.

"I have to go."

She placed the tray of food down on the bed and stood there staring at him. "I don't understand, Lucas. What's the matter?"

He snapped. There was no other way to describe it, but something deep inside Lucas finally broke. Maybe it was because he'd kept all of his anger and frustration bottled up and it was just time to let it out. Or maybe this was his way of getting out of a situation that he didn't have the courage to do on his own.

Snatching up the paper from the bed, he shoved it at her. Emma looked at the story Lucas had indicated, and once she was finished reading, she looked at him quizzically. "I still don't understand, Lucas. You're in the paper, it's a nice story. No big deal. Why are you so upset?"

"You don't understand!" he started out, his voice louder than she'd ever heard it. "This is why I don't go out. This is why I live where I do! I don't want people prying into my life, speculating about my injury!"

"But you have an injury, Lucas!" she yelled back. "If you don't want people speculating on it, then have the surgery and get it fixed!"

With a growl of frustration, Lucas snatched the paper back from Emma. "What good will that do? Will it make me a quarterback again? Will it give me my career back? Geez, Emma, I can't even have a full night of sex with you without needing therapy on my knee afterward!"

Although his words were full of rage, Emma couldn't

help but laugh. "Seriously?" she mocked. "Most guys would want a medal for that kind of stamina, Lucas, and not look at it like it's a bad thing!"

"This isn't a joke, Emma," he warned. "This is—"

She cut him off. "*This,*" she snapped, taking the paper back again, "is an article about how a former football star stopped and signed some autographs for some fans. *This,*" she said again with emphasis, waving the paper in front of his face, "is a positive story about how your fans have missed you and just want to make sure that you're doing okay."

"I'm not that guy anymore!" he yelled. "Don't you get it? I don't want to be associated with that!"

"Why?" she demanded. "What is so horrible about being associated with Lucas Montgomery, the athlete? Huh? Tell me, Lucas! Those kids thought you were a hero!"

"Because that man is dead, Emma!" he roared. "He's gone, he's never coming back, and now I'm just some guy sitting at a desk, pushing papers around! That's not a hero, that's a nobody." His breathing was ragged and he just wished that Emma would let him be. Taking a deep breath he waited for her next attack. He was ready for it.

What he wasn't ready for was the look of utter disappointment on her face. "You're a coward, Lucas," she said with an amazing amount of calm. "I've said it before and I'll keep saying it. It's not you, exactly, that's cowardly, it's your actions. You have the ability to make this right. Have the surgery, Lucas. Do the world a favor and stop this pity party and have the damn surgery."

"It won't change anything, Em," he said in a voice devoid of emotion. "I'll still never be that guy again."

"You know what? Nobody cares if you're ever that guy again. Be somebody else. Go into coaching, go into league management, go into broadcasting or whatever it is that the guys in the booth do! You have a ton of options, Lucas, and you've cut yourself off from all of them because you're too scared to try. You want to play it safe in your little mountain cave, cut off from the world, and you know what? That's the guy you should be trying *not* to be."

With the newspaper still in her hand, Emma walked over to their now cold breakfast and threw it down on top of the plates before scooping the tray up. "I'll tell you what, Lucas, I didn't know you before your injury and I think that I probably wouldn't have liked you. Go on back to your hiding place; go back to living your empty shell of an existence. Me? I've got a life to live."

And with that, she exited the bedroom and went into the bathroom to do her own form of hiding until she was sure Lucas was gone.

Chapter 11

By the time Emma made it to the office on Monday, she was able to go for more than two minutes without thinking about Lucas and getting mad all over again. There was no doubt in her mind that he had driven all the way back to the mountains yesterday and that there was no chance of her running into him at the office.

By noon she had pretty much snapped at everyone who worked in the building and when poor, unsuspecting Rose asked her if she wanted her to bring back lunch, Emma turned on her too. "No, Rose, I do not want you to bring back lunch for me. I am perfectly capable of taking care of myself!"

Then she felt like crap because Rose merely nodded and walked away with her head down, a suspicious sniffle coming from her as she left the office.

"Emma? May I speak with you?"

Great, just what she needed, her boss calling her into the office. "Sure," she sighed and followed William into his office. Emma didn't wait for him to ask her to take a seat; she sat down where she always did and looked at him defiantly.

William arched an eyebrow at Emma. "Is everything okay, Emma? You seem a little on edge today."

That was the understatement of the year. How was she supposed to explain to him what was wrong when it was his son that had her ready to spit nails? Taking a deep breath, she faced her boss with something close to sincerity. "It's a personal matter, sir, and I'm sorry for bringing it with me to the office. I'll be sure to apologize to everyone after lunch."

William sat there and said nothing, simply watching Emma until she began to squirm in her seat. "Was there something else?" she asked, itching to get back to her desk.

"Lucas left for home yesterday," he stated blandly.

"Yes, well, that's what he does, right? He leaves." Emma was proud of the fact that he voice didn't crack.

William merely nodded. "It was nice having him here for the whole week last week. I was hoping he'd stay longer."

Emma sighed and looked everywhere except at her boss.

"Still, I guess it's progress." He hoped Emma would say something, anything, but she could barely make eye contact with him and that really told him all he needed to know. She was just as upset as he was about Lucas leaving. He hid the smile that threatened to cross his face. Emma was the key to keeping Lucas home where he belonged; now all he had to do was figure out how to fix whatever was going on with them so that Lucas would come back.

"Is there anything else you needed, sir? There's no one manning the phones since Rose is out getting lunch." It wasn't a complete lie and it was one that Emma hoped would get her off the hot seat.

"Thanksgiving is coming up," William said by way of response.

Emma hung her head and mentally counted to ten before raising her face to his. "Yes it is."

"Any big plans?"

"I'll be spending it with my parents and their families." When William looked at her funny, she explained. "My parents have been divorced since I was ten. They're both remarried with new families, and so the holidays are a bit hectic for me because I have to make sure I spend equal time with both of them."

"They love you, Emma; I'm sure they just want to share the holiday with you."

She shook her head. "Not really; it's more about annoying each other. This year I'll have dinner with Mom and her family and then go to Dad's for dessert. Mom will, of course, run late with dinner and then cry when it's time for me to leave. I'll arrive at my dad's late and he'll be annoyed because he knows my mom did it all on purpose just to ruin his Thanksgiving. It's a vicious cycle, really."

"Sounds exhausting," he said, relaxing into his chair and resting his chin in his palm.

"You have no idea. I long for the day when I don't have to run around on a holiday, when I can just do my own thing."

"I'm sure it's very stressful for you. Maybe you should take a couple of days to prepare yourself."

Emma made a face at him. "I'm beginning to get a complex here, sir. I've taken more time off in the last couple of weeks than I have in the last couple of years. Is there a problem with my work?"

William let out a hearty laugh. "Oh, no! For heaven's sake, Emma, how could you even think that?"

"Well, you've been trying to get rid of me an awful lot and—"

"No, no, no," he denied. "I just know that I've been

working you too hard and that if I don't nudge you, you won't take the time yourself. You've been a model employee, Emma, it's just that..."

Emma leaned forward in her seat. "Yes?"

"Well, I had hoped that by now you would have relaxed a little more around me and as my assistant, you'd feel comfortable calling me William."

She looked at her boss as if he'd lost his mind. Seriously? He was upset because she addressed him with respect? "Oh, I couldn't do that, sir. Sorry. I don't believe that I should be on a first name basis with my boss. You own the company, and as such, you should be spoken to with respect."

"What if I said that you had to call me William instead of 'sir' or 'Mr. Montgomery'?" he asked, carefully watching her expression.

"I'd fight you on it," she stated point-blank.

"I see." William studied her for another moment and then gave a weary sigh. "Well then, I guess there's nothing left to say. You'd better get back out there to the phones, and hopefully by the time Rose comes back, you'll be back to your usual sunny self."

"Thank you, sir," Emma said as she stood and then blushed.

"No worries, Emma," he said, a smile on his face. "Someday you'll be able to be a little less formal."

Emma sincerely doubted it but she smiled and went back to her desk, closing the office door behind her.

William sat back down in his chair and thought about their conversation. Emma really was the model employee, but he'd much rather see her in another position altogether, as his son's wife.

Lucas was miserable. It had been more than a week since he'd stormed out of Emma's place, and he'd spent most of that time cursing himself. Now he had to head to his parents' for Thanksgiving and try and pretend that he didn't remember that Emma lived only twelve minutes away from them, or that he'd rather spend the day alone with her than with a houseful of relatives.

It was only Tuesday morning, and Lucas knew that he could be at Montgomerys' offices by the afternoon, and maybe start paving the way to apologizing for reacting so badly to the story in the newspaper. Emma was right about what she had said. He was living a hollow existence and avoiding life.

He was hoping to fix that soon.

His mind made up, Lucas packed a bag and got the house closed up, not certain how soon he'd be returning. With any luck he'd be able to patch things up with Emma, spend Thanksgiving with both her and his family, and start easing his way back into living in the city again and coming to terms with being part of the corporate world on a permanent basis.

But when he arrived at the office, things didn't go as planned. For starters, Emma was nowhere to be found. He said a quick hello to Rose before heading into his father's office.

"Lucas!" William said with surprise. "I had no idea you were coming into town early. We weren't expecting you until Thursday. Your mother is going to be thrilled." He grabbed Lucas and hugged him before pulling back and studying his son's face. "What's the occasion?"

"It's Thanksgiving," Lucas said simply.

"Not yet it's not," William corrected. "Sit, sit. You feel okay?"

"Fine, why?"

"No reason, just thought maybe you were here for an appointment or something."

Lucas wasn't stupid, he knew his father was hoping, just as Emma was, that he'd just fix the problem and jump back in the game. "No appointments, Dad. I just thought I'd come home a little bit sooner. They were talking about snow up by me and I didn't want to take the chance of missing Mom's turkey dinner." It wasn't a complete lie; there was always a chance of snow in the mountains and, as Lucas had recently learned, his father didn't really pay attention to the weather reports.

"Smart man, Lucas. So, what are your plans while you're here? It's a holiday week so there's not too much going on here. As you can see, we're on a bit of a skeleton crew."

Lucas had noticed that but didn't want to ask specifically about Emma. He wasn't ready to answer any questions about what was going on with them until he had time to talk to Emma herself. "Well, I noticed that Rose is out there but I just assumed Emma was at lunch."

"No, she took the whole week off."

"Is she okay?" Lucas couldn't hide the alarm in his voice; ever since her accident and her return to work, Lucas hadn't bothered to ask how she was feeling or if she had any lingering effects from the concussion. He was such a bastard!

"Oh, she's fine. She had some personal matters to attend to with her family and was a little distracted so I told her to take the week off; it's a short week so we were fine."

"Well," Lucas began a little more calmly, "that's good. Hopefully she'll get things taken care of." He looked around the office awkwardly and wasn't sure what else he was supposed to do or say.

William watched his son with amusement. He was looking around just as Emma had the week before, doing everything humanly possible not to look directly at him. Two of a kind, just as William had hoped. "Well," William boomed, scaring Lucas out of his reverie, "I do have some work to do, so if you'll excuse me..."

"Oh, right. Sorry, Dad. I guess I'll see you at home later." He walked around his father's desk and gave him a hug before walking out of the office. He stood still for a moment, unsure of what to do with himself. Did he go to Emma's? Did he need to call first? Screw it, he wasn't going to obsess about it, he was just going to go and see her.

Only, he didn't.

She wasn't home.

Lucas sat and waited in his car for thirty minutes, but Emma didn't come home. It was only then that he realized that he didn't even know her phone number. He really was a piece of crap. What kind of man sleeps with a woman repeatedly and doesn't even bother to get her phone number? It was amazing that she hadn't brought that up in their last fight. She must think he considered her good enough to screw but not good enough to want to talk to once they were out of bed. He'd have to rectify that and soon.

Perhaps getting back into the swing of things and being amongst the land of the living wasn't going to be as easy as he had hoped. With nothing else to do, Lucas decided that the best place for him to be was at his parents'. He could settle in, visit with his mother, and then maybe, just maybe, find a way of getting Emma's phone number and seeing her tonight.

For something other than sex.

Less than two hours later, he had what he was looking for. Luckily his mother was having issues with her iPhone and while he was helping her with it, he'd scanned her list of contacts and found Emma's number. Leaving him alone while she went to make dinner, Lucas slipped into his father's study to make the call and smiled when he heard Emma's voice on the line.

"Hey, Em," he said, feeling more nervous than he'd been the first time he'd asked a girl out in the seventh grade.

"Lucas? Is that you?"

"Yeah, it's me," he said awkwardly. "Listen, I was wondering if you were free tonight."

She hesitated.

The silence was killing him. "Em? Are you still there?"

"I'm here," she said quietly. "I didn't realize you were in town."

"I got in this afternoon. I know it's short notice and all, but I just wanted to see you."

"I don't think that's a good idea, Lucas."

"Why?" His tone was deep and husky and Lucas realized that he wasn't sure what he'd do if she turned him down.

"Because whenever we get together, it ends badly," she said honestly. "I don't want to fight with you anymore, Lucas. I can't fight with you anymore."

"Well then, we won't fight," he said simply. "I never did get to take you out to dinner. I'll come by and pick you up, we'll go and get something to eat, and then maybe see a movie or something. We won't have time to fight. We'll be out in public and having fun." He was going for light and cheerful, but it didn't feel natural.

"You don't go out in public," she reminded him, her tone wary.

"For you, I'm willing to make an exception." Lucas heard her quiet laugh and knew he'd broken through her resistance. "What do you say, Em? I'll pick you up at seven and we'll go wherever you want."

It was tempting, far too tempting, Emma thought. Maybe with them being out in public she could resist falling into bed with him.

And maybe pigs would fly.

"I don't know, Lucas," she hesitated again.

"Please, Emma? I'll come over at seven. If you decide you don't want to go out with me, I'll leave," was all he said before hanging up, not giving her the opportunity to turn him down. It was a risky maneuver, he told himself, but deep down Lucas knew that Emma would be waiting for him. He'd have to be careful to show her respect and let her see that she wasn't merely someone he was sleeping with; she was more. They may have begun their relationship fast and out of order, but Lucas swore that by the end of the night, Emma would see that he was sincerely making an effort to show her how he felt.

Words may not be his strongest point but dammit, he sure as hell would show her in every way possible how much she was coming to mean to him.

Emma was ready at six thirty. She berated herself for acting like a giddy schoolgirl and yet that was exactly how she felt. Lucas was taking her on a date. True, he hadn't apologized for his outburst yet, but she was hopeful that at some point tonight that he would.

Where would they go? Where should she suggest they go for dinner? After their shopping debacle, Emma was more than a little cautious to avoid anyplace that was going to be too overwhelming for Lucas. She understood his fears, sort of, and wanted to respect his feelings. There was a small bistro on the outskirts of the city that would be perfect. A quick Internet search found the number and she quickly called, hoping that they wouldn't need reservations. Luckily because they were still dining fairly early, the restaurant had an opening, and no sooner had she confirmed their time but Lucas was knocking at her door.

Emma stood and took a few deep breaths before checking her reflection in the mirror by her front door. Her hair was loose and wavy and she wore an indigo blue jersey dress that clung to her just enough to be sexy but not too over-the-top. She hoped that Lucas would like it and when she opened the door and he openly let his eyes caress her from head to toe, she knew she'd made the right choice. Stepping back and inviting Lucas in, she was stunned when he leaned in and placed a gentle kiss on her cheek before handing her a bouquet of lilies.

"Oh, Lucas, thank you!" she said sincerely. "They're beautiful!"

"No, you're beautiful, Em," he said solemnly. "You take my breath away."

Well, how was she supposed to respond to that? Her initial instinct was to grab him by his expensive suit jacket and drag him into the bedroom, but then she remembered that they were going on a date and that all of the good and yummy parts of their relationship could be explored later.

The evening was everything Emma could have wished for and more. Their dinner was delicious and the conversation flowed. There was a small jazz trio playing softly in the restaurant bar and they sat and had coffee while enjoying the music. Lucas suggested a movie but Emma found herself to be enjoying simply talking to him, so they opted to stay longer at the bistro before heading back to her place.

Lucas parked the car in the driveway, unsure what he was supposed to do from here. He knew that he'd walk her to the door but if she invited him inside, he didn't know if he'd be able to resist. And would she even want him to? Unwilling to keep the debate going in his head, Lucas walked around to Emma's side of the car and helped her out before walking her to the door.

"Tonight was wonderful, Lucas, thank you," she said shyly, clearly unsure of what they were supposed to do next as well.

"Thank you for being willing to go out with me on such short notice."

Emma fumbled with her keys before finally sighing heavily, as if she'd just made a monumental decision. "Would you like to come in?"

"Are you sure, Em?"

Emma opened the door and stepped inside, holding the door open for him. "Yes, I'm sure."

It was all the encouragement he needed.

They continued to talk until well after midnight, seemingly unable to find a stopping point. They discussed their childhoods, their families, her career at Montgomerys, and Lucas even opened up about his football career. All in all, Emma became more and more entranced with the man, which was a dangerous thing. No, the more she learned about Lucas, the more she found that what she was feeling was not just a crush or an attraction, but that she was falling in love with him.

"You know," Lucas was saying, "I wasn't sure you'd agree to go out with me tonight."

"You didn't really leave me much choice," Emma replied, her tone seductively light.

He chuckled. "Well, I figured if I gave you too much time to think about it you'd probably tell me no." He stopped and studied Emma's face, her beautiful face with those expressive blue eyes that told him more than he should know. "I have no excuse for my behavior, Emma. My career is a very sensitive subject and I've gone to great lengths to keep my private life private. I'm not sure that's going to be something I can overcome right away."

"I do understand, Lucas. I just want you to see that everything people say or do or ask is not negative. The only one looking at you in a negative way is you."

In that moment, Lucas knew that she was right. If he was going to be able to move forward with his life and break free of the walls he'd built around himself, then he was going to have to change his entire mindset. "I wish I could tell you that I was going to change, and that what happened that weekend was never going to happen again, but I'm sure that at some point, old demons are going to surface and I'm going to struggle with it all again."

Emma reached forward and took one of his hands in hers. "No one expects you to change overnight, Lucas, or to be perfect. Just be you." The need to kiss him became too great and before she could question her own sanity, Emma leaned in and placed a kiss on Lucas's cheek.

Instantly he changed the angle of his head and gently captured Emma's lips with his own. When she sighed and leaned further into him, Lucas shifted so that he could take her in his arms and hold her close. "I've wanted to do that all night."

She hummed with pleasure. "Why didn't you?"

"Because I wanted to show you that I am interested in you, Emma Taylor, as a person and not just as someone I want to sleep with. Although I do. A lot."

Emma smiled against his neck and nipped at it. "That's good, Lucas, because I feel the same way." Raising her head, she met his gaze. "I really enjoyed tonight, getting to know you and just spending the time talking."

"And the sleeping with me?" he asked huskily.

"Oh, I enjoy that too. A lot." They continued to stare at one another and Emma knew what Lucas was asking without words. He was quickly becoming an addiction.

For far too long Emma had lived cautiously, never taking any risks or chances. Right now, she was willing to live a little dangerously and open her heart just a little more to the man sitting before her. He may not love her, he may very well break her heart and destroy her; but for tonight he was all hers and she was willing to live in the moment and take that chance.

Without a word, Emma simply rose to her feet and extended a hand to Lucas. Never breaking eye contact, he accepted her hand and came to stand beside her. Emma led Lucas to the bedroom and said a silent prayer that the risk would pay off.

Chapter 12

As predicted, Thanksgiving had been a nightmare. As much as Emma had hoped and prayed to be saved from it all, she got sucked into the same family drama that had been going on for way too long. For a brief moment, she had considered inviting Lucas to join her, but then thought better of it. No need to let her family be the ones to scare him off; she wasn't ready to lose him yet.

On the flipside, he hadn't extended an invitation to join him and his family for the holiday either. While Emma tried not to let her feelings be hurt by it, she knew that where Lucas was concerned, she was going to have to wait and be patient. After all, a month ago he hadn't even been willing to leave his home in the mountains for more than a day. At least now he was venturing out for nearly a full week at a time. It was progress.

Now as she was getting ready for work on Monday morning, she had to wonder if Lucas was going to be at the office. She had seen him just yesterday, but he had been contemplating going back to his place to check on things. He'd taken her out for lunch and they'd watched a movie on the television before ordering takeout, and he'd left at a fairly early hour.

She missed him already.

With a sigh of resignation, Emma knew that it was something she was going to have to get used to. Lucas hadn't made any real promises to her except that he would try to overcome his issues with his past. So far he was doing that, but the pace was more of a struggle for her. Why couldn't he just open up a little bit more and clue her in on where he saw them going?

Grabbing her keys and hoping to give the rental car back this week, she headed out the door with a smile on her face and a little hope in her heart.

"Lucas!" His mother beamed as he walked into the kitchen early Monday morning. "What a surprise! We thought you'd gone home last night."

"I'll probably end up back there today but Emma's car is ready and I figured I'd take her up there to get it later today. Hopefully Dad won't mind if she leaves a little early."

"Oh, of course he won't. After all, it's his fault that her car had to be repaired. I guess there was more damage than they originally thought."

"Why would you say that?" he asked.

"Well, it just seemed like it took a bit longer than expected. Three weeks is a long time for some minor bodywork."

Lucas looked at his mother and laughed as he shook his head. "Mom, her car went down about ten feet into an embankment and straight into a tree. The entire front end was messed up. It wasn't just bodywork that needed to be done but engine work as well. Plus, I wanted Bob to make sure it was in perfect running condition before Emma got it back. Apparently she doesn't follow up on tune-ups and oil changes the way she should."

"Hmm…" his mom said with a knowing smile.

"What? What was that sound about?" Somehow Lucas feared he wasn't going to like the answer.

"It's just that you've taken a lot of interest in Emma these last weeks, and now you're going through all the trouble of getting her car fixed and getting it back to her. Seems to me that you're going a little above and beyond here."

"Above and beyond what, Mom?" he sighed.

"Don't get snippy," she quipped. "We both know it's been a long time since you've done much of anything. For crying out loud, we practically have to drag you out of your precious mountain home to get you to come here once a month."

"Mom…"

She paid him no mind and went on. "All I'm saying is that I didn't think it was possible to see you make such a turnaround. But I have to give your father credit; he certainly knew what he was doing in sending Emma up there." Looking over at her son, she immediately realized what she had said and froze.

"What do you mean, Dad knew what he was doing?" Lucas asked cautiously. "What are you talking about?"

"It's…it's nothing. Your father always said that eventually you'd get tired of living such a solitary life and…"

"No, that's not what you said, Mom. You said that Dad knew what he was doing in sending Emma up there. He sent her to my place on purpose? Is that it?"

Her shoulders slumped and tears began to well in her eyes. "It wasn't like that, Lucas!"

"Then tell me what it was like! All this time it seemed a little odd that Dad was claiming to have a senior moment when he gave Emma the wrong address, but I let that go, and now you're telling me it was intentional? Why? What did he hope to gain by this?"

His mother sighed in resignation. "Sit down, Lucas," she began.

"I don't want to sit! I want you to tell me what the hell is going on!" he demanded.

"You were becoming more and more isolated and withdrawn, Lucas! We all know that you're not fully healed and to be honest, we all have wondered why you would want to stay injured!" His mother didn't raise her voice or lose her temper often, but she was making up for it all right now. "It was only a matter of time before one of us hit our breaking point and confronted you but we also knew, as your parents, that we would most likely end up pushing you further away, and I refused to let that happen."

"What does any of this have to do with Emma?"

"Your father noticed that the two of you seemed 'interested' in one another. It wasn't something that was obvious to anyone else, but your father is a people watcher and he just picked up on some clues from the two of you. He said the only time he ever saw you smile was when Emma was in the room. He knew that you'd never do anything about it, especially not with an audience, so he just sort of created a situation to bring the two of you together."

"In a blizzard? He was that inconsiderate to Emma that he risked her well-being over this?"

"You wouldn't come home, Lucas! You were drifting further and further away!"

"Did she know?" he asked suddenly.

"What?" his mother asked nervously.

"Did she know? Was Emma aware that she was being sent up to my place to lure me out of hiding?"

"Don't be so dramatic, Lucas," she snapped.

"Then answer my question," he said with a deadly calm that he certainly didn't feel. "Did Emma know why she was being sent to my place?"

She shrugged. "I…I don't think so."

"But you're not positive." It wasn't a question.

"You'll have to talk to your father."

Grabbing his keys from the kitchen counter he turned to walk away just as he said, "Believe me, I will."

Rage.

There was no other way to describe what he was feeling right now other than pure unadulterated rage. He'd been set up! By his own father! He knew his family was upset with him for moving so far away and for pulling back from them all, but to set him up like this was inexcusable!

And what about Emma? What was her role in all of this? He knew she'd had a crush on him before, but would that be enough of an enticement for her to become a willing part of his father's plan? All this time he'd been falling for her—maybe it was all an act on her part.

"Dammit!" he cursed, slamming his hands on the steering wheel. He didn't want to believe it was true; he wanted to believe that she was as unsuspecting in all of this as he was and that his father had set them both up.

His tires screeched as he pulled into his parking spot at the office. In record time he found himself standing, breathless, in his father's outer office, staring at Emma.

"Lucas!" she said, taking in his disheveled appearance. His breath was ragged, his tie was askew, and his hair looked as if he'd been running his hands through it in frustration. "Are you okay?" She made to stand and walk to him but Lucas held a hand out to stop her.

"Is my father in?"

"No, he had a meeting in Concord this morning. He'll be back by eleven. What's going on?"

Lucas looked around and saw Rose and some of the other employees staring at him. "I need to speak to you in my office. *Now*." He turned and walked away, not bothering to see if she would follow.

Emma mumbled a small "excuse me" to Rose before following Lucas to his office and shutting the door. He was pacing behind his desk, his entire body rigid with barely contained rage. "Lucas?"

"I'm going to ask you something, and I want an honest answer."

"Of course."

"In your job with my father, have you ever mailed anything to my home?" He stood still finally and looked at Emma.

"Yes, I have. Rose and I both handle sending out the paperwork."

"So then you'd know my home address."

"Lucas, what is this about? You're scaring me!" she pleaded.

"Just answer the question, Emma. Do you type up and print out the address labels with my home address?"

"Yes." Her belly felt queasy and a sense of unease

began to fill her. Emma wasn't sure where this was all leading but she was certain that it wasn't going to be good. "Yes, I've typed up your address before."

"Didn't it seem odd to you when my father sent you to deliver paperwork to him that he gave you my address?"

That's what this was about? He was still harping on the weekend that she'd shown up at his house? What in the world? "To be honest, it didn't occur to me that it was your address he was giving me. I was distracted with the task of getting up to the mountains before dark. I asked for an address to put into my GPS and he gave me one. I had no reason to question whose it was. For all I knew, you all lived on the same piece of property."

He had to hand it to her, her explanation made some sense. Then he remembered part of their conversation from the previous weekend when they'd talked about her career at Montgomerys and how she'd gushed on how much she respected his father and would do anything for him.

"Is that all, Lucas?" she snapped, unwilling to stand for this ridiculous interrogation any longer.

"You told me that weekend that you would do anything for my father. That you respect him as your boss and that you felt that you owed him for giving you a chance here when you were under qualified for the position of his assistant. Was that true?"

"You know it is. I'm not a liar, Lucas."

"That remains to be seen," he said and walked around his desk toward her. Emma took an immediate step back but Lucas reached out and gently grabbed her arm to stop her. "Did you know that you were coming to my house that night? Were you willing to seduce me into coming to work at Montgomerys full time?"

"What?" she demanded. "Have you lost your mind? Seduce you? If you remember correctly, I crashed my car into a tree! How seductive is that?"

"That was truly an accident, but I find it hard to believe that all of this happened—you showing up at my place, getting snowed in together, and the physical relationship that followed—were all just a random series of coincidences."

Emma yanked free of his grip. "I don't give a damn what you believe, and I don't know what brought this on, but I've had just about enough! I don't have to explain myself to you over this situation anymore, Lucas! Your father asked me to deliver some papers to him; he gave me an address and I went. If there was anything misleading or whatever about that, then it's on him, not me, and I am offended that you would accuse me of such things! I am damn good at my job and yes, I'm willing to do what needs to be done, but that does not include whoring myself out to the boss's son to entice him back to work!"

Without another word, Emma stalked from his office, slamming the door behind her. From Lucas's standpoint, it was a glorious exit, but she was just a little too defensive for his liking. He couldn't be sure if she was telling the truth or not and until he talked to his father, he wouldn't know for certain.

For a brief moment, panic set in. What if Emma was telling the truth? What if he'd just made the biggest mistake of his life and threw away the chance at a relationship with the woman he was certain he could fall in love with?

Emma was a complete wreck. Where had all of that just come from? What had happened between last night and this morning for Lucas to be so angry with her? Why was he accusing her of such horrible things? Carefully, she sat down at her desk and let out a shuddering breath.

"Are you okay?" Rose asked quietly from behind her.

Emma gave a weak smile. "I'm fine, thank you for asking, Rose."

Rose returned the smile and walked away. Emma was thankful Rose didn't pry, but wasn't sure how it was going to be possible for her to work right now.

After several failed attempts at typing up a contract that William Montgomery had asked her to have ready for him, Emma finally asked Rose to handle it while she went to the ladies' room to try and get herself under control. Her heart was still racing and actually hurt. How could Lucas think that she was with him because of his father? Hadn't she showed him time and time again what he meant to her?

She splashed some cold water on her face and sat in one of the upholstered chairs that were in the executive washroom while she collected her thoughts. The only way she was going to get to the end of this was to confront Mr. Montgomery and see what was going on. She had wanted to keep her relationship with Lucas private, but apparently something was out in the open and there was no way Emma could sit back and let anyone think that she was for sale.

With a steadier disposition, Emma left the security of the washroom and headed back to her office, where she heard a heated argument going on in her boss's office.

"You sent her up there to lure me to work, Dad! Admit it!" She heard Lucas shout.

"I'm not going to lie to you, Lucas. I didn't know what else to do! You wouldn't listen to me or your mother or your brothers so yes, I thought that maybe Emma might be able to convince you to come back to work!"

"Why would you think that Emma could succeed where all of you failed?"

"Because I saw the way you looked at her and the way she watched you, dammit! I was desperate and I used that to my advantage, but I will not have you talking to me like I'm some sort of criminal! I'm your father and you will talk to me with respect!"

"I'll talk to you any way I damn well please," Lucas snapped, his voice full of contempt. "You manipulated me for your own personal reasons. You didn't care about the time that I needed to heal or what I wanted..."

"You weren't healing! You stopped going to therapy and you passed on the other surgeries..."

"How the hell do you know about that?" Lucas demanded, his voice going deadly calm. Emma had to strain to hear him. "Did Emma tell you about that?"

"No, of course she didn't. I make it my business to know everything, Lucas. Do you think I wouldn't try to find out why my once friendly and outgoing son was suddenly hiding away from everyone? Why you wouldn't be around anyone for more than a few hours a month?"

"So you talked to my doctors? That's unethical of them and you!"

"No, I talked to your coach. He filled me in," William said calmly. "Lucas, I never wanted things to come to this but I didn't know what else to do! These last few weeks, having you home, have been wonderful. Your mother and I are just thrilled to see you actively participating in life again!"

"Did Emma know?"

"Did she know what?" William asked cautiously.

"Was Emma in on the plan to go up to my house and lure me home?"

William hesitated. "No, she was not in on any of it. I set her up and sent her up there blindly on the pretense of bringing me those papers."

"I don't believe you," Lucas said honestly. "I can't believe that as close as you and Emma are that you would set her up like that. What were you hoping would happen once she got there? There was a blizzard coming, for crying out loud!"

"I knew we were expecting some snow but I didn't realize how much," William said wearily. "I figured she'd get up there, it would be snowing enough that you wouldn't want her out driving in it, and she'd be forced to stay the night."

"To what end, Dad?"

"You'd have no choice but to talk to her, interact with her. I could see every time you were here that you wanted to, but you wouldn't allow yourself. So I did what I could to make sure that you…"

"Slept with her?"

William winced and then looked ashamed. "You make it sound crude, Lucas. That wasn't how I intended it."

"Wasn't it? You sent her up there to seduce me into coming home. Well, the joke's on you, Dad, because I'll be damned if I'll let you or Emma manipulate me. From now on, I'll work from home only. I'm done with this bullshit."

"Don't take this out on Emma, Lucas! She had nothing to do with it—it was all my doing!"

Lucas looked at his father and saw the distress on his face. "You don't get it, do you? I've had people making my life decisions for two years now. The decision never to play football again wasn't mine; the decision not to have any position in the NFL wasn't mine. And you went and took away the decision on whether or not I wanted to work here with you or to have a relationship with Emma."

"So you'll walk away from your family and her just for spite?"

Lucas didn't respond. He stormed from the office and didn't even notice that Emma was standing beside the door, tears streaming down her cheeks.

Without conscious thought, Emma walked into William's office. "Is it true?" she asked, her voice shaking.

William looked up at her with utter devastation on his face. "Which part?" he asked wearily.

"All of it," she demanded softly. "You set me up to make Lucas move back home."

All he could do was nod.

"I can't work for you anymore," Emma said, feeling more in control than she had moments ago. "You not only risked my life by sending me out into that storm on a fool's errand, but you used me to fight a battle that wasn't mine and you used my emotions against my will. I can't work for someone like that."

"Emma, let me explain…"

She held up her hands to stop him. "There's nothing left you can say. I think you'll understand if I don't give two weeks' notice."

William knew at that point he'd lost.

Everything.

"I'll make sure Rose is up-to-date on what I was working on, and then I'll be leaving."

"You don't have to quit, Emma. Take a few days to calm down and then we can talk."

"It won't make a difference. But I have one request, sir," she said boldly.

William cringed at the title she'd always called him by. He hated the formality, he hated the stiffness in her spine, and the fact that he was responsible for putting it there. "Anything."

"This conversation that we're having? You are not to share it with Lucas. This is between you and me. He has enough issues with you right now and I don't need to be any more a part of them than I already am."

"I really wish you'd reconsider…"

Emma smiled sadly. "You know, I once told Lucas how much I respected you and felt like I owed you so much because you took a chance on me when you promoted me to be your assistant. But now? I can't trust you. I don't think I'll ever be able to look at you and not remember what it is that you cost me."

"And what was that?" he asked quietly.

"The chance at a life with the man I love." And then she was gone.

Chapter 13

THE HOLIDAYS HAD PROVEN TO BE A GREAT distraction, but as Emma stood in her kitchen in early January, she wasn't sure what was going to distract her now. It had been over a month since her departure from Montgomerys. The awkward situation had only been prolonged due to the issue with her car. She'd been on the verge of calling for a cab when Jason Montgomery had quietly taken the phone from her and offered to take her to pick her car up. As much as she wasn't feeling too kindly toward any of the Montgomerys, Jason had played no part in what had gone wrong.

He'd been the perfect gentleman on the two-hour drive and made sure he steered clear of any talk of business or of his family. He'd been content to talk about her plans for Christmas and New Year's and then about their mutual interest in books. All in all, what should have made her feel better, only stood to make Emma feel worse. She really had loved the Montgomerys and knew that, in time, if Lucas had only given her the chance, she would have fit in with them better than she ever had with her own family.

Damn him.

The thought of job hunting over the holidays had not been appealing and Emma was silently thankful for the severance pay that had appeared in her bank account. She'd wanted to decline it and tell William Montgomery what he could do with his money, but it had allowed her the time she needed just to wallow in her own misery until she was ready to look for work.

Luckily, the week before Christmas, a fairly perfect job had opened up, as if it was created just for her. Her favorite bakery was looking for help. Emma only found out about it because she was craving brownies but didn't want to be bothered making them herself.

The small bakery was a family-owned business and Emma had frequented it enough that she knew the owners well. They had discussed baking techniques from time to time, and so when the holiday orders were becoming too much for them to handle and Emma had walked in on her brownie quest, they had asked her if she'd consider helping them out.

It was a godsend.

The crowds had been plenty and the work kept her so busy that most days she came home too exhausted to think. But now with the busy season over, Emma was certain that it was time to move on and find a more permanent position. The thought made her sad, because as much as she enjoyed working in the corporate world, baking was really a passion for her, and now she had the time to dedicate to it. Maybe it was time to change careers?

As much as that thought appealed to her, she couldn't afford to live on a part-time baker's salary. Maybe she should look into a business loan and starting her own bakery? Then she thought of her bosses and realized she'd be their competition, and she didn't want to do that to them.

Sighing, Emma realized she was back to square one. What to do?

"Emma? Would you mind watching the front for

a little while so I can go to the bank?" her boss, Mrs. Dupre, asked.

"Of course," Emma replied with a sincere smile. Straightening her apron, she walked out to the front of the bakery and came to a dead stop.

"Emma? Is that you?"

"How are you, Mrs. Montgomery?" Maybe the floor would open up and swallow her right now, Emma thought. She hated the thought of any of the Montgomerys looking down on her career right now and acting smug, like leaving their company had been a mistake.

"Oh, I'm doing fine. Sort of…"

"What can I help you with? We have some fresh-from-the-oven muffins over here," Emma said brightly, indicating the shelf with the oversized muffins.

"Actually, what I need is enough dessert for say… two hundred people."

"What?" Emma gaped.

"Well, next month is mine and William's thirty-fifth wedding anniversary. We're having a big party at the country club but I absolutely detest their desserts. I've made an arrangement with them that we can bring in our own dessert caterer but I'm having a hard time finding one that makes the things we want."

"Okay," Emma said, forcing the cheeriness into her voice. "Why don't you tell me what you're looking for and we can arrange a tasting for you to see if we can meet your needs."

Monica Montgomery looked at her with a combination of love and gratitude. "Actually, Emma, it's no accident that I'm here. Rose mentioned to me that you were here and I want you to do the desserts. You know how I have always loved all of the goodies you've made for me over the years, and that's what I want."

"I...I can't do that. You have to understand," she stammered.

Monica waved away whatever it was that Emma was going to say. "Emma, I may not look like much, but having raised three boys has taught me a thing or two about being firm. For starters, Margaret Dupre and I have been friends for ages. I always come here for baked goods and I always told her about how wonderful the things you made for me were. I wasn't the least bit surprised to find you working here."

Emma nodded but was unsure of what to say.

"I already talked to Margaret about my plans and she suggested you for the job mainly because she knew that you'd be good at it."

"I'm not going to take her customers from her. If you've come here for years, why hire me?"

"Oh, Emma," she said wearily, "you have created quite a hole in our lives. I don't think any of us realized just how big of a part of our family you were until you weren't there. William didn't just lose an assistant, he lost a friend. And I lost my brownie supplier." She laughed, and Emma couldn't help but join in.

"I know that you think things may be...awkward if you do this party for me, but I can guarantee you that I am the only Montgomery that you will have to see. You and I will work on the menu and you'll bring everything in before anyone arrives at the club. Please say yes, Emma. I would really appreciate your help with this. I trust you to help make this party special."

How was Emma supposed to say no to that? There was

a war waging within her and as much as she wanted to say yes—to give herself a shot not only at helping someone who had always been kind to her, but to take that first step toward changing her career—she just couldn't do it.

"I'm sorry, I really am, but I just can't. I'm…I'm just not ready to take that chance on seeing…"

"Lucas?"

Emma nodded and cursed the tears that were beginning to well up. "I know you said that I'd get in and out of there before I'd have to see anyone, but I just can't take that chance." She looked up at the older woman and smiled sadly. "I'm not ready to take that kind of risk."

Monica looked at Emma and her heart broke. Her family had done this to her. The once vibrant and joyful young woman was now emotionally devastated, and it was all her son's and husband's fault. She wanted to smack them both right now.

"Emma, tell me what I can do? How can I make this right?"

Swiping a stray tear away, Emma cleared her throat. "I wish there was something you could do, I really do. But this is just the way that it has to be."

Shaking her head, Monica refused to admit defeat. "No, I don't accept that. I'm going to be a bit of a brat right now and say what should have been said a long time ago." Squaring her shoulders, she looked Emma in the eye. "I'm not going to make excuses for my husband or for Lucas; that's not my place. In this whole rotten situation, you were the victim. I know Lucas likes to play that part, but this time he's out of luck. I was furious when I found out what happened when Lucas confronted the both of you and as much as it pains me, he hasn't come home since."

"Oh no," Emma gasped. "Surely you saw him for Christmas?"

The older woman shook her head. "Not a phone call or a card."

"That's horrible! Dammit," she said with disgust, "I cannot believe he would do that to you!"

A laugh escaped before Monica could stop it. "To me? Sweetheart, I didn't extend those to him either. I'm appalled by his behavior and I'm tired of tiptoeing around him. He's a grown man and it's time he took some responsibility for his actions. To that end I can say with great certainty that Lucas will *not* be at this party."

"No! He's your son! Surely you'll make up by the time the party comes around."

"It's doubtful, and you know what? There's a lot less tension with Lucas back in hiding. For far too long this whole family has been on edge trying not to do or say anything that would upset him and I'm tired of it. He's my son and I love him, but for two years we've all made him the focus of everything and it's time to move on to something else. William and I have had thirty-five wonderful years of marriage and as much as I'd like to stay mad at him, I can't. I want this party, I deserve this party, and I am going to have this party no matter what!"

Emma couldn't help but smile. "Good for you."

"That said, young lady, you are the only one I want to do the desserts. You don't have to worry about Lucas; there isn't a snowball's chance in hell of him making an appearance. You will most likely risk seeing William but I think that between the two he is the lesser threat to your well-being." She leaned forward and took Emma's hand. "You have no reason to be in hiding, Emma. If anything, you should walk into that club with your head held high that you stood up for what was right and refused to be a part of this ridiculous game."

As far as pep talks went it was a good one. Emma chewed her bottom lip as she thought about it. "I don't know that I can do all of the baking. My kitchen isn't big enough."

"Use this one." They both turned and saw Margaret Dupre standing behind the counter. She walked toward them and smiled. "Emma, you have a passion for baking and the energy to make it happen. I'm getting to the point where it's just a chore to me. Monica knows what she wants and you can make her party perfect. Use the kitchen here. I really don't mind."

"But...but..." Emma stammered looking from one woman to the next. "It just feels wrong to use your facility for this. I can pay you for the time!" she suggested but Margaret just waved her off.

"You want to know how you can pay me?" Margaret asked. "Do a fantastic job and promise me that when you are ready to admit that you want to do this full-time that you'll let me know, because I can't think of anyone better to take over this business for me."

Emma's heart was beating so wildly that she thought she was surely going to pass out. "Are you serious? I didn't even know that you wanted out!"

"I've been toying with it for a while but I didn't want to get serious about it until I found the perfect person who was going to love it like I once did. You can do that, Emma. You have a gift and the customers love you. Do this party for the Montgomerys and get the word out that you're taking over this bakery. The place will be packed with customers the way it used to be."

She didn't know what to say. It was all too much. It wasn't every day that you got handed what you wanted without really trying. It was too good an opportunity to pass up. She could handle seeing William and the threat of Lucas was gone. Emma turned to Monica Montgomery and smiled widely. "I'll do it!"

The weeks that followed were the kind that Emma thrived on. She was learning the business of running a bakery while meeting with new clients on catering special events. The Montgomerys' anniversary party was her first priority, and she was pleased with the progress they were making.

Besides a traditional yet customized cake that would be their centerpiece, Monica had requested at least a dozen different kinds of cakes, cookies, and pastries for her guests to enjoy. They had met several times to finalize the menu and Emma was thrilled with what they had decided upon. From cheesecake bites to truffles and gourmet cupcakes, Emma was certain that her desserts were going to be a definite hit with the guests.

The party was set for Valentine's Day weekend and although it was a little cliché, the Montgomerys had indeed gotten married on February fourteenth. She knew this as a fact because in her years working for them, she'd been responsible for making dinner reservations.

The thought of Valentine's Day was always depressing for a single woman, and it was even more so for Emma because she was spending the day ensuring the happiness of a couple who had been blessed with thirty-five years of marriage. She only wished that someday she'd get to hit that kind of milestone with someone.

"Any chance of there being any of those peanut butter mousse cupcakes?" a male voice said from behind her.

Emma whirled around and genuinely smiled. "Jason! How are you?"

"I'm good, thanks. Mom said that you were taking over this place and she brought home some amazing cupcakes yesterday and I must have eaten about half a dozen of them. Have pity on me, Em!" He laughed. "Are there anymore left?"

She laughed with him. Jason had always been so nice to her, and she realized that she actually had missed him. "For you? I think I can scrounge up a few." Emma turned and walked to one of her display cases and boxed up another half dozen for him. Handing the box to him, she waved his money away. "On the house."

"Emma, that's a surefire way to go out of business. Please, let me pay for these."

"Your money's no good here," she teased. "Consider them my gift to you for the day that you took me to go and pick up my car."

Jason rolled his eyes. "That's just crazy. It was Dad's fault that you needed to go and get the car. You don't owe me anything."

"Then consider them a gift to a friend," she said simply. "And promise not to share with anyone."

"Done!" he said. "The place looks great, Emma. Mom is so excited that you're doing the desserts for the party. But tell me the truth: Are these cupcakes on the menu?"

She laughed again. "They aren't, but I promise that the ones that are on the menu are even better!"

"Not possible, but I guess I'll just have to wait and find out." He looked around the shop again before facing

Emma. "Are you doing okay? I mean, this is a complete one-eighty from what you were doing at Montgomerys."

"I am more than okay. Baking was always something that I loved but never had the courage to think about as a career. Between your mom and Margaret, I'm making a go of it."

"Will I see you at the party?" he asked.

"Probably not. I'll be bringing everything over before any of the guests arrive. I'm just the hired help that day." It wasn't said with any form of malice, she was simply stating a fact.

"Well, that's just not right. I think you should get to stay and enjoy the festivities. If nothing else, you should get to sit and collect all of the compliments the desserts are going to garner!"

"You're sweet, but with the agreement that your mom has with the club, they will have people to do the serving and so really, all I need to do is drop everything off."

"Seems a shame, Emma," he said and then paused. "We miss you."

"Thanks, Jason. I miss everyone too," she admitted honestly. Emma knew that by everyone she was implying the office staff, but it was really more than that. If Jason caught on to that fact, he chose to say nothing.

"Well, maybe I'll see you at the party. I'll try to get there early just in case you need a hand."

"Take care of yourself," she said, hoping he realized that she wasn't encouraging him to visit with her again. The fewer Montgomerys she saw, the more intact her heart would stay.

Chapter 14

Valentine's Day dawned cold and gray. Snow was in the forecast, and Emma was more than a little nervous about transporting dessert for two hundred people. Her purchase of the bakery had been completed the previous week and one of the things she'd invested in was a delivery van. Her staff helped her load everything into the van and she had been assured that there would be staff at the country club to help her unload.

Since there was a chance that she'd be seen by some of the guests, Emma had chosen to dress up. Wearing a deep purple wool wrap dress that was cut modestly low in the front and had a full skirt, she felt that should she get caught staying longer than planned, she'd be able to blend into the crowd. For the transport and set up, she wore conservative shoes but had a pair of matching heels in her bag just in case.

Things went from bad to worse almost instantly. The club was short on staff and could only spare her a few minutes to move the heavier items into the catering hall. Emma glanced around and silently prayed that Jason would be true to his word and arrive early.

He did not.

Once the cake was set up as the centerpiece of the dessert station with the help of the few staff members she'd been able to utilize, Emma went to work on getting the rest of the desserts set up and displayed properly. She was halfway through when Monica and William showed up.

"Oh, Emma! Everything looks beautiful!" Monica gushed. "William, doesn't everything look wonderful?" Her husband nodded and simply smiled with gratitude at Emma. "How is everything going?"

"Well," Emma began, unsure if she should be the bearer of bad news.

"Is there a problem?" William asked.

"It seems that the club is a little short staffed today, so there wasn't enough help for me. I was able to get everything in but I'm afraid I'm a little behind on the setup. I was hoping to be done and gone by the time you had arrived." At the crestfallen look on William's face, she corrected herself. "Not because I didn't want to see you, but because I didn't want you to see things still being set up. I wanted everything to be perfect for your arrival."

"We certainly appreciate that, Emma," he replied. "Tell us what you need and we'll give you a hand."

"Oh, no! Please don't!" she cried. "It's your party and you shouldn't have to do any of this!"

"Nonsense. We were promised a full staff and I will be having words with the event manager over that. In the meantime, let's get this all set up."

As much as Emma wanted to argue, she wanted to get the setup done so she could leave even more. In less than twenty minutes, between the three of them, the table was completed and looked exactly as she had pictured it in her mind. She couldn't have been more pleased.

"Emma," Monica began, her throat clogging with tears, "it's more beautiful than I ever imagined. The cake is just…stunning." It was a multitiered cake, each layer a different flavor, and it was decorated with all the milestones from the Montgomerys' life together. "And all of the pastries…it's a cake lover's dream!"

"I'm glad you're pleased," Emma said, visibly relaxing for the first time in hours. "Now, you go and enjoy your party. Congratulations to you both." She turned to grab her bag when she felt William's hand on her arm. She stood and faced him.

"Actually, Emma, we were hoping you would stay and celebrate with us," he said shyly. "You were the icing on the cake, so to speak, in making this day be everything that my lovely wife envisioned, and it would mean a great deal to us if you'd stay."

"Oh, I don't know," she said, indecision weighing heavily on her mind. Part of Emma wanted to make a mad dash for the door, while the other looked around the room and marveled at what a spectacular party they were going to have.

"If it makes you feel any better, you can help cut the cake and serve when the time comes," Monica said.

"Oh, what the hell," she said. "Why not?" And just like that, she was swept up into a big embrace by the two Montgomerys who were flanking her. "Okay, okay, the two of you have a party to host and your guests should be arriving shortly. Let me go and freshen my makeup and put on my party shoes and then we can start celebrating!" She hugged them both and then went in search of the powder room.

"I thought she'd put up more of a fight," William said, watching Emma walk away.

"I think she misses you as much as you miss her. She

just needed to have the excuse to stay." Leaning over and kissing her husband, Monica smiled.

"What was that for?" he asked, his own smile spreading.

"For thirty-five wonderful years." William leaned in and kissed her properly. He could still make her swoon after all these years. "Now, let's go and greet some guests."

Emma was enjoying herself thoroughly. She didn't think it was possible, but she was surrounded by most of the Montgomery family and having a wonderful time. Both Jason and Mac had danced with her until her feet hurt, and she couldn't remember the last time she had laughed so much.

The dinner menu had been elaborate and it was almost time for dessert to be served. Excusing herself, she went in search of the event manager to see what role she needed to play in that particular part of the evening.

"I know you're a bit short staffed, so if you need me to assist in cutting and plating the cake, I'd be more than happy to help," Emma said.

"Thanks, Emma," the woman replied. "We got extra staff to come in so I think we're going to be okay. Sorry about earlier."

"It was no big deal; it's what I'm paid to do."

"Well, you were promised staff to help you, and you ended up doing the bulk of it by yourself—along with the Montgomerys." She cringed. "Not my finest hour."

Emma laughed. "No worries, we all know that sometimes things happen that are beyond our control. Besides, everything worked out and looks great."

"Your display is magnificent. I'd like to meet with you next week and see if maybe we can work out some other events together. The baker here is fine for small events, but we would love to have someone who could handle the more specialty end of it, and if this is what you can provide, we'd love to do business with you."

Emma was floored. An account like this would be huge for her business. Pulling a business card from her purse, she handed it over. "Give me a call. I think we can definitely work something out." They shook hands and Emma watched as the other woman walked away before doing a little happy dance in place and then hoped that no one noticed.

With a quick glance around, she straightened her skirt and made some last-minute adjustments on the dessert table when someone spoke from behind her.

"May I have this dance?"

Emma froze. It wasn't possible. There was no way this family could possibly lie to her again! And she fell for it! Dammit! Taking her time fanning some napkins and turning a few cupcakes to optimize their appearance, Emma finally turned around and faced Lucas. She couldn't make herself utter a word; she simply stared defiantly at him.

Lucas wasn't sure what to expect when he saw Emma, but the woman staring coolly at him was definitely not it. Clearly he had his work cut out for him. Without saying a word, he merely held out a hand to her and waited for her to take it.

"You're kidding, right?" she finally said.

One dark eyebrow arched at her. "About asking you to dance? No, I don't really kid about stuff like that."

"I'm not dancing with you, Lucas," Emma snapped.

Looking around the room, Lucas turned back to her and leaned in close. "People are watching. You don't want to make a scene, do you?"

Oh, she wanted to make a scene; she wanted to make a great big epic scene where she screamed the room down and raged at all of the ways the Montgomerys weren't to be trusted. Ever! But Emma saw that they, indeed, had an audience. She reluctantly took his hand and let Lucas lead her out onto the dance floor for the slow song the band was playing.

Her goal had been to remain silent but her curiosity got the best of her. "What are you doing here, Lucas?"

"I thought that would be obvious; it's my parents' anniversary."

Growling with frustration, Emma glared at him. "I know it's their anniversary. What I mean is everyone said you weren't coming, that they hadn't seen you in months. Why show up now?"

"As I said, it's their anniversary and I wanted to be here. And for the record, I have seen them."

"Figures," she mumbled.

"Excuse me?" he said, a smile tugging at his lips.

"I said it figures," she hissed. "Your family seems to excel at lying, particularly to me."

"And that's a bad thing?" he asked, spinning her gently as he tugged her a little bit closer.

"Yes, Lucas, lying is a bad thing and I don't appreciate it at all. I trusted your parents. I took this job because they promised that you wouldn't be here. I kept my word, but apparently they didn't feel the need to do the same."

"Well, maybe they did it for a good reason."

Emma pulled back slightly and stared at him as if he'd lost his mind. "And what could that possibly be?"

It didn't take much to pull her back into his embrace, and Lucas just let himself feel for a moment before speaking again. "Let me ask you something. Why did you quit Montgomerys?"

"Who said I quit?"

"Are you still working there?"

She rolled her eyes. "You know I'm not, Lucas. I couldn't possibly cater this event if I was. And what does that have to do with anything?"

"Why'd you quit?"

"It was time to move on," she said simply, wondering when the hell the band was going to finish the damn song so she could get out of this nightmare.

"Liar," he whispered up against her ear and smiled when he felt her shiver.

When she went to pull away, Lucas merely held her tighter. "Let me go," she demanded quietly.

"No." He felt more than heard her sigh.

"Lucas, now is not the time for this conversation. Please let me go."

"Tell me why you left Montgomerys."

"You're not going to let this go, are you?"

"The band was told to keep playing until I told them to stop," he said lightly, rubbing his cheek next to hers. "So really, the quicker you talk to me, the sooner those poor guys can get a break and people can have their dessert."

"You're a real bastard, you know that?"

"I never claimed to be otherwise."

"Fine," she huffed. "I heard your entire conversation with your father that day. I was horrified that he would do something like that and use me that way. I couldn't work for him anymore. I don't respect him."

"And why wasn't I allowed to know?" Lucas leaned back and looked into her face, amused at how her blue eyes, normally so full of joy, were now shooting daggers at him.

"Because it wasn't about you and it didn't concern you. I left because of what he did to me," she said adamantly. "And your ego is so huge that you would have thought that it was all about you."

"True enough, but a lie is still a lie, Em."

Now she looked at him with confusion. "Excuse me?"

"You're standing here right now, in my arms, and you're lying to me." He turned them again on the dance floor and smiled at the band before giving her his full attention again.

"How am I lying to you?" she demanded, struggling to put some distance between them.

"I think that you were angry with my father and rightfully so. But I think that you could have forgiven him."

"Then you don't really know me."

Lucas leaned in and nuzzled the side of her neck before whispering in her ear, "Oh, I think I know you better than you think. I believe that had I not gone off and had such a temper tantrum before talking to my father and if I hadn't accused you of such horrible things, you would have stayed on at Montgomerys. You would have made Dad grovel, but you would have stayed. I'm the real reason that you left and you didn't want to add more fuel to the fire between me and Dad."

"You're crazy."

"Maybe." He shrugged and lifted his face so he could look into her eyes. "But look me in the eye right here, right now, Emma, and tell me that I'm wrong. Tell me that I'm not the reason you left." His voice was low, but fierce, and Lucas felt that his entire future hinged on this one moment.

"What difference will it make? I'm done with Montgomerys: the company and the family." Emma's bravado faltered slightly and the longer she looked into Lucas's eyes, the more lost and confused she became. Lucas continued to watch her, and Emma felt as if all conversation around them had stopped. The band kept playing and all she wanted was to run and hide.

What was one more lie? Everyone else seemed to be okay with lying to her, why should she feel guilty about speaking one of her own? But she couldn't do it. "Lucas, I refuse to answer that question. Now stop the band, please," she said firmly and nearly fell to the floor as Lucas released her. His eyes were fierce, burning into her.

They stood there like that for what seemed like an eternity before Lucas turned toward the band and nodded his head. "Thank you for the dance, Emma," he said softly and then turned to walk away.

And that's when she noticed it.

"You're not limping," she said out loud before she could stop herself.

Lucas turned and looked at her. "No, I'm not. I don't plan on limping much in the future either."

Emma took a step toward him. "Why not?"

"I had the surgeries done," he said matter-of-factly.

"I've got a lot more rehab to go through, and there are still times when my knee gives me some trouble, but unless I really overdo it, I don't limp."

She was stunned. "Oh, well…good for you. I'm happy for you, Lucas. Really. Maybe now you can finally be happy." Knowing that at any moment she was going to burst into tears, she said a hasty good-bye before fleeing the room.

Running blindly down a hallway, Emma didn't stop until she found an empty parlor room. Quickly shutting the door behind her, she collapsed into one of the chairs and tried to catch her breath. She'd just pretty much made a spectacle out of herself in the middle of the party. She'd been in Lucas's arms and it had felt so good, something that she'd ached for, and she'd gone and walked away.

"I'm a damn idiot," she mumbled and slouched further into the chair.

"No, that's me, I'm afraid," Lucas said from the doorway.

Emma spun and looked at him. "What are you doing here?"

He chuckled and shut the door behind him. "I thought we already covered that. Twice. The anniversary party? My parents? Any of this ringing a bell?"

"I mean in here, Lucas? Why are you in here? In this room?" she asked, full of exasperation.

"Because it's where you are, Em," he replied. "That's where I want to be always, where you are."

No words had ever sounded sweeter, but she was afraid just to give in. "I'm still mad at you, Lucas," she admitted weakly.

"I know," he said softly as he came to kneel in front of her and placed a finger over her lips when she went to protest. "I said some pretty hateful stuff that I wish I could take back and erase. Do you think you might be able to forgive me some day?"

Emma stared deeply into his eyes and knew that she already had. The man had that effect on her. "Why did you have the surgeries? You were so set against them."

Leaning forward, Lucas rested his forehead against hers. "I was scared to. It was safe to stay injured because I knew what to expect. I was afraid of being disappointed again. Having the surgeries and still not being able to do the things that I wanted to? It was too much for me." He raised his head and looked at her. "Then all the things you said to me came to mind and you were right; I wasn't really living. I was going through the motions, and not very well. I wanted to be able to do all of the things that we did together without having pain. There were more things I wanted us to do together but we couldn't because of my limitations."

"Oh, Lucas, I don't want to be the reason you did this!" Emma cried, a lone tear streaming down her cheek. "You needed to do this for you!"

"Without you, Em, I'm nothing. I wanted to do this for us. I want to be the man who takes you dancing or hiking or skiing or on endless shopping sprees to furniture stores that are way too big for any normal person to go through on the average day," he teased. "I want to see what this new life has to offer me now that I'm okay with no longer being Lucas Montgomery, football star."

"I heard that guy wasn't all that," she said.

"He was certainly lacking in the most important part of his life."

"What part was that?"

"His heart, Em. For all of his athletic skills, he didn't have a heart and he certainly didn't have you." Not wanting to wait another minute, Lucas claimed Emma's lips with his own. It had been too long and he needed to taste her more than he needed his next breath. When they finally resurfaced, Lucas took a steadying breath. "Tell me I'm not too late, that I didn't wait too long. Tell me that we still have a chance for a future."

Emma ran a hand over his cheek, down the strong column of his throat, studying him, unable to find the words to tell him how much she was feeling.

"I love you, Em. I have for a long time and I know I should have said it before. I should never have walked away from you or doubted what we had. I'm so sorry for that."

"I love you, too, Lucas," she whispered, completely in awe of how much she actually did. "You scare me to death with how strong my feelings are for you and it nearly killed me when you walked away."

"I'll never leave you again, I swear it. Tell me you forgive me," he pleaded.

Emma leaned in and kissed him again. "There's nothing to forgive. We both needed time to be able to get to this place."

"I don't know about that. I've been miserable without you. So many times I wanted to come and see you, but I didn't want to do it until after I'd had some time to heal."

She sighed. "I wish I had been there to help you," she

said sadly. "I would have helped you, Lucas. Who was there for you?"

"My brothers. It took me a little while to get things right with my father but pretty much as soon as Jason took you to get your car, he came to my house and pretty firmly put me in my place. I couldn't even argue with him because, like you, he was right. I made the call the next day and got the surgery scheduled."

"But your mom said…"

"I know," he said, stroking a hand down her cheek, wanting nothing more than to keep touching her. "The truth is that I didn't see them for a long time. I went to New York to have the surgeries and didn't tell anyone where I was going because I didn't want anyone coming to see me. I had to do this for myself. I missed Christmas and New Year's, but all with a good reason."

Emma shook her head.

"Don't be mad at them. They didn't mean to mislead you; they were just letting me handle this my own way. You know I'm not good with social graces," he said with a smile, reminding her of the time she had accused him of that. "I promise to get better."

"I don't want you to get better, Lucas. I love you just as you are."

Standing, Lucas held his hand out to Emma and helped her to her feet. "I would be honored if you'd accompany me back to the party, Em."

She turned and glanced out the wall of windows. "Oh, look, it's snowing!" she said with wonder.

Lucas led her to the window and then stood behind her and wrapped his arms around her middle. "Then I think we should head to your place."

Emma turned her head and looked at him questioningly. "Why? I don't think it's supposed to accumulate too much."

"Doesn't matter," he said, holding her a little tighter. "The thought of possibly getting snowed in together is too good an opportunity to pass up."

Unable to help herself, Emma grinned. "Well then, we better get going. I'd hate for one of us to end up in another ditch and have to spend any time recovering."

"Darlin', the only recovering you have to worry about is from our making up for lost time."

Emma totally liked the sound of that.

Epilogue

"You're looking pretty smug over there, Dad," Lucas said as he adjusted his tie.

William lifted his champagne glass to his son and smiled. "I'm not going to lie to you, I'm feeling pretty smug."

"Yeah, yeah, yeah… We've already thanked you enough for your interference."

"You make it sound like a bad thing. All I did was give the two of you a little push in the right direction. You may have figured it out eventually but I'm not getting any younger and I want grandchildren."

Lucas rolled his eyes. "Really? You're going to start with that today? It's our wedding day; we're focused on getting down the aisle and going on a much needed honeymoon, and you're starting the grandchildren guilt trip already? Isn't that Mom's job?"

"Oh, don't worry; she's champing at the bit, too. I just beat her to it."

"Lucky me."

William stood and helped Lucas finish with the tie he'd been fidgeting with for almost ten minutes. "You're not nervous, are you?" he finally asked.

"What if I hurt her?"

For a moment, all William could do was look at his son with a combination of amusement and sympathy. "We all get hurt at some point in a relationship, Lucas. It happens a lot in a marriage. Even the best ones have someone getting hurt at one point or another. The key is to apologize when you do hurt her and learn from your mistakes. No one expects you to be perfect."

"I want to be perfect for Emma; she deserves that."

"Son, do you know your future wife at all? Has Emma ever asked for perfection?" Lucas shook his head. "All she wants is you. Be yourself and that will make Emma happy."

Deep down, Lucas knew his father was right. In the six months since his parents' anniversary party, there hadn't been a day that had gone by where Lucas didn't say a prayer of thanks that Emma had given him another chance. Their wedding was set in motion before they had gone to bed that first night while the snow was gently falling outside.

"Hey, are you ready?" Lucas turned to see Jason standing in the doorway and Mac crowding the space behind him.

For once, Lucas didn't need to think about his answer. He was ready for whatever the future had in store for him, and looked forward to the endless possibilities of a future with Emma.

Prologue

William Montgomery was feeling pretty good about himself. As the orchestra played, he watched his youngest son Lucas dancing with his new bride, Emma. They made a beautiful couple and as far as William was concerned, his role as matchmaker was a complete success.

Looking around the room, he saw that everyone was laughing and smiling and having a good time. It filled his heart with joy. This time last year, Lucas was a brooding loner who had cut himself off from just about every aspect of life. But thanks to William's interference, and the help of Mother Nature, Lucas had found himself and fallen in love with the beautiful Emma Taylor, now Emma Montgomery. William had no doubt that there'd be a grandchild in his near future.

A server came over to refill his champagne, and William smiled at him. Why hadn't he thought to do this before? He had three sons who seemed content to stay single. Well, now he had only two to worry about. Mac and Jason were both over by the bar talking with some business colleagues. Why were they talking business when there were eligible women in the room?

William sighed wearily. His sons seemed clueless where women were concerned, at least as far as he could tell. Not that he thought either of them was living the life of a monk, but it would be nice if one of them had a girlfriend.

Or at least a date for their brother's wedding.

"Stop frowning, William, it's our son's wedding." His beautiful wife of thirty-five years came and sat down beside him, placing a gentle kiss on his cheek. "There's nothing to frown about today."

"Says you," he mumbled.

"What could you possibly have to be unhappy about? Emma and Lucas are deliriously happy and in love. The wedding is lovely and everyone is having a good time."

"Look at them." He motioned to their sons by the bar.

"What about them?" she asked.

"When are they going to find women and fall in love and get married?"

"Oh, William, for crying out loud. We're not even done with this wedding and you're already trying to plan the next one?" she laughed.

"I just want to see them happy."

"Who says they're not?"

"Do you remember Lucas a year ago?" he asked, taking his eyes from his sons to focus on his wife.

"You cannot compare Jason and Mac to what Lucas was going through; the situations are completely different."

"On some levels, yes. But basically they are too wrapped up in business to have relationships. I don't want them to work their lives away. They deserve to have the kind of love that Lucas and Emma have, and that you and I have."

She smiled and cupped a hand to her husband's cheek before leaning in and kissing him softly on his lips.

"What was that for?"

"For being wonderful."

He smiled. "I know that for a while Lucas wasn't thrilled with me for interfering in his life, but maybe this time—"

"Don't you dare!" she scolded. "You were lucky where Lucas and Emma were concerned. They already had feelings for one another. You just had to nudge them along. Neither Jace nor Mac are in that position."

"Not yet," William said, turning to kiss his wife again and then watching as she stood to go and talk with some of their guests.

William Montgomery was feeling good about himself right now. He had a purpose and a plan was beginning to form. All he needed was for lightning to strike twice.

Chapter 1

"SHE HAS TO BE MARRIED."

"Excuse me?"

"Whoever it is that we choose, she has to be married." Jason Montgomery was adamant on this point. There was no way he was going to get caught with someone else looking to snag the wealthy boss.

"This is about Lucas, isn't it?" The head of human resources eyed him with a mix of suspicion and humor. In her late fifties, Ann Kincade had been with Montgomerys for almost twenty years and had watched William Montgomery's sons grow up. "Honestly, Jason, you are making a big deal out of nothing."

"Am I?" he asked incredulously. "Ever since Lucas and Emma got together, I have gone through four different assistants. Why? Because now they all think they can hook up with the boss."

"That's a slight exaggeration, Jason," she admonished.

"Is it?" He stood and began to pace his office. "First there was Rose—"

"Rose got promoted to being your father's assistant when Emma left. That had nothing to do with you."

Jason sighed with frustration. "That wasn't what I was going to say. When Rose moved over to the main suite, you replaced her with Janice."

"She was a very nice woman. Great organizational skills."

"She was a damn stalker who I found watching me through the bushes at home with binoculars!"

"Okay, I'll give you that one. But then there was Lynda—"

"Cougar on the prowl. She didn't want to work; she wanted to find a rich, *younger* husband to take care of her."

"And her typing skills sucked."

One of Jason's dark eyebrows arched at that comment, but he said nothing. "Then there was Claire." He stopped and stood in front of Ann, his arms crossed over his chest. "Do I even need to remind you of that little debacle?"

Ann looked down at her pile of files in her lap. "I still think it wasn't what it looked like."

"The woman was sprawled out on my desk in her underwear. How could that be misinterpreted?" he shouted. A growl of frustration escaped before he could stop it, and he raked a hand through his hair. "Now I have this trip coming up that I need to take an assistant on and I don't have an assistant! I'm walking around on eggshells here because I feel like everywhere I turn, there is someone looking to marry me!"

"We'll have to put an ad out and look for male assistants," Ann suggested.

"There's no time for that, and what if he's gay?"

Ann let out a hearty laugh before she could help it. "Oh, Jason, do you hear yourself? Now you think that men are going to be after you, too?"

He sat back down behind his desk and put his face in his hands. "I'm going crazy here, Ann. I have a lot to do to prep for this trip. There's a lot riding on it and I can't

spare the time to fend off women who are hoping to be the next Mrs. Montgomery."

"Is it absolutely necessary for you to have someone go with you?" she asked seriously.

"It's a long trip, with meetings set up with dozens of potential clients. I need someone to be with me taking notes and organizing contracts and getting them back here to the office. I can't do it all myself. As it is this went from a ten-day trip to about three weeks. What am I supposed to do?"

"That's a long time to ask anyone to travel with you, especially if they're married. No one is going to want to be away from their spouse for three weeks."

Jason frowned. "Damn, I hadn't thought of that."

Ann started sorting through the employment profiles she held in her lap. "As of right now there are no male candidates. You could always take one of the junior execs with you to—"

Jason shook his head. "No, the ones I talked with can't be spared for that length of time."

"What about a temp?"

Again he shook his head. "I need someone with a working knowledge of the company. I won't have time for hand holding and training. I need someone who can step right in and get to work. I've got less than two weeks before I leave and I'll need every minute of it to get organized."

Placing the files down on Jason's desk, Ann stood and frowned. "What you're asking is impossible."

"I'm relying on you to make it possible," he countered.

"Jason, be reasonable."

"I would love to be reasonable, Ann, believe me.

Right now there is nothing about this situation that makes things easy for me, either. I cannot afford to take someone with me who 'accidentally' shows up in my bed or worse, makes a spectacle of themselves at a corporate event. I don't want to lead anyone on or give them the impression that they are with me to play corporate wife!"

She stared at him until Jason started to feel like he was going to squirm. "I'll see what I do, Jace, but I can't make promises."

He nodded and then she was gone.

Maggie Barrett did her best to live her life under the radar.

Getting called into the boss's office did not fit with that motto.

She had barely stepped into the executive suite when William Montgomery's assistant Rose told her that Mr. Montgomery was expecting her. With a heavy sigh, and a straightened spine, she walked through the doors.

"Maggie!" William Montgomery boomed. "How have you been?"

Taking the seat he indicated, Maggie sat down and swallowed the nervous lump in her throat before responding. "Fine, sir. How are you?"

"Great, can't complain," he said with a sincere smile and then he reached for a folder that was on his desk. His expression turned slightly more serious as he read the contents. Quietly he closed the folder and studied Maggie. "Ann tells me that you were offered a promotion."

Maggie nodded. "Yes, sir, I was."

"And that you turned it down."

Again, she nodded.

"Care to tell me why?"

"I'm perfectly happy with the position I have."

"You are overqualified for the position you have, Maggie; you and I both know that. Now why don't you tell me why you really turned down the job as Jason's assistant." His tone was firm but gentle.

Her shoulders sagged slightly. "You know why I took this job, Mr. Montgomery. I'm not looking to be anyone's assistant ever again. I'm very happy working in customer service."

"Answering phones all day is maddening," he replied. "The move up to an assistant would mean that other people would be fielding the calls, and you could do the kind of work that you are more than capable of doing."

It probably wouldn't look good for her to cry in front of her boss. Not that he hadn't seen her do that before, but it wasn't something she wanted to repeat. "I appreciate your concern, Mr. Montgomery, I really do. I'm just not willing to be put into that type of situation ever again. I can't." Her voice trembled on the last word and Maggie silently cursed herself for showing weakness.

"Maggie," he began hesitantly, "I am not the type of person who throws his weight around. I think you know that about me." She nodded. "We have a situation that you are the only one qualified for. I'm not asking you if you want the position, I'm telling you that I want you to take the position."

Maggie's head snapped up as she stared at him with eyes wide. "But you know why—"

William held up a hand to stop her. "Believe me, I remember quite well why you feel the way you do and I think that by now you should know that I am one of the good guys. Have I ever done anything to make you doubt me?"

Silently, Maggie shook her head.

"Have I asked anything of you in all of the time you've worked for me?"

Again she shook her head as she stared down at the floor.

"I wouldn't ask this of you if it wasn't important. You are the only person I can trust for this assignment."

Raising her head, her brown eyes filled with tears, she asked, "Why? Why me?"

William sighed. "Ever since Lucas and Emma fell in love, Jason has had sort of a target on his back. We can't seem to keep an assistant for him. He's been stalked, propositioned…you name it, these women have done it. Most men would be flattered, but Jason takes his work very seriously and he needs someone who'll do the same."

"I still don't understand how this involves me."

"When I took you in with Montgomerys, Maggie, you asked me to do what I could to protect you, right?" She nodded. "One of the things that I did was lie for you. As far as anyone in the company knows, you are a married woman. You and I are the only ones here who know differently."

Maggie considered his words. "So you think since everyone believes me to be married that I'm a safe bet for Jason's assistant?"

"That's exactly what I'm thinking. Jason isn't looking

to seduce anyone and he certainly isn't looking to be seduced. I would think that you, more than anyone, can understand his position."

She blushed. Maggie tried never to think about the way that she had come to work for William Montgomery, and in the three years she'd been here, this was the first time they'd referred to it. "I can respect the situation, sir; I just don't feel comfortable—"

"Maggie?" he interrupted gently. "It's time. You've hidden yourself down in customer service long enough. I hired you without knowing a damn thing about you: the woman I met needed help, and I gave it. I'm asking you to return the favor."

How could she say no to that? The man had given her a safe haven, a job where she didn't feel hunted, or that she was there for any other reason than her work. "How can I be sure I won't find myself in the same situation I was in when you met me?"

William's expression softened as he looked at her. "Maggie, I give you my word that you will never, ever find yourself in such a position. Not with Jason and not with anyone here at Montgomerys."

She stood and looked down at her boss. A simple nod of her head was the only response she gave.

William rose to his feet and faced her. "If at any time, for any reason, you feel like something isn't right, I want you to promise me that you'll call. I'll believe whatever it is you tell me and I'll get you out of there, okay?"

Again, all she could do was nod.

"I'll let Ann know to get the paperwork started. I'll also let Rose know that you'll be working with her the rest of the week to get acquainted with things up

here and arrange for you to meet with Jason." A wild look of panic crossed Maggie's face and William made a quick decision. "We'll meet with him together, you and me, okay?"

Maggie took a steadying breath and agreed.

Then silently prayed that she hadn't just made the second biggest mistake of her life.

Trapped.

That was the only word that came to Maggie's mind as she frantically tried to figure a way out of the situation. She could either go back upstairs to the hotel room that her boss had reserved for the two of them—unbeknownst to her—or she could sleep on the street.

Martin Blake had been the model boss; for a year she'd been his executive assistant, and never in her wildest dreams could she have imagined that something like this would happen to her.

Maggie looked around the lobby—in search of what, she didn't know. She had no money, no form of transportation, and no form of ID. Martin had seen to that. They were three thousand miles from home on the other side of the country. He was smart to choose now to hatch his disgusting plan. There actually was a conference going on, but Martin had very little interest in it; his focus was seducing Maggie.

She felt sick. Any moment she was sure she was going to be ill. Collapsing on one of the opulent sofas in the hotel lobby, tears began to fall. "What am I going to do?" she cried gently, knowing that no one was there to answer her.

"Excuse me, miss," a gentle voice asked. "Are you okay?"

Tears streaming down her face, Maggie looked up and saw a man, probably in his late fifties, staring down at her, his face one of calm concern. Who was he? Did Martin send him to find her?

"I...I'm fine," she lied.

The man sat down at the opposite end of the sofa, not wanting to scare her more than she obviously was. "Are you sure? Is there someone I can call for you?"

The thing was, there wasn't anyone Maggie felt she could call about this situation. She didn't want to alarm her family; she had no close friends who would be able to pay for a flight home for her—especially when she had no ID to present when she got to the airport. Shaking her head, a fresh wave of tears began to fall.

"Whatever it is, I'm sure it will be okay. Please, tell me what's going on? Do we need to call the hotel management? The police?"

As much as Maggie had wanted to say yes, Martin's taunting words came to mind. As she had been clawing to get out of the hotel room he mocked, "Go ahead and call the cops or hotel security. I'll just tell them we had a lovers' spat and you are trying to blackmail the boss. I believe they call that extortion, and it's a crime, Mags."

"No!" she cried, coming back to the present. "No, please...no one needs to call the cops or security. I'll...I'll be fine."

The man looked at her with obvious disbelief. He had a briefcase at his feet and he reached for it, pulling it into his lap and opening it. Without a word, he handed her his card. "I'm William Montgomery. I'm from

Charlotte, North Carolina. That's where my company is, too. It's been in my family for three generations and, God willing, it will go to my sons and they'll carry on long after I'm gone. I've got three sons; always wanted a daughter, though," he said lightly.

"I don't normally come to these conventions; seems like a great waste of time. Most of the attendees are here looking for a break from work, not to learn more about how to do their jobs more effectively." He sighed wearily and then smiled. "We drew straws, my sons and I, to see who would come and check this place out. I lost." He gave a light chuckle and felt relief when Maggie gave a small smile. "I'm too old for nonsense like this. Conventions are a young man's game."

William looked around the lobby, clearly unwilling to leave her in such distress.

"Although, most of the young men I met here today need to learn a lot more not only about business, but about respect in general." Maggie nodded and wiped at her tear-streaked face. William reached for a handkerchief in his pocket and handed it to her. "I don't know about you, but it certainly makes me lose a little bit of faith in this generation."

"I agree," Maggie said softly.

William couldn't help but smile. He wanted so badly to help this woman but she was clearly spooked. Something had happened and he may not ever find out exactly what it was but he knew that he had to get her out of the hotel and to someplace where she'd feel safe.

William smiled at her. His manner was fatherly, caring—nothing at all like the way Martin had treated her. "Listen," he said calmly, "how about we go

over and have a cup of coffee? The café over there is still open."

"Oh, I can't," she said nervously. "I don't have my wallet with me."

"It's my treat." When Maggie hesitated, William quickly added, "You'd be doing me a huge favor. I've done nothing today but talk to a bunch of upstarts with overinflated egos."

Maggie thought about it for a moment and realized that maybe it would be okay to join him for coffee. She hadn't had anything to eat since they'd left Virginia on the early morning flight—Martin hadn't allowed her to eat all day. Sadistic bastard.

She stood and said a quiet, "Thank you."

William towered over her petite frame. "It's my pleasure, Ms..." He left the words dangling.

"Maggie," she said finally. "Maggie Barrett."

"Well, it is a pleasure to meet you, Maggie Barrett," he said, his tone nothing but friendliness, and Maggie knew in that instant that things just might work out all right.

True to his word, William had set the wheels in motion to get Maggie settled into her new position. Within an hour, he had all her belongings transferred to the executive floor, and from where he stood in his office doorway, he could see her working with Rose. After lunch, they would sit down together with Jason and get things really moving.

It did his heart good to see Maggie up here working where she belonged. He hated pushing her into it, but deep down William knew he'd let her hide out too long.

What that bastard had done to her back in California so long ago had been traumatic for sure, but William also knew that Maggie had too much to give to spend her life hiding away from everything and everybody.

When William had offered her the position with Montgomerys, Maggie had been shocked and more than a little apprehensive. Desperate to help her when she was so clearly in need, he had vowed to meet her every wish in order to get her to agree to work for him.

She had wanted a low-profile position; he gave her one. She needed to get her belongings from where she lived in Virginia to someplace new in North Carolina. William paid for the move and put her up temporarily in an executive apartment that the company owned until she found a place of her own. He'd sent people to get her car and had taken care of ending her employment with Martin Blake without letting anyone within the man's company know where she was going.

William Montgomery was very thorough in everything he did, and if keeping this woman under the radar for a little while meant keeping her safe, he'd do it.

Her final request was that no one know that she was single. While William didn't think that would deter some men, he knew that no one within his company would dare approach Maggie in an unprofessional manner. So he'd agreed to her request and no one was the wiser. Luckily, it wasn't something that came up very often. According to his human resources manager, Ann Kincade, Maggie was a virtual loner. She was pleasant to work with, but never engaged in any outside activities with her coworkers, mostly keeping to herself.

For a moment, William felt remorse at forcing her

so clearly out of her comfort zone, but then he thought of how well it had worked last year when he'd done the same for his son Lucas, and silently prayed that he would have similar results.

Maggie sensed William's stare, looking up and giving him a weak smile. By now, she knew her boss could be trusted and was sure that his son would be no different, but she wasn't happy that this promotion, this shift in her life, was not her decision. It was going to take a little while to adjust to it.

Working with Rose was no hardship; the woman knew her job and was easy to talk to. The job itself had some challenges that were actually related to her skills, but for the most part, the biggest challenge was going to be in trusting the man she was going to assist.

Maggie had seen Jason Montgomery often enough around the building. He was certainly an attractive man and his mere presence seemed to bring out sighs from the women working around her. That always irritated Maggie. She was never going to show any outward signs of attraction to anyone. No matter how attractive that six-foot-tall, dark-haired, dark-eyed package was!

Looking back, she knew that she hadn't had any attraction to her former boss; she had genuinely liked Martin as a person. Somehow, however, he mistook that feeling for sexual interest, and thought that gave him the right to seduce her. Just the thought of it now, years later, made Maggie sick to her stomach.

"Are you okay?" Rose asked.

Shaking her head to clear it, Maggie looked at her. "Sure. Why?"

"You just had a weird look on your face and you

kind of went pale." Rose looked at her watch. "Why don't we stop here and break for lunch. I have you and Mr. Montgomery scheduled to meet with Jason at two o'clock. You'll have an hour for lunch and then about thirty minutes after you get back to get organized and write up any questions you have for him. Will that work?"

"Yes, thank you," Maggie said with a smile, relieved that Rose didn't push her for more of an explanation. Walking to her desk, Maggie picked up her purse and a notebook. Her plan was to start making notes now on the things she wanted to discuss with Jason Montgomery.

Stepping onto the elevator, the first and most important question came to her mind. *Are you a pervert who plans on mistaking a simple smile for an invitation to sexually harass?*

Chapter 2

"WHAT?"

"Is there a problem? I think the question was fairly simple."

Jason looked at the woman sitting across from him at the conference table and then to his father. "This is some sort of joke, right?"

Maggie looked at him, her brows furrowed. "I don't think this is a joking matter, Mr. Montgomery. The question speaks for itself. Are you the kind of man who can tell the difference between someone being polite and someone offering an invitation?"

"What the hell kind of question is that?" he yelled and then turned to his father. "Seriously? This is who you think is the best option to work with me?"

William was barely able to contain his mirth. "She meets and actually exceeds all of your requirements, Jace. She's got the computer skills, organizational skills, and customer service skills that will prove useful on your trip, plus she has years of experience as an executive assistant."

Jason narrowed his eyes as he heard his father's words. "If she's so qualified, why has she been working in customer service all this time?"

Maggie had had enough. "If you have a question about my qualifications, Mr. Montgomery, please address me. I am more than capable of answering *your* questions."

Jason couldn't help but take note of her obvious dig at his inability to answer her earlier question. "Fine," he bit out. "If you have all of these qualifications, why haven't you been assigned to anyone in all of your years with Montgomerys?"

"I was a bit burned out after my last assignment with my previous employer and wanted something a little less stressful."

"And you think that now you're ready to handle the stress again?" he asked.

Her first response was to say no and hope that he'd let her leave and go back to her quiet position three floors down, but she knew she had made a promise to William. "Yes, I believe that I am more than capable of taking on this assignment."

"Ann tells me that you're married. How does your husband feel about you taking on a position that will have you traveling for the next several weeks?"

Maggie was not a very good liar but said a silent prayer that she'd sound believable. "My husband travels a great deal for his job, so we both have no issues with this trip." That sounded plausible, didn't it? She looked over at William and saw his slight nod of approval.

Jason looked over Maggie's resume and personnel file. "This is not in any way, shape, or form a pleasure trip. We'll be working long hours and meeting with a lot of people. It is imperative that you be able to keep up the pace and keep notes on all of our dealings and get whatever information is needed back here to Rose for her to begin processing. Is that going to be a problem?"

"I can assure you," Maggie began, "that I am highly organized and I don't have any issues with the long

hours. It will be a refreshing change of pace after doing the eight-to-five schedule."

"We'll have no regulated schedule," Jason countered. "Some days we may be up at dawn for an early morning meeting, other days we may not be meeting with anyone until the late afternoon. When we're not in scheduled meetings, we'll be working together on organizing the data we've collected, planning ahead for our next clients, or traveling. Maybe all at one time. Will that be a problem?"

Maggie shook her head. "As I said, I believe I am more than up for the challenge."

"It won't leave you a lot of personal time. You'll be more than compensated for all of the overtime and I will try to make sure that you're not overwhelmed, but I won't have time for someone who feels the need to make constant calls to home or has a jealous or needy spouse who needs to call you several times a day."

"That won't be a problem," Maggie said firmly.

"Be sure that it's not, Mrs. Barrett," Jason said with equal firmness.

William chose that moment to interrupt. "I think the two of you have more than enough to get started on. I do have some calls to make, so Jason, why don't you take Maggie to your office and let her get started going over all of the client files?"

Jason nodded and stood. Maggie did the same. "Maggie, if you have any questions, please feel free to come and see me, okay?" William said gently and Jason had to wonder at the exchange. His father was notoriously kind to all of his employees, but Jason sensed that there was something different about Maggie. He was about to comment on it when Maggie turned and headed for the door.

"Jason?" his father said quietly.

Jason saw that Maggie had exited the office, and he turned and looked at his father.

"Maggie is exactly what you're looking for. If you push, she's going to push back. You won't have to worry about her like you did with the others. She's going to do a good job for you on this trip."

At the moment, Jason wasn't so sure. While he could appreciate Maggie's credentials, he had a feeling that their personalities were going to clash, and that was almost as inappropriate as some of his former assistants' behavior. "I hope so, Dad. There's a lot riding on this trip."

"That's pressure that you've put on yourself, Jace. You wanted to try for this expansion, and while I think it's a great idea, I don't want it to consume you to the point of pushing yourself so hard that you forget to live a little."

"What the hell does that mean?" Jason snapped.

"It means that you have a great work ethic and a desire to see the company succeed. Just don't forget that Montgomerys isn't your whole life."

There were times when his father spoke like Yoda, and right now Jason didn't have the time to delve any deeper into what he was saying. He had to get Maggie acclimated with his project and make sure she was completely prepared when they left in two weeks for their whirlwind trip.

Jason had done a damn good job. Sitting on the private plane that was getting ready to take off, he looked over at Maggie and smiled. They had worked long hours

for the last two weeks, and she was just as familiar with every aspect of this project as he was. She was smart, inquisitive, and well versed. He knew without a doubt that she was going to be an asset to him on this trip and that he wouldn't have to spend precious time explaining things to her, because she clearly understood exactly what it was he was trying to accomplish.

Not once during the previous weeks had there been an issue with the long hours. At first Jason was sure that her husband was going to put up a fight; after all, Maggie had been working fairly regular hours for so many years, so this was quite an adjustment. But just as there'd been no complaint from the husband, Maggie hadn't complained either.

They'd worked side by side from eight in the morning until sometimes as late as ten at night. Jason found that after their initial clashing during their interview, they both seemed to come to understand each other and had formed mutual respect for one another. Conversation flowed when it was needed and at the same time, they were both comfortable working in silence. For having worked together only two weeks, they were seemingly in sync. Jason wasn't used to that.

"If we don't hit any delays we should be in Chicago by ten. I called and confirmed the town car, and since we'll have missed most of the morning traffic, we should be at the hotel by eleven," Maggie was saying as she glanced at their schedule on her tablet. "We're meeting the Claremont people at one, so once we're checked in, we can have lunch brought up to the rooms and be ready to go by twelve thirty." She looked up at him. "How does that sound?"

"Good," Jason said distractedly. Meetings like this didn't normally stress him out, but this plan for expansion that he had made him a little edgy. "Did we leave the evening free or did you pencil something in?"

"I left it free just in case they wanted to meet over dinner. I didn't want to over-schedule us on our first day," she said lightly. "I've researched several restaurants in the area and the one at our hotel would actually be perfect for a meeting. I can call in a reservation now if you'd like, just in case?"

She was very efficient; that was what Jason admired most. Maggie was certainly making his life easier already. "Let's wait and see how the afternoon goes. For all we know they can be exhausting and not people we want to work with. In which case, we'll just have a quiet dinner and discuss our next plan of attack."

Maggie laughed. "Sounds like a plan. I'll just mark these places for future reference."

While she was busy tapping away on her tablet screen, Jason studied her. With her blonde hair pulled back into a severe ponytail and her brown eyes downcast, Maggie seemed to do her best not to stand out. Jason had to wonder a little at that. While he could appreciate her professional manner and her obvious desire not to draw attention to herself, he couldn't help but wonder why. Most of the women he knew, both in business and in his personal life, did things to make themselves look attractive. Maggie, on the other hand, wore little to no makeup, dressed ultraconservatively, and did her best to blend into the background. This was exactly what Jason had said that he wanted, but the more he got to

know Maggie, the more he had a feeling that she wasn't presenting her true self.

Their captain announced their turn for takeoff and Jason watched Maggie's response. Her white-knuckled grip on the seat told him that flying was definitely not her thing. While most of their travels were going to require flying, there were going to be some shorter legs that he had planned a rental car for. He was sure that Maggie would be relieved on those days.

"Not a fan of flying, huh?" he asked, hoping to distract her.

"No, not really."

"It's not so bad," he said in a soothing tone. "The key is to just relax."

"Easy for you to say," she mumbled and heard Jason laugh.

"Look, don't focus on what you're feeling, focus on me."

Maggie's eyes went wide. "Excuse me?" she said, indignant.

"I mean, talk to me about this meeting today. Talk to me about the weather. Talk to me about what you think of my tie," he suggested.

"Your tie?"

"Sure. Whatever you need to talk about, we'll talk about," he said and smiled at her confused look. "So what do you think? Stripes? Is it a good look?"

He was teasing her and for that Maggie was relieved. In their time working together, they had gotten along much better than she had expected. They had always kept things on a business level; this light side of him was a pleasant surprise. His dark eyes twinkled and she felt

herself relax. "I'm not normally a fan of stripes, but they aren't overly obnoxious."

"Stripes are obnoxious?" he asked.

"They can be. Think of prison stripes."

That made Jason laugh again. "Well, I can guarantee you I will not be going for the prison stripe look. Ever."

"Good to know," Maggie said and realized that her stomach no longer felt so queasy and that they were no longer climbing. She loosened her grip on her seat and looked out the window. "Is that it? We're done with takeoff?"

Jason smiled at her. "See? A little distraction always works." The next hour passed quickly, and soon they were in the car and heading for their hotel. Check in went like clockwork. Jason was glad they had adjoining rooms. They were only going to be in Chicago for two days, but it would make things easier if Maggie was close by when he needed her help.

No sooner were they settled in their rooms than lunch was being delivered. While Jason had been checking them in, Maggie had been taking care of ordering their food. Jason knocked on the door dividing their rooms and Maggie unlocked it and let him in.

"That was fast," she commented as she reached for her briefcase.

Jason stopped her. "Whoa, we're going to eat lunch like normal people and not talk business for the next fifteen minutes, okay?"

Maggie more than readily agreed. They had been talking business for weeks and she felt like if Jason were to fall ill, she would be able to handle any and all of his meetings because she knew the details so intimately. To

be able to have a few minutes reprieve to eat and relax sounded like heaven.

Jason had set up their food at the table in his room and waited for Maggie to sit down before he joined her. "I hope you had enough time to get at least a little settled into your room."

Maggie waved him off. "I don't plan on getting too comfortable. It makes it easier when it's time to leave if I haven't taken everything out."

"That makes sense. Did you have time to call home?"

"What for?" she asked without thinking.

Jason arched a dark eyebrow at her. "I thought you would check in with your husband and let him know we arrived safely."

"Oh," Maggie said, forgetting for a moment that she was supposed to be married. "I texted him. He's at work so I just figured we'd talk later tonight."

It sounded believable enough, but Jason had to wonder how good a marriage she had if they spent so much time apart and didn't seem to mind it at all. If he was married, he'd certainly be uncomfortable with his wife traveling with another man! What was wrong with Maggie's husband?

Clearing those thoughts from his mind, Jason took a bite of the BLT Maggie had ordered for him and then asked, "Have you ever been to Chicago before?"

She was delicately eating a chef's salad and held a finger up while she finished chewing before answering. "Actually, I haven't. It was never on my radar as someplace I wanted to see and I'm not really focusing on it now, since we're not here to sightsee."

Practical, Jason thought, and for just a minute he

felt bad about not making any time to show her some of the sights. It seemed like Maggie led a very quiet, sheltered life and it made him a little sad for her. With a husband who seemed to lack any interest in her and Maggie's quiet acceptance of it all, it just didn't sit well with Jason.

"Are you a baseball fan?" he asked. Maggie shook her head. "Oh, well, I thought maybe we could maybe find time to tour Wrigley Field, but if that's not something that interests you..."

Maggie gave Jason a serene smile. "I don't expect you to entertain me, Jason. We're here to make Montgomerys grow. That's not going to happen if we're off playing tourist."

While he should be happy that she wasn't looking for any personal attention from him, there was just something about her demeanor that was unsettling. Jason made another mental note to delve a little deeper into this as their trip went on.

"You're right about that," he finally answered. "I always tell myself that I'm going to take the time and go and see a game but I never do. Are there any sports that you do enjoy?"

"Hockey."

Jason almost choked on his sandwich. "*Hockey?* Seriously?"

Maggie looked at him with confusion. "What's wrong with hockey?"

"Nothing, nothing at all, it's just that I thought for sure you would have said something like tennis or golf."

She laughed out loud and Jason found that he enjoyed the sound of it. "Why on earth would you think that?"

"Well, for starters, you're a fairly conservative woman. Hockey is a loud, obnoxious, violent sport. I just can't see you standing up and screaming at a game."

"Well, believe me, I have done my share of screaming. I think hockey has got to be one of the most challenging sports there is to play. There's so much going on and it's just fascinating to watch."

"Who's your favorite team?"

"The Rangers."

"New York? You're a *New York* fan? Aren't you from Virginia?"

"What does that have to do with anything? Virginia doesn't have a hockey team and the Rangers are awesome!"

"How many games have you gone to?" he asked, still in disbelief that they were even having this conversation.

"Not nearly enough," she said lightly. "I've only gone to New York twice and I was a teenager. My dad took me to a game at Madison Square Garden and it was amazing. Then last year, I managed to go and see the Rangers play the Hurricanes in Raleigh."

"Is your husband a hockey fan, too?"

"What? I mean, yeah, sure. He's okay with it."

"Raleigh's not that far away. I'd think that you would try to go more often."

"It's three hours of driving each way. To go to a game would make it a two-day event and I just don't have that much time to invest, you know? Besides, there's something magical about seeing a team play on their home ice. The vibe at the Garden is completely different from what I felt in Raleigh."

Jason tucked that bit of information away as he glanced at his watch. "If we're going to get everything

done, we need to finish up here. The car will be back for us in fifteen minutes. Will that be enough time for you?"

"I'm ready," Maggie said dismissively, pushing her unfinished salad aside. "All I need to do is grab my briefcase. I've got everything we need for today in there, organized and ready to go."

Finishing his last bite of sandwich, Jason rose from his chair, went in search of his own briefcase, and then turned back to Maggie. "So what do you think? Do I stick with the stripes or do I need to change?"

"Don't be such a chick, Jason," she said teasingly as she stood. "You look fine." Maggie turned and walked into her room to grab her things. Jason realized that her opinion really was beginning to matter.

It was well after eight when they were finally riding the elevator back to their floor at the hotel. Maggie leaned back against the wall and sighed. "I didn't think they'd ever stop asking questions. I mean, in every scenario I played out in my mind, none of them went like this."

Jason faced her as he leaned against the opposite wall. "I know what you mean. I think I sort of zoned out there after a while." He scrubbed a weary hand over his face and let his head fall back. "And as if that wasn't enough, what was with the dinner they brought in?"

"Oh, I know, right? I thought Chicago was known for its good food! I have no idea where that stuff even came from."

"Want to order some real food for us, or do you want to go down to the restaurant to eat?" he asked.

"Honestly, I want to kick off these shoes and crawl

into bed." Maggie stopped and considered what she was saying. "Okay, maybe I have the energy for some ice cream, but nothing more than that."

Jason chuckled. "I may order a pizza."

That piqued her interest. "Pizza? I could stay awake for some pizza."

"Atta girl," he said, still laughing. They arrived at their floor and headed for their rooms. "Why don't you go and relax and I'll call you when the pizza gets here."

"Bless you," Maggie said as she practically fell through her door. Within minutes she had stripped out of her business attire that was beyond uncomfortable after such a long day and changed into a pair of yoga pants and a T-shirt. Certainly Jason didn't expect her to be dressed in her work clothes all the time, did he?

She pulled the clip from her hair and massaged her scalp. Working longer hours was taking a little more getting used to. During her stint in customer service, her workday was relatively short compared to what she was doing now, and staying in such a severe look was getting uncomfortable. Staring at her reflection in the mirror, Maggie considered what else she could do with her hair to make it look professional without killing her scalp. Running her fingers through her long hair, she shook it out and found that she felt much better. It was almost nine o'clock when Jason knocked on the door.

"Pizza delivery!"

Maggie opened the door to him and smiled. "Do you want to eat in here or are you already set up in your room?"

Jason couldn't speak. For a moment he could only stare. The woman he had come to know these last weeks

was gone, replaced by someone completely different. With her hair loose, Jason realized just how long it was. It was wavy and thick and wonderful, and he found himself itching to reach out and touch it to see if it was as soft as it looked. She had bangs that were wispy and light and seemed to drag his attention to her expressive brown eyes.

Eyes that were staring curiously at him right now.

Oh, right. Pizza. "I've got everything set up inside," he said gruffly and then turned back toward his room. "I had them send up some drinks, too. I wasn't sure what you wanted so I got a variety."

"I probably shouldn't have anything with caffeine this late, but there is something to be said for a Coke with pizza."

"A girl after my own heart," he said and then realized how awkward that was. "What I mean is…"

Maggie laughed. "It's okay, Jason. I know what you meant." She sat down and helped herself to a slice of the deep dish pizza and groaned with delight at the first bite. "Now that is food," she said with a sigh.

Jason held in his own groan. With her new look and the near orgasmic sounds she was making while eating, he was starting to sweat. She was his assistant and she was a married woman! He should not be noticing all of these things about her and yet he couldn't seem to stop himself.

"Aren't you going to have any?" she finally asked.

"What? Oh, yeah, sorry. I guess my mind is still on the bizarre meeting from today."

"Please, no more talk about business," she pleaded. "I think I'd just like to forget that today even happened."

"I couldn't agree more," he mumbled.

"So does that mean Claremont is off the table for prospective clients?"

He nodded. "I don't think we could meet each other's needs. I'd rather cut my losses now and move on to what's next."

"I'll email Rose in the morning with an update. Our next appointment isn't until ten tomorrow and then our flight to Ohio is after dinner."

Jason merely nodded again. He couldn't focus. He wanted Maggie to finish her pizza and go to her own room. His mind was spinning in a dozen different directions—none of which were business related—and he needed to get his thoughts back on track. Knowing he was being rude, Jason grabbed up another slice and stalked over to the other side of the room, sitting down with his laptop and doing his best to ignore Maggie. Maybe she'd get the hint and leave.

Within minutes, she did. With a quiet "good night," she closed the door between their rooms and Jason heard the lock go into place. That's when he let himself breathe again. If this was how he felt after one day, how the hell was he going to survive for another twenty?

They were airborne once again the following evening, and Maggie could tell that Jason wasn't pleased with their trip so far. Neither meeting had gone as they had hoped and Maggie could only pray that Jason wasn't going to let this get him down.

"Well, tomorrow's another day," she said to break the silence.

Jason merely grunted in response.

She decided to make another attempt to draw him out. "Neither of them are what Montgomerys is looking for. I'm glad we got them out of the way early and now we can move on to something better."

Jason glared at her.

Okay, now what? "I've been doing some research on our group for tomorrow. They have a similar history to Montgomerys, and Nick Austin, their CEO, is a huge football fan. I bet we can spend some time talking about Lucas to break the ice a little."

"I'm not using my brother's former career to schmooze anyone," he snapped.

That was it, she'd had enough. "Look, I know you're not happy right now with the way things have gone so far, but none of it is my fault. I didn't research the people to meet with, you did. I came into this whole thing late in the game and I don't appreciate having you snap at me for things that aren't my fault!"

Maggie snapped shut the book she was reading and turned to look out at the sun setting in the sky. The view was spectacular, but it did little to ease the tension she was feeling right now at Jason's miserable attitude.

Jason knew he was being a jerk and it wasn't fair to be taking out his anger on Maggie, but he was beyond frustrated. Between the miserable meeting yesterday, and the confusing way she'd made him feel last night, the very last thing he'd needed was another round of miserable meetings today. So far this trip was a complete disaster and it had only just begun!

Not wanting to alert his father to the problem that was brewing, Jason had asked Maggie to wait before sending

anything into the office. While he could tell she wasn't in complete agreement with him, she'd done as he asked and merely saved the information on her computer until he wanted it sent.

How about never, he thought to himself.

They would be landing late in Cleveland and Jason knew there'd be a town car waiting to take them to their hotel. By now, all he wanted was to be alone. His tie was choking him, his head was pounding, and he had no desire to make small talk anymore. Tomorrow would be here soon enough; they'd have to go back into schmoozing mode and do their best to kiss up to another group of potential clients that might be worse than what they'd dealt with in Chicago.

Maggie stayed silent for the remainder of the trip and during the ride to the hotel. When Jason handed her the key to her room, she took it and quietly followed him into the elevator. "Look, Maggie, I'm sorry I snapped at you earlier. I know none of this is your fault. I just had so much hope for this trip and none of it is going like I planned."

"It's okay, Jason," she said meekly. "I know you have a lot on your mind. You don't need to add worrying about me to the list."

"Dammit, Maggie, that's not what I'm saying!" he yelled and then caught himself. "Let's just meet up in the morning down in the restaurant for breakfast. Maybe a good night's sleep will help."

They stepped off the elevator and Jason noted that this time Maggie's room was across the hall from him. "Good night, Jason," she said softly, her eyes not meeting his, and Jason felt ten kinds of crappy.

~

She had to admit, a good night's sleep did seem to help. But then again, she hadn't had the opportunity to speak to Jason yet. For all Maggie knew, her good mood was going to be shot right to hell before her first cup of coffee.

They met up at eight in the restaurant and Jason took great care to be fastidiously polite. He held her chair for her, asked how she slept, what she wanted to order, did she want anything special... By the time he unfolded her napkin for her she was ready to scream.

"Okay, enough!" she said. "Look, we were both on edge last night, but today is another day. Not all of these meetings are going to garner the results that we want, but we can't let it freak us out. We've got another two and a half weeks to get through and we'll never make it if we get into a funk when things go wrong."

Jason took a deep breath and then seemed to relax. "You're right. I know you're right. I'm just a damn perfectionist and it's been a long time since things didn't go exactly as I had planned."

She reached out, placed her hand on his, and then gasped. Before she could pull her hand away, Jason's eyes met hers. Had he felt it too? It was like a spark, a warmth that wasn't there before and now suddenly was. "Um, you shouldn't be so hard on yourself, Jason. I'm sure there are going to be a lot more successes than disappointments on this trip. You can't take it personally."

Pulling her hand away, Maggie scanned the room for their waitress and prayed their food would arrive quickly. She needed the distraction.

"Did you tell your husband what a jerk I was?" he asked sheepishly. Honestly he didn't want to talk about the man Maggie was married to, but he needed to remind himself of the fact that she was, indeed, married. Especially after whatever has just passed between them.

"You weren't a jerk, Jason," she said kindly. "You were disappointed."

"That doesn't answer my question," he returned. "Did you tell him?'

"It didn't come up," she said, averting her eyes.

Luckily their food arrived and Maggie put all her attention on that. "I have to admit, I don't normally indulge in a big breakfast but sometimes it's a real treat."

Jason nodded. "I don't normally eat a large breakfast either, but when I'm on the road I try to just in case I end up missing lunch due to a meeting. Back at home, if we're deep in work mode, Rose makes sure that food comes in. I can't guarantee the same thing when I'm relying on somebody else's timetable."

"I can only hope we don't have any more mishaps like that meal at Claremont's. I think I'd rather skip eating all together than have to eat food like that again."

Jason agreed.

Within an hour they were climbing into a cab and heading for their first meeting of the day. "Remind me again how tight a schedule we're on today?"

Maggie pulled out her tablet. "Okay, we've got a ten a.m. with Nick Austin, a one o'clock lunch meeting with the Smith Group, and then we have to head back to the hotel and change because we've got the charity auction at the Rock and Roll Hall of Fame. I've got your tux and my gown with the concierge to be pressed and ready to go.

We have a limo picking us up at seven so we should have plenty of time after lunch to go over the two meetings and get a little time to relax before heading out for the night."

Jason was exhausted just thinking about it. "I really packed the schedule, didn't I?"

Maggie laughed. "Just a little."

"If it had been you doing all of the planning, what would you have done differently?"

"So far?"

That didn't sound good. "With the whole trip," he answered.

"Well, I understand you're trying to maximize your time and really, you've done that with military precision."

"But…"

"But," she chimed in, "you didn't leave a lot of time for incidentals."

"Like what?"

"Well, let's say that this meeting with Nick Austin is going well and we need more time with him. We don't really have it because three hours after the start of our meeting, we're due to start another one. I would make sure that we worked in four-hour time blocks, nothing less."

"Okay," he said slowly. "How often do I give us less than four hours?"

Maggie scrolled through their itinerary and frowned. "Quite often. You have several appointments right on top of each other, and then other times you have up to eight hours between appointments. I realize sometimes that's all that is available, but it is going to have us in and out of the car a lot more than is effective."

"I didn't even think to look at it that way. I was more concerned with getting the appointments made than

thinking about how efficiently I was spending my time." His tone was slightly defensive and he hated feeling like he'd made a mistake.

"It's okay, Jason. This was something you needed an assistant for. It's all going to work out just fine; some days it will seem like an adventure," she teased.

They pulled up to their first appointment and Maggie gave him a beaming smile. "Ready?" she asked.

"As I'll ever be," he said as he exited the vehicle.

They arrived back at the hotel at three thirty and Maggie already felt as if she'd run a marathon. The first meeting had gone extremely well, and their lunch meeting was pleasant enough, but the client was going to require a little more time before he signed with Jason. All in all, she was pleased and knew Jason was, too.

"I'll call the concierge and make sure our clothes are back up to us by six," she said as they walked toward their rooms. "Is there anything else you need before then?"

"I think we're good for now. What are you going to do with yourself this afternoon?"

Maggie thought for a moment. "Well, since there isn't much for me to do with the files for today, I'm going to send what I have to Rose and then maybe catch a nap, then take my time getting ready for tonight. What about you?"

"I've got some files I want to look over and a little research I want to do, but a nap certainly sounds appealing."

Smiling, Maggie took out her key card, turning toward her door. "Listen," Jason said suddenly. "Why don't you make an appointment with the hotel salon and go and get pampered for tonight?"

Maggie looked at him as if he'd lost his mind. "Excuse me?"

"You've been putting in some long hours and have had to deal with an extremely grumpy boss, so why don't you take a little time for yourself?" His words were spoken lightly.

The thought was both appealing and unnerving at the same time. Was this how it was going to start? Was Jason going to woo her with spa treatments and special favors in hopes that she would feel indebted to him? The thought made her frown but when she looked up at his face, which looked genuine and sincere, she knew he was nothing like her former boss.

"Are you sure?" she asked hesitantly.

"Of course I am," he said. "You've got nothing to do for a couple of hours, so call down and see if they have an appointment and do whatever it is that women do before they have to go to some formal charity event."

She laughed. "Honestly, I have no idea what that is! I've never gone to one before."

"Seriously? I would've thought that with your previous employer or even with your husband that you would have done something similar at some point."

At the mention of both the fake husband and her disgusting ex-boss, Maggie's stomach turned. Jason saw the look on her face and instantly stepped forward, concerned. "Maggie? Are you okay?"

"I'm fine," she quietly lied. "Let me see if they can squeeze me in for something." She opened her door and then turned back to Jason. "Thank you. I appreciate your generosity."

As the door closed, Jason wondered, not for the first

time, just what went on in Maggie's mind. There were times she was outgoing and friendly and seemingly full of joy, but it didn't take much to make her completely shut that side down. He was getting a little tired of not knowing what the trigger was, but he had a sinking sensation that it had to do with her marriage.

And that thought bothered him more than he was willing to admit.

At six forty-five, Jason knocked on Maggie's door. His tux had arrived promptly at six o'clock and he was dressed by six fifteen, so he found himself just pacing in his room with nothing to do. The limo would be downstairs in five minutes and he hoped that Maggie would be punctual. He knew her to be so when it was for work, but most women Jason knew tended to take a lot longer to get ready when it was for a social event.

When Maggie opened the door, Jason felt his jaw drop. She was stunning. In a navy blue strapless evening gown that hugged her petite, curvy body, she took his breath away.

"I wasn't sure quite how formal I needed to be," Maggie said as she tried to read Jason's expression. "I thought that this was understated enough to be formal and classy." She wished Jason would say something, anything.

When they had originally discussed this event, all Jason had told her was to bring "some sort of gown." That wasn't much to go on. Maggie had researched previous events for this particular charity and then had done some major damage with her Visa card. The gown was a knockoff of a Christian Dior gown that some

actress had worn to the Screen Actors Guild Awards, and though she normally didn't go for such a bold and sexy look, Maggie had simply fallen in love with it.

Down at the spa she had gotten a manicure, pedicure, and facial before getting her hair done. Gone was the severe ponytail of the workday, and in its place was an elegant chignon with a few loose tendrils that curled along the side of her face. All in all, she had been pleased with the look, but Jason's hard stare had her second-guessing herself.

"Jason?" she finally asked. "Are you okay?"

He quickly shook his head as if to clear it and then cleared his throat. "Yes, I'm fine, sorry. You look lovely. Are you ready?"

It was the first real compliment Maggie had received from a man in over three years and it made her blush. She ducked her head slightly as she turned and shut the door, then managed to walk a few steps ahead of Jason to the elevators. They rode down in silence and Maggie felt a little in awe of the stretch limo waiting for them.

She turned an inquisitive eye to Jason. "Tell me again why we needed a limo?"

He smiled. "This is a big event," he said simply. "It required a limo."

Whether that was true or not, Maggie didn't know, but in that moment she realized how big a difference there was between her regular, ordinary life and the life of the wealthy Montgomerys. She felt a little inferior, but knew that was of her own doing. The Montgomerys never flaunted their wealth or their position and if anything, they were beyond generous. For this one night she

was going to enjoy seeing how the other half lived and pretend it was nothing out of the ordinary for her.

That thought lasted until they pulled up to the venue and she found herself more than a little starstruck by the crowd. As they made their way up the red carpet, Jason stopped and shook hands with many people, always introducing her, but after a few minutes, he stopped and pulled her over to the side.

"I know this is a little overwhelming, but you have nothing to be so nervous about," he whispered in her ear and felt Maggie shiver.

"I'm not nervous," she lied and then heard him chuckle as he seemed to pull her a bit closer.

"You're glued to my side, Maggie. I can feel you shaking and I can hear it in your voice every time you speak. Take a deep breath and relax, okay?"

She lifted her eyes to his and nodded. They were standing way too close; she was plastered to him, but not in an uncomfortable way. It had been a long time since she had let any man get this close to her physically, and she found that with Jason, she didn't mind it all.

His dark gaze was burning into hers and Maggie licked her dry lips, forcing herself to take a small step back and look away. "So," she said, expelling the breath she had been holding, "are we ready to head in?"

Honestly, Jason needed another moment before he felt he was truly in control of his thoughts, but he didn't want to scare her. He simply nodded and took her hand, leading her up to the main doorway.

Soon they were swept into the crowd and drinking champagne, Jason doing his best to meet up with the people that he wanted to while keeping track of Maggie

at his side. They sat down for dinner and Jason managed to make some new contacts. Maggie was savvy enough to put all of their information into her iPhone for future reference without being overly obvious about it.

Once dinner was over, the actual charity event presentation began. There were several performances by some big name artists in the music industry and then the actor who had organized the event gave a twenty-minute speech imploring the guests for their support. By ten o'clock, everyone was back to mingling, and Jason caught Maggie watching the couples dancing with a wistful look on her face.

Unable to help himself, he placed his champagne glass down on the nearest table and intently walked toward her. At his approach he asked, "Would you like to dance?"

Her eyes went wide with delight. "Are you sure? Don't you have more people to talk with?"

"I think I've done more than my share of talking tonight and even came out a little ahead. Besides, what kind of man would I be if I didn't make time to ask a beautiful girl to dance?"

She hesitated. He thought she was beautiful? This was probably all kinds of against the rules, slow dancing with her boss, but at the moment, it was all that Maggie wanted to do. Another downside to her self-imposed exile: she missed the simple act of human contact.

"What do you say, Maggie?" Jason asked again when she didn't respond to his initial request.

"I would love to," she said, placing her hand in his. There was that same jolt she'd felt when they'd touched at breakfast but it didn't scare her this time; instead, she embraced it.

They joined the couples out on the floor and simply swayed to the orchestra. "I can't even remember the last time I went dancing," Maggie said as she aligned herself with Jason. "It may have been my senior prom."

All sorts of thoughts raced through Jason's head. What about her wedding? Her honeymoon? Wasn't that the sort of thing couples did? He thought of his brother Lucas and his new bride Emma and the way they had danced at their engagement party and wedding. Hell, Jason may not be an expert on married couples, but he sure as hell knew that they danced! He was just about to make a comment on it when he felt Maggie snuggle a little bit closer and sigh.

His body was on high alert. She felt very good in his arms, and without conscious thought, he wrapped his arm around her to pull her even closer, surprised when she didn't resist. Jason rested his head on top of hers and simply enjoyed the feel of her, the smell of her, the way her hair tickled his chin.

He was treading into dangerous territory here and yet couldn't seem to find the will to care. Luckily the orchestra moved smoothly into another slow song and he was treated to having Maggie close for another few minutes. Then what? The smart thing to do would be to thank her for the dance and then find a colleague or two to talk to but that thought left him cold.

Jason knew what he wanted, knew what he needed, knew without a doubt that it would be a mistake, and still couldn't bring himself to care. Lifting his head, he reached up and placed a finger under Maggie's chin so that her eyes met his. Her sexy, slumberous expression matched his own and he cursed himself as he lowered his lips to hers.

Chapter 3

The moment Jason's lips touched Maggie's, he knew he was in trouble. It was perfect. He felt her slight tremble before she lifted her arms around his neck to pull him in closer. Jason wanted to devour her right then and there but kept his touch soft and gentle so that if she wanted to pull away, she could.

But she didn't.

If anything, Maggie seemed to be doing her best to drag a deeper kiss out of him. Jason wanted to oblige, he really did, but this was not the place. With a growl of regret he raised his head, his breathing ragged. "Maggie?"

Slowly Maggie opened her eyes and then he watched as reality slowly set in, shock and embarrassment crossing her face. "*Ohmygod,*" she gushed and ran from his embrace.

Jason stood motionless for a moment, not sure what he was supposed to do. Why had he given in to temptation? He was stronger than that! They had more than two weeks to go on this trip and he could *not* afford to screw this up and scare Maggie off. Dammit! Looking around, he noticed that no one was paying any particular attention to him, so he made his way off the dance floor in search of his assistant.

It didn't take long to find her.

Standing in the far corner of the lobby, Maggie tried

to catch her breath. Dear lord, what had she done? She'd kissed Jason! She'd kissed her boss! What was she supposed to do now? Her mind raced frantically and her first instinct was to call William and tell him that she needed to leave here immediately. But once she took a moment to think that through, she realized she was the one who was at fault here, not Jason. Maybe she had misread his intentions? No, he was definitely the one who initiated the kiss, but she was the one who had practically devoured him.

Maggie was sure her face was twenty-seven shades of red and almost jumped out of her skin when she heard Jason say her name softly from behind her. Reluctantly, she turned to face him.

Before he could even say a word, Maggie held up a hand to stop him. "That was completely unprofessional of me and I don't know why it happened." When Jason tried to speak again, she continued on. "Let's just say that I got a little swept up in the moment and it won't happen again."

"Maggie..." he began.

"Honestly, Jason, I'd rather not talk about it." She looked around the lobby and noticed that people were starting to leave. "Are there more people that you needed to talk to or would you mind if we called for the car?"

Jason stared down at her skeptically. There were a million thoughts racing through his head. Caught up in the moment? That's all it was to her? *Hell no!* There was more to this than she was letting on but the harder he stared at her, the more her bravado seemed to be failing and he felt like he was wordlessly bullying her. "No," he said finally. "I think it's been a successful evening. I'll call for the car."

Within twenty minutes, they were back in the limo and on their way to the hotel. Maggie was going to try for small talk, but she couldn't seem to find anything to talk about. They were going to be leaving Cleveland in the morning and had a flight to Boston. Their itinerary had them spending three days in Boston and then they were heading to Manhattan for four days.

Right now all Maggie wanted was a day to herself to figure out what in the world was going on with her. She had been so confident in her ability to stay in control after the way things had gone down with Martin Blake that she never gave a thought to what would happen if she was the one attracted to her boss.

She thought those feelings were long dead, ruined by a man who trapped her like some sort of prey. For some reason, Jason Montgomery was bringing feelings out in Maggie that she wasn't ready to deal with. Being in such close proximity to him was certainly not helping the situation.

A cry of relief nearly escaped her lips when they finally arrived back at the hotel. Maggie noticed once they were in the lobby that Jason wasn't behind her. She stopped, turned, and saw him standing still, watching her. "Jason?"

"You go on up, Maggie. I'm going to go grab a drink in the bar." He motioned to the hotel lounge behind him. "Why don't we plan on meeting down here to grab the car for the airport in the morning?"

"That sounds fine," she said quietly, knowing that Jason was probably trying to figure out how to get rid of her for the remainder of the trip. "I'll see you in the morning." With that, she walked quickly and got on the elevator just as the doors were beginning to close.

~

Jason was a wreck. Three shots later and nothing was making sense. He gave a mirthless laugh as he paid the bar tab and made his way to the bank of elevators. Why did he think more alcohol was going to help clear his mind?

Maggie had given him hell from the get-go about not mistaking a smile for a come-on. He could live with that. But was he mistaking her kiss for something more than what it was? Hell, what was it? He never should have given in to the urge to kiss her but she had looked so damn desirable that he couldn't resist. And if she wasn't married? Well, he wouldn't have spent the last hour in the hotel bar, that was for damn sure!

Married. Jason had never in his life pursued a married woman. Never. How was he supposed to stay on this trip with her if he was attracted to her? How were they supposed to go back to the way they worked together only earlier today with this kiss hanging between them? Hell if he knew.

Once up in his room, Jason ripped off his tie and jacket and stalked the interior. He couldn't afford to let Maggie leave. She was too important to what he hoped to accomplish business-wise on this trip. But if he was going to survive the next couple of weeks, he was going to have to put some strict parameters on them so that they weren't in any more of these situations.

Booting up his tablet, he pulled up their itinerary. They had three days scheduled in Boston and then four in New York. The Boston meetings were going to be lengthy, but were in large groups and in offices; no

chance of slow dancing and drinking there. Once in New York their schedule was a little more open, and with a weekend in the middle, they'd have a day or so with nothing to do. That could pose a problem.

What if he told her to call her husband and Jason would fly him in for the weekend? Maybe seeing the two of them together would be just what he needed to put everything in perspective and remind him of why he needed to keep his distance.

The plan was perfect. Sighing with relief, he stripped and got ready for bed. Tomorrow when they were en route to Boston, he'd surprise her with his idea. Maybe Maggie was just missing her husband and that was why she'd kissed him.

Lying down, Jason turned out the light, staring at the darkened ceiling and thinking about Maggie's lips on his and the man who had the right to kiss them any time he wanted. His final thought as sleep claimed him was, *Lucky bastard.*

They were airborne and Maggie was pulling up the files that she wanted to review with Jason when he finally spoke. "Listen, I was thinking, we're scheduled for three days in Boston but realistically, we can be done in two. That means we can hit Manhattan by Saturday morning and then we don't have any meetings until Monday. Why don't you call your husband and I'll fly him up for the weekend?" He was quite proud of himself for thinking of it, but the look of pure horror on Maggie's face had him reconsidering.

"What?" she cried. "Why? Why would you do that?

We have a schedule to keep and there's no time to just change things around like that. It's not necessary, really. We have a lot to accomplish and you're not paying me to have a weekend getaway."

Wow, protest much? "I just thought since we've been working so hard that maybe you would appreciate having a bit of a break. Most people at least get the weekend off. I honestly thought you'd like the idea," he said hesitantly.

"Well, it's not necessary. I am being well-compensated for working long hours on this trip and there's no need for you to go out of your way to change anything. If you would like to use the free time to do… whatever, then please feel free. I don't need to be entertained. We have enough work to keep me busy."

"Maggie, you're taking this all wrong," he said, leaning forward in his seat. "I'm trying to do something nice here."

"You treated me to a spa treatment yesterday. You took me to an amazing event at the Rock and Roll Hall of Fame last night. I actually got to stand next to John Lennon's guitar! I'm traveling around the country to places that I've never seen before while staying at luxurious hotels, and I'm getting paid for it!" Her words were a little more clipped usual.

Jason held up a hand to calm her down. "Okay, okay, I get it. Geez, it was just a thought. I'm sorry I brought it up." He watched as Maggie slowly calmed down, and now his curiosity was piqued even more. From what he'd learned so far, this mystery husband never danced with her, never traveled with her, apparently never called her, and she didn't have any inclination to spend time with him.

Hmm… That could also explain last night's kiss. Frustrated wife? Bored with her husband? Jason felt ill. It didn't sit right with him. Even if Maggie wasn't happily married, it didn't give him the right to hit on her or for her to use him as some kind of substitute.

Who was he kidding? She wasn't using him for anything. She nearly left skid marks trying to get away from him, and even now was sitting as far away from him on the private plane as humanly possible. It was wishful thinking on his part that she was the one interested in him and not the other way around.

With the determination he was known for, Jason decided that the only way to keep his sanity was to push all personal thoughts of Maggie from his mind and focus on the business at hand. He was feeling confident about the upcoming meetings. He had to get his head back in the game if he wanted to move Montgomerys into a tax bracket that they'd never even dreamed of.

"I can't believe that went so well," Maggie was saying on Friday evening as they took a cab back to their hotel. "That had to be the shortest meeting in history."

"Well, it helped that Dennis Michaels had more pressing matters to attend to," Jason said as he texted his brother Mac with an update.

"He should never have kept that appointment with us! His wife was in labor!"

Jason laughed. "We corporate types never like to miss an appointment," he teased. "Besides, it's their first child and those are notoriously slow in arriving."

Maggie nodded in agreement. "Well, between this

meeting being over way earlier than expected and everyone else being so agreeable and ready to sign on the dotted line, we are actually ahead of schedule." She leaned back in her seat and sighed. "I wish all of our meetings would go like the ones here in Boston. Any chance we can put in a request for that?"

"If only." Jason hit the Send button on his phone. "I don't know about you, but as much as I've enjoyed our time here, I'm anxious to hit New York City and spend some time there. You up for a late night drive?"

"What about our flight tomorrow?"

"I'm tired of flying. I'll get us a car and we can grab something to eat on the road. It's a four-hour drive and—"

"We won't get in until close to midnight, Jason!" she said incredulously, even though the thought was appealing. "Why don't we wait to fly tomorrow?"

"Because the flight isn't until noon and then we'll miss half the day there. There's so much to see and the weekend is wide open. The weather is supposed to be beautiful, and I want to walk around and eat pizza and grab hot dogs from a street vendor, shop a little..."

"You shop?" she asked, clearly amused at the thought.

"Yes, I do," he said simply. "And there is no place better to shop than New York."

"I don't know about that, but I will admit that I'm looking forward to the food."

"Is that a yes, Maggie? Ready for a road trip?" he asked excitedly, forgetting about his earlier intentions of keeping his distance.

"Oh, what the hell!" she said with equal abandon. "It beats watching another night of bad cable."

"Atta girl."

Jason knew how to make things happen. Within the hour there was a rental car waiting for them at their hotel and they were packed and ready to go. Maggie had made arrangements to get sandwiches for the trip from the hotel restaurant, and by seven o'clock they were on the road.

Jason had been on the phone most of the time they were getting ready, and Maggie had to wonder who he was talking to. By the time they were hitting the I-90, Maggie had their food and drinks situated so Jason could eat and drive. They talked amicably about some of the sites they hoped to see, and while secretly Maggie was thrilled to have the free time to explore New York City, she knew she couldn't let herself get too carried away. She was on company time no matter what Jason said.

By the time she saw the lights of the city, Maggie was sleepy and yet too excited to close her eyes. There was so much to see and do, and she felt the energy of the city consuming her already. Soon they were deep in the heart of the city, and she nearly choked when she saw where they were.

"The Four Seasons? We're staying at the *Four Seasons*?" she squealed. "That wasn't on our itinerary, Jason!"

He laughed as he climbed from the car and smiled at the valet who was helping Maggie out. "Well, our hotel couldn't accommodate us for tonight, so I made some calls and got us in here. You're not disappointed, are you?"

Maggie burst out laughing and nearly fell over. "Yes,

Jason, I am extremely disappointed that I have to stay at one of the top luxury hotels in the world. Damn you." She barely got the sentence out before breaking out in a fit of giggles again.

Jason walked around the car and grabbed her hand, something that felt far too natural, and led her into the lobby. "Now behave yourself," he teased as he walked to the desk to check them in.

"Welcome to the Four Seasons, Mr. Montgomery. We have two rooms waiting for you for five nights—"

"Five nights?" Maggie interrupted. "You completely canceled the other reservation?"

Jason nodded. "This is where I really wanted to stay anyway," he said simply.

Maggie felt like a country bumpkin. She was dressed casually, and even in her best clothes she had brought with her, she felt hyperaware of the fact that she was completely out of her element here.

Jason saw the apprehension on her face and questioned it.

"I wasn't mentally prepared for this, Jason," she said quietly. "I don't belong here."

"Nonsense," was all he said as he accepted their room keys and followed the bellboy to the elevators. It was late and Jason was exhausted. He had a lot to accomplish this weekend—hopefully relaxing and maybe figuring out what was behind his assistant's apprehensiveness whenever the subject of her husband came up. Even though he had promised himself he'd stay focused strictly on business, he wouldn't be satisfied until he knew the truth about the woman who was beginning to consume all of his thoughts.

Chapter 4

ONCE AGAIN THEY HAD ADJOINING ROOMS, BUT HAD agreed to sleep in on Saturday morning since they had arrived late the previous evening. Maggie was completely on board with that plan because she was totally exhausted and the bed in her room was the most comfortable one she had ever slept on.

As much as she had planned on sleeping late, she woke up at a conservative nine o'clock and ordered herself some breakfast. The thought of calling Jason and seeing if he was awake crossed her mind, but she was kind of enjoying the little bit of space and freedom she had.

Since their flight to Boston, they had gotten back on track. The kiss was seemingly forgotten. Out of sight, out of mind, she supposed. But at night? It was the highlight of all of her dreams. Sure, during the day Maggie was able to play the part of the engrossed executive assistant, but once she was alone with her thoughts? They were filled with one Jason Montgomery. Even now when she closed her eyes she could feel his lips on hers, the way his strong arms had embraced her, the smell of his cologne…

Dammit.

Taking the time to shower in the magnificent spa-quality bathroom, Maggie felt that she would be just fine spending the day in there! The knowledge that she had

five days to luxuriate in this kind of atmosphere was making her giddy.

By eleven she was dressed, ready, and more than a little anxious to go outside and explore the Big Apple. She called Jason's room and was surprised when he told her he'd been up since seven waiting for her call. They agreed to meet down in the lobby and Maggie told him she was more than willing to let him play tour guide.

Dressed in jeans and sneakers, Maggie was ready to walk for however long Jason planned. "Was there any place in particular that you absolutely want to see?" he asked as he put on a pair on sunglasses and walked out the front door of the hotel.

"Everything!" Maggie said with a bright smile. "I'm just excited to have a day to do this!"

"Remember that you said that," he said with a wicked grin, took a moment to get his bearings, and then took her hand and led her out onto the streets of New York.

Four hours later, Maggie found herself ready to drop. She collapsed on a sidewalk café bistro table and just tried to catch her breath. "Okay, I know I said that I wanted to see everything but I didn't really mean it."

Jason sat down opposite her and ordered them each a sparkling water. "Don't quit on me now. We've barely scratched the surface!"

"Scratched the surface? Jason, I am dazzled by all that we've seen, but surely we can catch a cab for some of it."

"It's not the same..." he said sweetly.

"We've seen Times Square, we've walked in Central Park, we've eaten pizza and hot dogs." She stopped to breathe. "Then there was Rockefeller Center and

Radio City Music Hall… I think I am done for the day. I may need to go and soak my feet in my tub-slash-swimming pool."

"Well, you could do that but if you do you're going to miss out on the best part," he teased.

She glared at him. "Best part? You mean we haven't seen the best part yet? What are you holding out on me?"

"Well, I was able to make some calls this morning and I got us two tickets to the Rangers game tonight!"

"No way!" she said excitedly. "Seriously? You're not joking with me?"

"I would never joke about tickets to a sporting event. It wouldn't be right."

"Damn straight it wouldn't. *Oh my gosh*! We're going to Madison Square Garden! I'm going to see the Rangers play on home ice!" Maggie began to babble, asking Jason a dozen questions in a row about the rest of their day.

"Slow down there, slugger," he joked. "We'll head back to the hotel so you can rest for a little while and then we can grab dinner someplace and then…"

"Dinner someplace? Are you crazy?" Maggie looked at him as if he'd lost his mind. "We are going to have the full game experience, and that includes eating from the concession stands in the Garden."

He wanted to laugh and tease her some more about the whole thing, but honestly he found her reaction to such a simple thing as a hockey game refreshing. Some women would fish for a nice dinner out before the game or want to avoid the game altogether, and yet here was Maggie, completely over the moon because they were going to eat hot dogs at Madison Square Garden so she could cheer on her team.

Yet another reason he was finding it hard to not be drawn to her.

"I cannot believe that you got us tickets," she said as she sipped her water. "This is the best day ever!" Taking a quick swallow, Maggie placed the glass down and looked at Jason. "Thank you. In case I forget to thank you later, I just want you to know right now how much this means to me."

If her words didn't say it, her eyes certainly conveyed it. "You are more than welcome, Maggie. I have to admit, I've never been to a game at the Garden, so you'll have to play tour guide this evening."

"Deal," she agreed readily. "Now, let's agree to take a cab back to the hotel so we can rest up for later."

Jason stood and then playfully pulled Maggie to her feet. "Deal."

The transformation was remarkable, and Jason found that in a crowd of eighteen thousand screaming hockey fans, he was speechless.

Somehow between the time he had dropped Maggie off at her room and the time they met to leave for the game, she had gone from mild-mannered assistant to rabid hockey fan! Her hair was loose and she wore a New York Rangers sweatshirt with jeans and sneakers, and if he listened closely enough, he could almost swear that she had suddenly picked up a New York accent.

"Off sides! *Off sides!*" she yelled at the top of her lungs as she jumped to her feet and Jason sat back and smiled. "Dammit," she muttered as the play was stopped and the crowd settled a bit. Without taking her eyes from

the ice, Maggie reached for her beverage and then sat down on the edge of her seat.

While Jason had the urge to say something, anything, that would allow him to interact with Maggie, for all intents and purposes, she didn't even realize he was there. Talk about an ego buster.

In between periods, they trolled the Garden to purchase more snacks and beer and Maggie was content to take it all in. When she did talk to Jason, it was about the game, the players, the building itself and although it wasn't a topic that he felt overly informed about, he was happy to watch Maggie enjoying herself.

By the third period he could tell that her voice was raw from all of the yelling, but when the final buzzer rang out and she turned and jumped into his arms in celebration, Jason knew that he was in serious trouble.

It had been a perfect night for Rangers fans, with a 4–1 victory over Philadelphia. As the final buzzer sounded out, Maggie jumped up along with the thousands of other fans to cheer and then jumped into Jason's arms. He caught her easily and found her excitement and enthusiasm to be contagious. "We won!" she cried. When she realized what she had done, she disentangled herself from Jason and joined the throngs of people walking from their seats. Maggie was simply glowing with victory as they exited their row. "That was amazing," she gushed. "Wasn't that a great game, Jace?"

He agreed. "I have to admit, there is definitely a vibe here in the Garden I can't imagine feeling anyplace else. New York fans are something else."

"You know it." Making their way through the mass exodus was time-consuming, and finally Maggie just stopped and dropped into a vacant seat. Jason stood for a moment in confusion.

"Are you okay?"

Maggie looked up at him. "What? Oh, yeah, I'm fine. It's going to take a while for the crowd to thin out, so I figured what's the rush?" She sighed and looked around the grand arena. "Think of the history of this place," she said in a near whisper. "How many games, events, and concerts has it seen? The number of people who've been here…it's amazing."

Jason sat down in the row in front of her and looked around. He'd never even given a thought to where he watched his sports, but the look of wonder on Maggie's face had him contemplating her words.

"I know it sounds silly and a bit clichéd, but it would be amazing if these walls could talk," she said softly, more to herself than to Jason. With a quiet sigh, Maggie stood and stretched. "Ready to fight the crowds once again?"

Jason stood. "I think we'll be okay; it's pretty empty in here already." Wordlessly, they walked up the steps to the nearest exit and he noticed how Maggie took one more wistful look over her shoulder before walking through the doors. He wished there was something he could say, something insightful, but decided just to let her have her moment.

They were outside finally and Maggie was a bit chilled but the thought of finding a cab seemed daunting. Jason read the indecision on her face. "It's not as hard as it seems. The trick is to walk a couple of blocks and then hail one."

Maggie nodded. "That makes sense." They walked silently up Seventh Avenue toward Times Square. The city was so alive, there was something so magical about it at night. How had she lived so long without experiencing so much? The way she lived had never really bothered Maggie before, but now? Traveling with Jason? She realized there was an entire world out there that she was missing out on.

Before she knew it, Jason had stopped and a cab was pulling up beside them. She climbed in and listened as he told the driver where to take them and then sat back, watching the city streets speed by. She didn't realize that she'd let out a sigh until Jason spoke.

"Did you want to walk some more?"

"Oh, no, it's just that there's so much to see. My feet are a bit sore and I know taking a cab is the right choice..."

"But..." he prompted.

She smiled, "But, I like to think that I'm superhuman and could handle walking the mile and a half back to the hotel."

Jason chuckled. "Well, if we hadn't walked so much today I might have considered it but I'm not as superhuman as I'd like to be either. I think tomorrow my body is going to be cursing me."

Maggie laughed out loud and Jason joined her. When they arrived back at the hotel, they commiserated like an elderly couple about all of their aches and pains, and Maggie was having a fit of the giggles by the time the elevator stopped at their floor.

Outside of her door, she took a deep breath and turned to face Jason. "Thank you so much for such an incredible night. It was absolutely the best."

He arched a dark brow at her. "Seriously? It was hot dogs and fistfights!"

"Are you crazy?" she laughed. "It was a chance to do something that I've always wanted to do! It wasn't about the food, per se, it was about the entire experience. I finally got to experience a night at the Garden as an adult who got to scream and yell and watch her team win!" Maggie caught herself before she flung herself at Jason and hugged him again. She was starting to like doing that too much.

With a steadying breath, she opened her door. "Anyway, it was a fabulous night, Jason. Thank you for making the time for us to do this." Her tone was serious, as was the expression in her eyes. She stood there staring at him for a long moment and almost caved and leaned toward him, something that he seemed about to do himself, when she took a step back. "Good night," she whispered and went into her room and closed the door.

Jason stood in the hallway staring at Maggie's door for far longer than he should have. He was confused and disappointed and didn't know why. It was the sound of voices coming off of the elevator that finally had him moving to his own room, and once inside he was too keyed up to go to sleep.

Glancing at the bedside clock, he noticed that it was barely eleven. It was late, but not too late to call the one person who could possibly shed a little light on who exactly Maggie Barrett was.

Kicking off his shoes, Jason pulled out his cell phone

and scrolled through his contacts until he found who he wanted, then relaxed on the bed and waited.

"Jason?" his father said by way of greeting. "Is everything okay?"

"Hey, Dad," he said easily, the sound of his father's voice bringing a smile to his face. "I'm fine. I just wanted to check in and see how you were doing."

"At eleven at night? Lucky for you I'm in the study and your mother is upstairs reading, otherwise she'd think there was some sort of terrible emergency that had you calling so late at night."

"Stop with the theatrics, Dad," Jason chided softly. "I know it's a bit late but..."

"Are you sure everything is okay? Is it the meetings? Are they going all right? I haven't seen any red flags in what you've been sending in."

"No, no...it's not the meetings; everything is fine there."

William was silent for a moment. "So where are you now? Still in Boston? You're due in New York on Monday, right?"

"Actually, we're in New York now. We drove down late last night after our last meeting and decided to relax this weekend." Jason couldn't hide the smile in his voice. "I took Maggie to a hockey game tonight."

"Hockey?" William said with disbelief. "Why on earth would you take Maggie to a hockey game?"

Jason laughed. "Believe it or not, she's a fan. For a woman who is quiet and unassuming during the day, she is a rabid hockey fan when she's watching her team play. It was quite an eye-opening experience."

Something in his son's tone caught William's

attention. "So she's a hockey fan? Who would've guessed? I can't imagine her sitting there in one of her conservative outfits, hair all pulled back, yelling and cheering for her team."

"There was no conservative outfit, Dad. She wore her hair all loose and wavy and a pair of jeans and a New York Rangers sweatshirt… She fit right in. She was like a kid in a candy shop. We ate hot dogs and pretzels and drank beer and Maggie said it was the best night." Jason sighed. "I never met a woman who was content just to eat hot dogs and drink beer."

William was glad Jason could not see him grinning like the cat that had eaten the canary. "Not all women want to be wined and dined, Jace. Maggie's a sensible girl with simple tastes. I'm sure she's unimpressed with the whole concept of spending a lot of money frivolously."

His father's words made sense, but Jason had a ton of questions that he needed answered if he was going to figure Maggie out. "No, you're right; Maggie's definitely not impressed with money. We're at the Four Seasons and she just about freaked out on me for spending the money."

William chuckled. "Sounds just like her. How did you end up there? That wasn't on your itinerary."

Jason explained about how their last-minute change of plans had dictated the change in hotels. "The thing is, I never gave much thought to where we stayed. All our lives we've stayed at some of the finest hotels in the world and to me, they're just a place to sleep, but the look of awe and wonder on Maggie's face when we walked in? It was priceless." An image of that face came to Jason's mind. "Then she was embarrassed

because she didn't think she was good enough to stay here."

"Well, I hope you convinced her otherwise!" his father scolded.

"Of course I did! Geez, what do you take me for? An idiot?" Jason sat up and raked a hand through his hair. "Look, there are some things about Maggie that just don't...fit."

William waited. And waited. "Like what?" he finally asked.

"Okay, for starters, there's the fact that she's even on this trip with me."

"Why is that a problem?"

"It goes back to that initial interview. Why has she worked for us for so long and I'm just now seeing her and hearing about her? How could you leave her down in customer service for so long when she is clearly such an asset to the company?"

"It wasn't my decision to make, Jason. Maggie didn't want to be an assistant; she was happy working in a low-pressure job. It was what she wanted."

"But why? She's so talented and intelligent! What happened at her last job to make her want to hide away in a mindless position?"

"That's not for me to discuss with you. Have you asked her?"

"What? No!" Jason nearly shouted, frustrated that his father wasn't giving him any information at all. "Look, you seem to know Maggie very well and I'm asking you to help me fill in some blanks!"

"Jason, she's your assistant. You work with her every day. Surely you must have some down time where

you're not talking about business. Why don't you ask about her personal life?"

"Because when I do she…changes. I can't quite explain it, but any mention of her personal life and she just sort of goes blank. I tried inviting her husband up here for the weekend and she nearly bit my head off!"

William stifled a laugh. "I think maybe you're overexaggerating, Jason. Why would she be mad about you inviting her husband to come to New York for the weekend?"

"That's what I'd like to know! If you ask me, this guy must be a world-class jackass."

"Why?"

Where did he even begin? Jason stood and began pacing the large room. "Okay, first of all, he let her come on this trip."

"And that makes him a jackass? If you remember correctly, you specifically asked for a married assistant who would travel with you. We found you one! How could that be a bad thing?"

"It's not that it's bad, not really, but he just doesn't seem to care that she's away. From what I can tell, he doesn't call Maggie and she doesn't call him. Doesn't that seem odd to you? You call Mom every day!"

"Well, your mother and I aren't like a lot of married couples. Maggie's young. I'm assuming her husband is young as well. How do you know they aren't calling one another?"

"Because I never see her on the phone!"

"Are you sharing a room with her?" William asked innocently.

"Dammit, Dad, you know I'm not! Why would you even say such a thing?"

"I'm just saying, Jace, that you have no idea what she's doing in her room when she's away from you. For all you know she's curled up in bed right now, all relaxed and sweet-talking her husband."

That image lodged itself in Jason's mind and made him angry. His hands were clenched at his sides and he wanted to walk across the hall, kick down Maggie's door, and see if that was the case. His father's voice was the only thing stopping him.

"You can't get angry at Maggie for doing what you asked," William sweetly reminded his son.

"What the hell did I ask?"

"You made it clear that you didn't want to waste time dealing with a needy spouse. Sounds to me like she is following your rules, not spending her work hours on the phone and keeping her personal life separate from your business hours."

When his father said it, it made sense, but to Jason it still didn't seem to fit. "Okay, sure, fine, I guess that could be the way that it is," he said finally.

"But…" William prompted.

"We went to a benefit the other night," Jason began, "and we danced." For a brief moment Jason swore he could still feel Maggie in his arms, and then remembered that he was supposed to be proving a point to his father. "And she said the last time she danced was in high school at her prom."

William let out a hearty laugh. "Son, I'm sure you're trying to tell me something but for the life of me, I don't know what it is!"

"Married couples dance, Dad! At their wedding, on dates, or whatever," he said defensively. "How is it that Maggie could be married and not have danced since high school?"

"Maybe her husband's a poor dancer?"

"Or maybe he's just a jerk," Jason countered. "Look, all I'm saying is that the guy seems to show absolutely no interest in Maggie. Any time we go anywhere or do anything it's like she's…living for the first time! I have to be honest with you, Dad, I'm worried about her."

"Well, Jason, to be honest right back at you, it's you I'm worried about."

"Me? Why?"

William let out a dramatic sigh. "You asked for an assistant who wasn't going to come on to you. We found you one. You asked for an assistant who is married. We found you one. You basically wanted a completely uncomplicated business companion who had no interest in you personally and yet here you are, attacking Maggie's personal life. She's your assistant; she's nothing to you. Leave her personal life alone, it's none of your concern." His tone was mild but his words were meant to provoke.

"What the hell is the matter with you?" Jason snapped. "Maggie's more than just an assistant to me! She's…" And then he caught himself and wished that he could take his words back. Dammit.

"Jason," William said, suddenly serious. "Maggie *is* just your assistant, right? You haven't done anything to change that, have you?"

His father knew him too well and Jason knew that lying would be pointless. "It wasn't supposed to be like

this," he admitted quietly. "I liked her work ethic, I enjoyed our conversations, and then we started this trip and suddenly…I'm getting to know Maggie and I feel… connected to her somehow. I look forward to spending time with her and getting to know her, and then I have to remind myself she's married and I realize I'm no better than all of those women who've worked for me these last months."

"You are nothing like that, Jace," his father replied solemnly. "How does Maggie feel?"

Once again, Jason knew it would be pointless to lie. "I think she maybe feels the same way but…she's married, Dad. I would never, ever do anything to jeopardize her marriage."

William took a deep breath and slowly let it out. "Talk to Maggie," he said simply.

"To what end, Dad? She's married; she's my assistant. There is no way this can end well."

William repeated his words. "Trust me."

If only it were that easy. "It's getting late," he finally said, suddenly feeling mentally and physically exhausted.

"Think about what I said, Jace."

"I will, Dad. Thanks for talking with me. Good night."

Jason powered down his phone, stripped, and climbed into the king-sized bed. Flipping the lights off, he rested against the pillows and stared into the darkness, wondering just what he was going to do about this situation.

He was a man used to being in control, a man who knew how to overcome every obstacle thrown in his path. Unfortunately, this was not a simple case of

overcoming some red tape in a business deal or appeasing a difficult client.

This was about his heart.

This was about Maggie's marriage.

This was about a situation that would leave somebody hurt. And Jason didn't want to be responsible for that.

He had to force himself to put his focus back on his business, to remember that Maggie was off-limits no matter how much she tempted him. But most important, Jason had to remember that for the first time possibly in his life, he wasn't going to get what he wanted.

Chapter 5

FIVE MORE DAYS.

Jason stared out his hotel window overlooking the Atlanta skyline and let out a weary sigh. Those first few days immediately following the hockey game had been the hardest of his life. While being a hardass had never been a problem for him before, it was suddenly one now when the one he was being hard on stared back at him with sadness and confusion written in her big brown eyes.

It had taken every ounce of strength he possessed not to cave in.

Not that he had been mean, no; Jason had gone into extreme workaholic mode and spent every waking moment doing nothing that wasn't directly related to Montgomerys and the expansion project. They could probably go home right now and skip these last few days of meetings—things had gone so well as they'd traveled down the East Coast that Jason didn't feel they'd be missing out on anything. He had more than enough business to make him happy.

But no, being the ultimate planner and perfectionist, and knowing that he always finished what he started, Jason knew he had to get through these last five days even if it killed him.

And it just might.

To her credit, Maggie never outright questioned

Jason on his abrupt change in behavior. When they'd met for breakfast that Sunday morning in New York, he'd made sure that he was deeply entrenched in his agenda for their upcoming meetings. He'd questioned her lack of preparedness and had actually sent her back to her room to get her laptop so that she could get some work done after their day off.

For the nine days that had followed, Jason had worked like a man possessed. He was up before dawn on most days and would utilize the hotel gym before starting work. By the time he met up with Maggie daily, he had already gone through an hour of the only physical release he could manage. He pushed his body to its limits every morning and then did the same to his brain throughout the day until he fell into an exhausted sleep every night.

And still it wasn't enough to take the edge off of what he was feeling for her.

Jason was careful to keep them from participating in any social settings as they had early on in their trip. Although he had a couple of charitable events on their agenda, he'd managed to exclude Maggie from them under the guise of needing her to prepare contracts and reports that were vital to their project.

Well, he laughed at himself mirthlessly, they weren't vital to the project quite as much as they were vital to helping him keep his distance. And his sanity. Maggie never argued, and actually seemed relieved not to have to traipse along with him everywhere he went. While Jason knew deep down that he should have taken his father's advice and actually talked to Maggie, he just couldn't bring himself to do it.

Five more days.

It might as well be a damn lifetime.

Turning from his view from the top floor of the Loews Atlanta, Jason took a look around the room. It was beautiful; it was luxurious. It was far too big for a man alone. The king-size bed only emphasized that he was sleeping alone and he didn't like it. If he really wanted to, there was no doubt Jason could go out and find company for the evening.

But he didn't want company, he wanted Maggie.

Dammit.

The bedside clock showed it was nearing midnight and Jason was too keyed up to sleep. He couldn't wait to get back to Charlotte: back to his own home and his own bed and his own life. Maybe once he was back in his own surroundings this obsession would end. Maybe once they were back to working in the office and not spending so much time with only one another for company, Jason would be free to pick up the phone and call a woman for a date without wishing she were someone else.

Maybe he would lose his mind before they ever got home.

Five more days.

Maggie was miserable. While Jason was doing exactly what he was supposed to be doing—being her boss—she missed the camaraderie that they had shared early on in the trip. She kicked herself daily for letting her guard down and allowing herself to have feelings for him.

In her own defense, Jason Montgomery was an incredible man. He was kind and funny and intelligent,

the type of man who really took an interest in you when he wanted to. And for a couple of days there, he seemed to really want to know Maggie.

Then he didn't.

She was certain it was her own fault. After all, here she was, a supposedly married woman who couldn't seem to stop throwing herself at him. She was the exact thing Jason had been trying to avoid on this trip. It was no wonder he barely looked at her. He was probably trying to think of ways to send her home and possibly move her back to the customer service department.

That thought was more than a little depressing, and Maggie let out a sigh. It was late and she was sitting alone in her hotel room curled up in a chair. Not that long ago, if anyone had told her she'd be staying in a luxury hotel and working as an executive assistant for an attractive man, she would have snorted with disbelief. Add the fact that she was the one attracted to the boss and not the other way around, and she would have laughed out loud. And yet here she was.

They had less than a week left on the trip. Three days in Atlanta, two in Miami, and then it was back home. What would happen then? She couldn't imagine Jason would fire her immediately. No, they still had a lot of work to do on this expansion project once they were back at Montgomerys. But once the project was wrapped up and it was back to business as usual, then what? Could she go to his father and request a transfer back to her old position?

Maggie stood and walked over to her mini fridge, pulling out a bottle of water and taking a long drink. She didn't want to go back to her old life, not really.

The woman she had been before this trip was a scared woman, a shell of a person. She wasn't living. She'd had no friends. These last weeks with Jason opened her eyes to how much there was to do and see, and she was missing it all because of the actions of one person. Maggie was done letting that bastard have any control over her life.

Placing the water on her nightstand, Maggie went about the task of getting ready for bed. Walking into the bathroom, she turned on the light and then took a long hard look at her reflection. She was too young to hide away from life any longer. While she didn't have a clue what to do about Jason and her feelings for him, she did know that when they got back home she was going to start getting involved in things. She'd finally accept some of those after-work invitations her co-workers were always extending. Maybe she'd join a gym, take a class or two, and start going out more.

Reaching for her toothbrush, she couldn't shake the image of the person she wanted to go out with the most.

Jason.

"You have to let that go," she scolded her reflection. "He's your boss and that's all he is ever going to be. He thinks you're married for crying out loud. How are you going to explain that one?"

She'd really backed herself into a corner. At the time it had made perfect sense, but now that she was ready for a change, Maggie realized one little lie was going to complicate her life in a major way.

For now she had no choice but to continue with the ruse. It had kept her from doing something completely foolish with Jason, and as much as she hated to admit

it, it was probably for the best that they hadn't fallen into bed together on this trip. It would only make things more difficult and confusing when they got home.

Unfortunately, the image of Jason in bed had her heart racing. Maybe it would have been worth the difficulty and confusion—even if it had turned out only to be for one night.

She slipped into her pajamas and turned out the lights as she climbed into bed. It was ridiculously large for one person and although it was a complete luxury, Maggie had a feeling it would even be more decadent to share it with someone.

Rolling onto her side, she couldn't help but punch her pillow out of frustration before settling in for yet another night filled with dreams of the one man she wanted but couldn't have.

Chapter 6

THEY'D MADE IT THROUGH THE ATLANTA MEETING and were landing in Miami. Jason spent most of the flight on the phone with his brother Mac while Maggie typed up last-minute contracts at Jason's request.

They checked into their hotel and rushed up to their rooms without exchanging a word. Maggie had just enough time to freshen up her makeup before Jason knocked on the door to signal that the car was waiting. She sighed with irritation. Did he really think one word from him would have her throwing herself at him? Couldn't he at least have the common decency to say something to her that wasn't directly about Montgomerys? It was getting beyond rude and Maggie wasn't sure if she'd be able to make it through another day like this.

When Maggie stepped out of her room, Jason was already halfway down the hall. She practically had to run to catch up with him at the elevator, and when they stepped on and he hung up the phone, Maggie stamped her hand over the emergency stop button and faced Jason full of fury.

"What the hell?" he snapped.

"You know, Jason, I think I deserve a little more common courtesy than a knock on the door beckoning me to follow you."

Jason pinched the bridge of his nose and inhaled

sharply. "We don't have time for this right now. We have an appointment to get to."

"Oh, I get that, Jason; believe me, I do. What I don't get is why I'm being treated like some sort of leper or something! I've been working my butt off for you on this trip and in the last week you have been impossible!"

His eyes finally met hers. "Rude? Look, I don't know what you were expecting on this trip, but I've been treating you like an employee. We are on this trip to work. I'll admit that I got a little sidetracked back in New York but then I realized it was a mistake. I hired you to be my assistant; not my date, not my friend. You are an employee of Montgomerys and you were chosen for this position because you meet certain criteria."

"Because I'm *married*?" she said snidely, wanting nothing more than to smack his face and make him stop using that condescending tone on her.

"That was partially it. You were qualified for the job that I needed done. I told you from the get-go this wasn't a pleasure trip and I think for a while there the lines were getting blurry." It was the most honest statement he'd ever made to her and the look of horror on her face had him wanting to take it back.

Maggie took a step back from Jason and lowered her eyes to the ground. "I see," she said quietly. Reaching beyond him, she gently hit the button for the lobby and was relieved when they started moving. "I'm sorry if I did anything to make you uncomfortable, Jason. That was never my intention."

With a growl of frustration, Jason reached out and hit the stop button himself and then caught Maggie by the arms when the elevator car jerked to a halt. "Maggie,

look at me," he said gently. When her eyes met his, they were wary and sad, and Jason felt like a school yard bully. "It wasn't *you*, okay? I just think it's better for us to stay focused on the project because when I let my guard down…"

Maggie couldn't help it, she leaned into him. "What?" she whispered.

Jason was only human. The feel of her, the smell of her perfume, and those big brown eyes looking up at him were his undoing. "I find it hard to forget that I shouldn't do things like this." And he lowered his mouth to hers. Maggie responded to him instantly and Jason thought he was going to lose his mind. Her lips were so soft, so pliant, and when she let out a sigh and relaxed into him, he took a step forward and pressed her back against the wall of the elevator.

He feasted on her lips like he'd been dying to for weeks as Maggie ran her hands up his neck and into his hair, anchoring him to her. Jason's tongue teased at Maggie's bottom lip and when she opened for him and touched her tongue to his, he thought he'd go up in flames. Jason wanted to tell her how much he wanted her, how much he'd been thinking about her and how he wanted nothing more than to cancel their meetings for today and go back upstairs when…

"Is everyone okay in there?" A voice was speaking to them through an intercom in the elevator and they broke apart instantly.

"Um…yes," Jason stammered. "We're fine." He reached over and set the elevator in motion again. "Thank you," he said out loud to whoever was speaking to them, knowing there was probably a camera that

caught all of that on tape. There was no way to claim a mechanical issue. They'd just have to step out into the lobby and pray that no one said anything.

They arrived on the main floor of the hotel and walked out to the waiting car. As they pulled away from the curb, Jason spoke without looking directly at Maggie. "I'm not going to apologize for that," he said simply.

"I'm not asking you to," she replied. There was so much that she wanted to say and that she wanted to ask, but now was completely not the time. They were wrapping up this trip and had two important clients to meet with today. The timing of all this really sucked.

"So," she began, getting her head back where it belonged, "Dennis Caprese is up first this morning. I've talked to his assistant several times in the last couple of days and per all of your preliminary talks with him, I've prepared the contracts already so that should everything go our way, he can sign today."

Jason nodded. He didn't give a damn about business and meetings right now. All he could think about was that kiss. Shouldn't she be outraged? Shouldn't she be demanding he not touch her again? He had been speculating for far too long about her marriage, and it just didn't sit right with him that Maggie wasn't putting up more of a fight. It didn't fit. The woman he had come to know had morals and was pretty traditional in her views and beliefs. It didn't match up with the image of her as a married woman. Jason had no doubt that she wasn't the kind of woman who would have an affair.

Then why did she kiss him with such urgency?

Why did it feel like she would gladly have let him

take her right there in the elevator, and to hell with the consequences?

And why did he want to tell the driver to turn the car around so that he could test that theory out?

"Here we are, sir," the driver said, interrupting his thoughts. "I'll stay close by so you can call me when you're done."

Jason mumbled a word of thanks and exited the car, Maggie close behind him. All of his wonderings and naughty thoughts would have to wait. They had meetings to get through. But once business was done, so was all of the tippy-toeing he'd been doing.

Jason was going to get some answers.

Tonight.

Their second meeting was over by four, but Alan Cummings, the CEO of AC Industries, invited them out for dinner. Jason had wanted to refuse, but Cummings wasn't one hundred percent on board yet and he figured that a few more hours in the man's company could only help their situation.

Maggie assumed Jason would send her back to the hotel to get started on paperwork and was surprised when he told Alan they'd both be there. Maggie looked at him quizzically, unsure why he wanted her to go with him when there was a mountain of work to do. Jason read the question in her eyes and simply said, "There will be plenty of time to get it all done when we get back to North Carolina."

She wanted to argue that she needed to get started while it was all fresh in her mind, but the reality was she really needed a little time away from Jason. After the

kiss they'd shared earlier, he seemed to fill all the space around her. She could feel him, smell him, and found it hard to concentrate with him so close by.

But she didn't say a word. Instead, Maggie merely nodded and stayed put in the conference room of AC Industries until it was time to leave. "Do you need to go back to the hotel before dinner?" Jason asked.

"I wouldn't mind doing that, but it's completely up to you. Mr. Cummings seemed set on an early dinner so I don't think it would be worth the rush to go across town and back again."

"Apparently he does a dinner like this once a month with several clients so we won't be one-on-one with him. I guess if nothing else I may get to network a little bit more," Jason said casually.

"That would be great, Jason, but then maybe it would be best if I didn't go. I'll only be in the way, and no one else will have their assistants with them, so—"

"Nonsense!" Alan Cummings said as he walked back into the room. He was a tall man with a booming voice, and Maggie nearly fell out of her chair at the sound of it. "I have a couple of other out of town clients meeting us tonight and several of them have their assistants with them. And even if they didn't, Maggie, I would hate to not be a proper host and not include you."

She smiled at him but still didn't feel up to spending any more time talking business. A little alone time back in her room to unwind and think about what had happened earlier in the elevator was what Maggie most wanted to do, but clearly that wasn't going to happen. "Thank you," she said finally and stood when he indicated that they were ready to go.

Back in the town car, they rode over to a restaurant on the water where AC Industries hosted their monthly events. Maggie loved the sound and smell of the ocean and wanted nothing more than to kick her shoes off and go down on the sand to enjoy the feel of it between her toes. Unfortunately, Alan and Jason were waiting for her, so she smiled sheepishly and walked with them into the restaurant.

Within an hour Maggie's head was spinning. They had met well over two dozen new people, had enjoyed hors d'oeuvres and several glasses of wine. All she wanted to do was sit down to a hot meal and finish the day, but Jason was working the room, deep in conversation. There was no way for her to get his attention and ask to leave without seeming rude.

Finally, dinner was announced and they were seated at a table for eight. It was some of the best seafood Maggie had ever tasted. Jason inquired if she was enjoying her meal, but once his eyes met hers—for the first time since the elevator—all thoughts of food left her mind. The heat in his eyes clearly matched her own and it was all she could do to nod her head. "Everything's delicious," she whispered.

Jason stared at Maggie's lips and thought of how delicious they had been earlier in the day. He suddenly found himself without an appetite for food, ready to be done socializing. They had an early morning meeting with one last client and then an afternoon flight home. He needed to get through this last night and right now, all Jason wanted to do was to take Maggie by the hand and drag her back to the hotel and to hell with the consequences.

"Jason!" Alan Cumming's voice shouted from across

the room. He turned and faced the man. "There's someone here I want you to meet!"

With a sigh of resignation, he excused himself and stood, but not before giving Maggie an apologetic look. She smiled serenely back at him; she understood. Once he was across the room and swallowed up into the crowd, Maggie decided to take advantage of the time and walked out onto the back deck of the restaurant that led out to the beach. There were several other guests mingling out there, so she knew no one would pay too much attention to her.

Once outside, the sound of the waves crashing and the view of the sun setting were just overwhelming. Unable to resist, she headed down the wooden steps that led to the sand below, kicked off her shoes, and started toward the water. It felt better than she had imagined. She couldn't remember the last time she had been to the beach, and it was just heavenly to stand still and let her senses take it all in.

"I see that you've loosened up some, Mags," said a voice from behind her and Maggie froze. *No, it couldn't be!* Slowly she turned around and gasped in horror. There, standing before her was her former boss, Martin Blake.

"Martin," she said as calmly as she could, even though she felt as though she was about to be sick.

"I see you're still giving the come-on to your boss," he said snidely. "Tell me, will you go back to the hotel and cry foul again?"

She wanted to punch him in his smug face. "There's nothing to cry foul about," she said crisply. "I finally work for a man who knows the difference between someone being polite and someone issuing a come-on."

She was rewarded when his expression faltered slightly. "Plus, I haven't had to fight my way out of a locked room to get away from someone who is no better than a rapist."

Martin's expression turned to pure fury. "You little *bitch*," he sneered. "You led me on for months and then you had the audacity to run out and play the victim?"

"I *was* a victim," she fought back. "I never led you on; I never wanted you to touch me. *Ever.* You're disgusting and I hope never to see you again." She spat the words at him and then turned and walked away with her head held high until she was around the front of the restaurant. Then she nearly crumpled to the ground. Her heart was racing and she felt ready to retch.

Never in a million years had she expected to see Martin Blake again, and right now all she wanted to do was get in the car and leave. But she'd have to go and find Jason first. The thought of going back inside and chancing another run-in with Martin was overwhelming. She gulped in several breaths and tried to calm herself.

"Maggie?"

Suddenly Jason was standing in front of her and gently pulling her to her feet. "What happened? Are you okay? Are you sick?"

She had never been so grateful to see anyone in her life. Well, that wasn't completely true. The last time she had felt this way it had been William Montgomery saving her. "Can we leave?" she asked a little too urgently, clutching the front of Jason's shirt for support. "Please?"

"Of course," he said and pulled her into his embrace. "What happened?"

"I don't want to talk about it right now. Can we please just go?"

Jason pulled back and looked down at Maggie's face. She was pale and her eyes glistened with unshed tears. Something was wrong. Something had happened, and while he wasn't going to push her right this minute, he knew he wouldn't rest until he found out. He led her to their waiting car and they rode back to the hotel in silence. Once inside, he let Maggie walk to the elevator while he headed to the concierge desk and ordered some tea to be sent up to her room.

He joined her moments later, and when they arrived up on their floor, he took the room key from her, opened her door, and followed her inside. Jason could be patient when he needed to be, but right now he felt anything but. He stood back and watched as Maggie kicked off her shoes and placed her purse and briefcase on her desk before collapsing in the oversized chair next to the window.

"Maggie?" he asked softly. "What happened back there? Did someone upset you?" By now he had figured out she wasn't sick. There'd been no signs of that on the ride back to the hotel, so his next thought was that someone had caused this. "You can trust me, Maggie," he said when he saw the hesitation on her face.

"Three years ago your father saved my life," she said in a voice devoid of emotion. "I worked for a big company as an executive assistant and I was away at a conference with my boss." Maggie stared out the window. "I had no idea that my boss had no real interest in the conference; he had brought me there to seduce me."

Jason felt fury rising inside of him. He tried to think

of every face he had seen tonight and figure out who had done this to Maggie. His thoughts were interrupted when she continued to speak.

"I was so naive. I honestly had no idea what was going on. He had booked all the travel arrangements when that was normally my job, and instead of questioning it, I was thankful to have had one less thing to do." She grew silent for a moment and collected her thoughts before going on. "We arrived in California and I was so excited because I had never left the East Coast. When we got to the hotel, he checked us in. Again, I didn't see anything wrong with that. I had never gone on a business trip before, so to me, it was all completely on the up-and-up."

"Maggie, you don't have to..."

She faced him briefly. "No, it's okay, Jason. I want you to know." Maggie turned to look back out the window again. "It wasn't until we got up to the room and he closed the door behind me that I realized that something was wrong. He was so quick; one minute we were talking business and the next all of my personal belongings were snatched from me. He laughed and said how he'd been planning ways to get me alone for months. I tried to leave; I was clawing at the door as he was clawing at me. When I finally got free he told me that if I went to the management or to the police, he'd tell them it was a lovers' spat and that I was blackmailing him for money. I knew they'd believe him over me. After all, he was a big-time executive and I was a nobody."

"That's not true, Maggie," Jason protested, but she wasn't listening.

"So I left the room and got down to the lobby and realized I had no place to stay, no money, and no ID.

That's when your father found me. He was so nice." She stopped and smiled at the memory. "I was so scared and he just sat with me in the lobby on the sofa and told me about himself, about his family, and then he offered to buy me a cup of coffee. He showed me his ID. By the time we were done with coffee, he had worked out a way to get my belongings back and offered me a chance at a new life and a new job."

Jason couldn't help but smile. That was his dad. William Montgomery took care of others and it was just one of the reasons that people loved him. He thought back to his first meeting with Maggie and how he had sensed that there was more to the relationship between her and his father and now he understood it.

Standing, Maggie walked over to her mini fridge and pulled out a drink for each of them. Jason waved her off. "I asked the concierge to send up some tea for you. It should be here any minute."

She smiled sadly at him. "You are so much like your father, Jason," she said softly. "You take care of people."

"I only hope that I can be like him. Dad's an incredible man."

"You're more like him than you think." They were interrupted by a knock at the door and Jason walked over and let the uniformed server in. He set up the tray with tea and an assortment of fresh fruit and cookies on the table. Jason tipped and thanked him and then went back toward Maggie. She poured them each a cup and they sat in silence for several minutes, each absorbing all that had been revealed.

"He was there tonight?" Jason finally asked, breaking the silence. "Your former boss?"

"Yes."

"Did he speak to you?"

Maggie nodded. "When Alan called you over after dinner, I went outside and walked down to the beach. I just wanted a few minutes to feel the sand between my toes." She gave a mirthless laugh. "I never heard him approach. I was just standing there enjoying the sunset and the ocean breeze and then there he was. He asked if I was going to lead you on back at the hotel and then cry foul."

"Son of a *bitch*," Jason muttered and then stood and began pacing the room. "Why didn't you come and get me?"

"I had to face him, Jason. I have been hiding for three years. I never saw him again after your father found me in that lobby. If I was ever going to be free of this…this nightmare, I had to face him. I did my best, I really did. I held on to my dignity and didn't let him bully me and then I walked away with my head held high. By the time you found me, I just crumpled. I held it together as long as I could."

Her voice broke on the last word and then the tears finally fell. Jason was instantly at her side and he pulled her close. For the first time in three years, Maggie finally let herself cry openly in front of another person. Maybe now it would finally be over. Maybe now she wouldn't have to feel like an idiot. Or a victim. She had gotten away from Martin before he was able to do anything, and she knew now that she had done nothing wrong. It was a relief. She had let him have three years of her life, and now she was free.

She cried into Jason's shirt, and when she realized what she was doing and made to pull away, he simply held her closer. "Your shirt," she whispered.

"Don't worry about my damn shirt," he said gruffly and led her over to the bed. Gently he sat her down and

then went over and closed the drapes. "I think you've had enough today. A good night's sleep will help a little, I hope." He smiled down at her. She was still dressed in her black pencil skirt and white blouse, but her hair was mussed up from her walk on the beach and all that had happened afterward, and her makeup was practically gone, and yet she was still the most beautiful woman he had ever seen.

"Sleep in tomorrow. I can handle the Hardwell people on my own," he said as he took a step away from her.

"That's not necessary, Jason," she protested and stood up. "You hired me to do a job and—"

"To hell with the job, Maggie!" he snapped and then cursed himself when she winced. She'd had a traumatic night and yelling at her wasn't helping. He took a calming breath. "Look, it's just that I know you've had an emotional night and I want you to rest and relax. I don't want you to have to be looking over your shoulder in case this guy shows up anyplace else, okay?"

She nodded and Jason took a step toward her and gave her a gentle shove to make her sit down again. "Try and get some sleep, Maggie," he said softly.

"I doubt I'll get much sleep. If I close my eyes, I'll just see him," she said sadly. "I'm probably going to channel surf for a while."

Jason sat down beside her on the bed and took her hand in his. "You have to at least try and sleep."

Maggie turned to him and gave him a weak smile before shaking her head. "It took months before I was able to close my eyes and not see his face after it happened. I'd sleep with the TV on just so that I wouldn't hear his voice in my head."

"Where was your husband during all of this?" Jason asked although he really didn't want to know.

Maggie didn't understand the question at first. Husband? What husband? In all of the turmoil, that little white lie had been forgotten. How was she supposed to respond? What would a husband do? "Um, we weren't married yet but whenever I let it get to me, he would just hold me until I fell asleep." She hoped that's what husbands did but right now, she couldn't find the strength to care.

Jason nodded and released her hand. A million thoughts were racing through his mind, but first and foremost, he wanted to be the one to hold her until she fell asleep tonight. It was beyond inappropriate and he knew he could never voice that out loud. Maggie had been through enough tonight with her previous boss without having to worry about her current boss harassing her, too.

"I wish there was something I could do or say right now to help," he admitted. "I don't think I've ever felt so helpless in my life. Thank you for trusting me with this, Maggie, but I have to tell you, I want to know who it is and go after him and beat him senseless for what he's done to you!"

Jason stood and was about to walk away when Maggie reached out for his hand and pulled him back to her. "That won't help anything, Jason. And I should be the one thanking you."

"For what? For making you go to that damn dinner? You said you didn't want to go and I forced you. That means it's my fault this happened, Maggie! Do you know how that makes me feel?"

She knew exactly how he felt, because it was written all over his beautifully expressive face. Without thinking, she reached out and cupped his face in her hands. "Jason,

you have nothing to be sorry for." She held her gaze steady with his, willing him to see how sincere she was. "No one could have predicted this happening. Thank you for being there when I needed someone, and thank you for sitting here with a near-hysterical woman and calming her down."

Jason reached up and placed his hands over hers before pulling them away from his face. Her touch was killing him. "I wasn't there when it really mattered, Maggie," he said, his voice gruff with emotion.

"You're here now," she whispered. "And I don't want you to go."

He stared down at her. What was she saying? "Maggie…I…"

"I don't want to be alone," she admitted. "I just want…I need…"

"What?" he asked so softly that she almost didn't hear him. "What do you need? Anything, Maggie. Anything you need, I'll do." He took a step closer.

She took a steadying breath. "Will you hold me?"

As if she were made of spun glass, he carefully enveloped her in his embrace. "Yes," he whispered into her hair and just reveled in the feel of her wrapped in his arms.

"Stay with me tonight, Jason."

He leaned back and looked down into her face. "I don't know if that's such a good idea."

She gave him a small smile, stepped out of his arms, and turned to pull down the comforter on the bed and turn out the bedside lamp. "I trust you, Jason." She sat down on the bed and reached for his hand. "I just need you to hold me."

Jason kicked off his shoes, removed his belt, and joined her on the bed. There they lay, completely clothed, and clung to one another for the rest of the night.

Chapter 7

Jason woke first. They were still wrapped around one another as they had been last night, and he found that he could get very used to waking up with Maggie in his arms. Her hand was resting right over his heart; the hand that bore the ring of another man.

"Dammit," he whispered and then gently tried to disentangle himself from her. Maggie let out a small sound of protest and when Jason was standing and looking down at her, her eyes fluttered open.

"What time is it?" she whispered.

"It's almost six," he said, trying hard not to let the anger he felt at himself show. When Maggie made to rise he held up a hand to stop her. "Go back to sleep, Maggie. It's early yet."

"I have to pack and we've got the meeting at nine and..."

"I'm going alone. I told you that last night. You can stay here and pack. I'll send the car for you around eleven and we'll head to the airport."

"I can be packed in fifteen minutes, Jason," she countered. "There's no reason for me not to go with you." She rose from the bed.

With a huff of frustration, Jason took a step back. "This isn't up for discussion, okay? I'm telling you, as your boss, that I am going to this meeting alone. I want you to stay here and make sure that everything is packed up and ready to go when the car arrives."

As if the "boss" line wasn't enough, his tone said it all. It was clipped and sharp, and was almost enough to make Maggie burst into tears. Again. "Fine," she said softly. "I'll make sure everything is taken care of." Before Jason could say another word, Maggie stepped around him, went into the bathroom, and closed the door.

He took the hint.

Silently leaving the room, Jason walked across the hall to his own room. Once the door was closed behind him, he slumped against it and cursed himself. What the hell had he been thinking spending the night with Maggie? It was all innocent, but did it really make a difference? She was another man's wife and he had no right to spend the night in her bed. And the fact that she was his employee only made it worse.

Jason always considered himself a reasonable, level-headed man, and yet right now he was feeling anything but. He could go to this meeting this morning without Maggie and it wouldn't be a hardship, but what was he supposed to do once they were in the car together riding to the airport? Or flying home? Hell, what was going to happen once they got back to the office? How could he possibly look at her, spend time with her knowing that he had crossed so many lines with her?

If her husband came and kicked his ass, he would take it. It was no less than he deserved. Jason had never gone after a married woman. He'd never even given one a second look. That was a line he never crossed. He believed in the sanctity of marriage and never wanted to be the cause of someone's marriage breaking up.

Until Maggie.

What was it about Maggie Barrett that had him

breaking all of his rules? She was supposed to be the answer to all of his problems, but had ended up causing a whole lot more.

Jason dragged himself away from the door and went about the task of packing. It would be good to get home and sleep in his own bed tonight. The thought of this trip finally being over was more of a relief than he ever thought possible. He needed to get his head back on straight, and maybe by the time they returned to the office on Monday he would have an answer for how to work with Maggie *without* working with Maggie.

It was early and he was organized, so the process of packing took little to no time and Jason found himself sitting on the edge of the still-made bed wondering what the hell to do next. Reaching for his phone, he decided that he needed to talk to someone other than Maggie.

He decided to call the one person who would understand what he was dealing with better than anyone else.

"Somebody better be dead or dying for you to be calling this early," Lucas said sleepily into the phone.

"Good morning to you, too, Brother," Jason said, forcing the chipperness into his tone.

"Jason?" Lucas asked, coming a little more awake. "What's going on?"

"Look, I'm sorry to be calling so early in the morning but…I've got a situation on my hands and I need some advice."

"Give me a minute to get out of bed so I don't wake Emma," he said quietly and Jason could hear the rustling of blankets as Lucas got up.

"I wouldn't have called so early if…"

"No worries, Jace," Lucas said. "Are you home already? Did everything go okay on the trip?"

"Everything is fine with the trip. We head home today after lunch."

"Okay, if it's not about the trip, then what's up?" Lucas asked around a very loud yawn.

Jason sighed. Where to begin? "You know how I've been having problems keeping an assistant ever since you and Emma hooked up?"

Lucas laughed. "You did make for some unforgettable stories. Personally, I thought that all of the women would go after Mac; after all, he's the next in line to take over Montgomerys."

"What does that have to do with anything?" Jason snapped. "I'm the better looking one."

That only made Lucas laugh more. "Sure, you keep telling yourself that. Most women are looking for money *and* power. Mac has got that."

"I've got that," Jason mumbled.

"No, Brother, you're the typical middle child. You do your best to stand out and believe me, with two such spectacular brothers, I know it can't be easy for you!" Lucas was clearly having fun. It had been far too long since they'd just bantered like this.

"Why did I bother calling you?"

"Beats me, but believe me, I'd rather be back in bed with my beautiful wife than sitting here listening to you whine about...wait, what did you call about?"

"I was getting to that!" Jason snapped and then let out a huff of frustration. "How did you deal with your feelings for Emma in the beginning? You know, with her working for us?"

"Wow…" Lucas began, "I don't know. I struggled with it. A lot. When we were snowed in at my place, that was the biggest hang-up for me. I mean, I didn't want to cross a line with her or have it come back that I had sexually harassed her or anything, but she let me know that it wasn't about work or Montgomerys. She was attracted to me."

"Yeah, but…when you both came back to work, wasn't it awkward?"

"Well, yeah, a bit, but that was because I still had the mind-set that I didn't want a relationship. I had to get my head on straight and I didn't want to drag Emma down with me. I was in love with her, but I thought it was better to stay away. Only I couldn't."

"Would you still have felt that way if Emma had been involved with somebody else?"

"Oh, shit, Jace… What have you done?"

"Nothing!" he replied defensively. "At least, nothing that bad."

"How bad?" Lucas asked.

"My assistant…Maggie?"

"Did you sleep with her?"

"No, not really…"

Lucas growled. "It's a yes or no question, Jace. Did. You. Sleep. With. Her?"

"Well…"

"Isn't she married? Wasn't that part of your criteria, that the person who went with you on this trip be married? How could you do that?"

"I can't explain it, Lucas. That's why I'm calling you. It's a freakin' mess and I don't know what to do!"

"Start at the beginning and tell me everything that

happened. I can't get you out of trouble if you start leaving crap out."

So Jason told Lucas about their trip, from the kiss at the Rock and Roll Hall of Fame to their spending the night together fully clothed in Maggie's bed. Then he waited for Lucas to say something. After several tense and silent moments, Jason finally spoke. "Well? What am I supposed to do?"

Lucas let out a pent-up breath. "You need to talk to Maggie, man. You have to know what she's thinking. I mean, you can't just assume that you're both on the same page. A lot of what happened sounds like you were caught up in some weird moment and last night? Well, that was just a bad situation and it can all still be strictly platonic. But she's married, Jace. There's no way around that one."

"What do I do when we go back to work on Monday?"

"You're going to have to talk to her. If you're feeling awkward, chances are that she is too. She may not want to stay on as your assistant, but you can't just make that assumption and transfer her; you could be looking at some sort of human resources claim on that one."

Jason preferred to think that Maggie wouldn't go that route. Then again, he also preferred to think that Maggie wasn't really married, or was maybe in the process of leaving her husband, so his conscience could be clear.

"That is not a conversation I want to have," Jason admitted.

"Believe me, I didn't want to have to admit to Emma that I was afraid to get involved with anyone but once the words were out, it was like a giant weight had been lifted." Lucas paused for a minute. "The thing is, Jace,

I can tell you about me and Emma all day long. She wasn't a married woman. We were two single people who were attracted to one another. You and Maggie may very well be attracted to one another, but do you really want to pursue something with her? What about her husband? How would you feel if you found out some other man was hitting on your wife? And it was her boss? You can talk to her about where she'd be comfortable working, but I would strongly advise you not to pursue this relationship."

Jason knew his brother was right and he knew these were things that he needed to hear. He had no idea how he was going to go about working with Maggie, seeing her every day and not acting on his feelings, but he was going to have to find a way.

"I know you're right, Lucas. I just needed to hear somebody say it out loud to me."

"I'm sorry, man. I know you were kind of hoping for someone to give you the okay to have your cake and eat it, too. But that's not going to be me. Hell, I hope it's not anyone. You need to get home and put an end to this."

"I will. And thanks, Lucas. I'm sorry I got you up so early."

"Don't ever apologize for calling when you're in need. Now if you'll excuse me, I'm going back to bed to kiss my beautiful wife awake and get on with my day."

"No need to brag," Jason mumbled.

"Hey, it's been a while since I had anything to brag about. I'm just making up for lost time."

It was hard to begrudge him that. They said good-bye and Jason was left alone with his brother's words. It was now after seven and Jason knew he had to get ready for

this last meeting and face Maggie and the decision he had to make.

~

Maggie had been ready and waiting in the hotel lobby at eleven o'clock when the car arrived for her. The driver informed her he had been scheduled to pick her up first and then go and get Jason. Once they had gone across town to pick him up, they were on their way to the airport.

"How did the meeting go?" she asked tentatively.

"Just as planned; he signed," Jason replied, checking his phone for voice mail or texts, anything to distract him from having to talk directly to Maggie. They drove in silence the remainder of the way to the airport and checked in the same way.

By the time they were seated in first class for their flight home, Maggie had had enough. "Look, I know this trip has been difficult for you because of me, but I have had enough of the silent treatment!"

Jason turned and looked at her. "Excuse me?"

"Oh, please, you heard me just fine. I'm sorry I have been such a burden to you. I know you thought you had hired someone who was professional and had her life together, and instead you got stuck with me. I'm sorry I had a meltdown last night and I'm sorry I crossed a few lines with you. But we still have to work together and that's kind of hard to do with you ignoring me!"

He could only stare. *She* was taking responsibility for crossing lines? Didn't she realize he was crossing them just as much? "Maggie, you had every right to your meltdown last night and it was because of me that it happened!"

She held up a hand to stop him. "I don't want to spend the entire flight laying blame. All I'm saying is that I want to keep working with you, Jason, but I can't if you're going to act like this." Her brown eyes were wide and pleading, and Jason wanted to put her mind at ease.

"I wasn't sure you'd want to keep working with me," he finally said. "I know I put a lot on you during this trip and I didn't always act like I should have. I honestly don't know if our working together when we get back is for the best."

There, he'd said it, put the ball in her court.

Maggie continued to stare at him. "Oh," she said quietly, disappointment marking her features. "I guess you could be right. I'm sorry you feel that way. I thought I had done a good job for you and..."

"No, Maggie, it's not that you didn't do a good job. You did a great job! On everything! It's just that...we seem to have a problem working...together. Do you understand?"

She didn't want to, and so rather than continue with this uncomfortable conversation, she decided to change modes and pulled out her tablet to go over his morning meeting. If Jason had wanted to pursue their original conversation, he chose to say nothing. They transitioned smoothly back into work mode and by the time they landed in North Carolina two hours later, Maggie felt confident that while she may not be working for Jason much longer, she had fulfilled her obligation to him and his father for this project.

They walked into the terminal. Maggie was determined to get to baggage claim and get home before

she let herself cry. A strong hand on her arm halted her progress. "Maggie?" Jason said softly as she turned around to face him.

This was it, she thought. He's going to give me the speech now so that there would be no scene at the office on Monday. As much as she willed it not to happen, tears began to well in her eyes. She took a deep breath in a feeble attempt to calm her nerves.

"I guess your husband will be here to pick you up," he said gruffly.

Her husband. She was getting damn tired of that lie hanging between them, but it was probably best to have that excuse to hang on to. "Yes, I'm sure he's waiting for me down in baggage claim."

Jason stared down into her face and swallowed the jealousy raging through him. He wanted the right to take her home. He wanted to tell her they didn't have to stop working together and be able to take her out on a non-work-related date. He wanted...all of the things he couldn't have.

"I just want you to know," he began, "that I couldn't have done this project without you."

She nodded her head, wishing he'd let go of her arm so she could walk away while her dignity was still intact. "I really need to go, Jason," she whispered.

"You never crossed any line with me, Maggie. That was all me. But I can't let you go before I say this."

"What?" she said, the words barely leaving her lips before his mouth claimed hers. Maggie quickly wrapped her arms around his neck and held Jason close to her. It was madness to be doing this in the middle of a crowded airport terminal, and yet she couldn't help herself. The kiss ended all too soon and Jason stepped away.

"That's why we can't work together anymore," Jason said, his breath ragged. "I want you too much to work with you every day and not have the right to do that."

Maggie made to speak but he stopped her. "Go, your husband must be waiting and it looks like a storm is moving in. I'll feel better knowing that you got home safely."

Everything in her was clamoring to tell Jason the truth, but she had to come to grips with what he had just admitted to. All this time, he had been just as attracted to her as she'd been to him! She reached up and stroked his cheek, unable to help herself, before turning and fairly running from him, disappearing into the crowd.

Jason meant to stay put and wait before heading down to baggage claim, but clearly he was a glutton for punishment. Keeping a safe distance, he only wanted to catch a glimpse of what the man who was married to Maggie looked like. He watched as she collected her bags and then headed out the door and into the rain. Was he waiting for her in the car at the curb to keep her from getting wet?

Carefully, Jason picked his way through the crowd until he could look out the long expanse of windows and see Maggie walking outside. She flagged down a cab and climbed in while the driver loaded her luggage. Where was her husband? Why was she taking a cab? Why had she lied to him?

Taking out his phone, he dialed his father's number and then went to claim his own bags. When his father answered, he immediately launched into inquisition mode.

"I know all about what happened to Maggie when you met her three years ago," Jason said by way of greeting. "Why didn't you tell me?"

William didn't miss a beat. "It wasn't my place to tell you. When I hired Maggie to come and work for us, she asked that I not talk about it and really, there was never a reason to. How was the trip? I'm glad she felt comfortable enough to share that with you."

"She really didn't have a choice," Jason said with a bit of annoyance.

"Why? What happened?" Jason relayed the events of the night before to his father. "Dammit, I had hoped that she'd never have to see that bastard again. Is she okay?"

"She was pretty shaken up by the whole thing and by the time we got back to the hotel, she told me everything."

"I never meant to lie to you, Jace. It was all part of her requests when she came to work for us. Maggie never wanted to be put in that kind of a situation again. Saying she was married just seemed to make her feel a little more…secure. I thought it was a crazy idea but if it made her—"

"Wait, wait, *wait*!" Jason interrupted. "Maggie's not married?"

Uh-oh. "I thought you said Maggie told you everything?" William said, sounding a bit sheepish at letting the cat out of the bag.

"She told me everything about her ex-boss, not about lying about being married!" he yelled. "Geez, Dad! How could you not tell me?"

"You were demanding someone who was married to go with you on this trip! Maggie fit the bill!"

"But she wasn't really married!" Jason countered,

not caring that he was starting to get looks from people around him in the airport.

"The lie served a purpose. Maggie was perfect for the position, but you didn't want a single woman. She didn't want to work for someone who was going to hit on her and that she couldn't feel safe with. It was what was best for everyone!"

"Dammit, Dad...do you have any idea..." Jason stopped as it all finally fell into place. Maggie wasn't married. They hadn't done anything wrong.

There was no husband.

"Jason? Are you there? Is everything all right?" his father asked frantically.

"I have to go. I'll talk to you over the weekend," was all he said before hanging up. Jason raced from the terminal and out to long term parking. He was soaked to the skin by the time he arrived there. Throwing his luggage into the trunk, he quickly unlocked the doors and climbed in. Now he just had to figure out where to go.

Whipping out his phone again, he quickly called the office and got Ann on the phone. "Hey, Jace! How was the trip?"

He had to be careful to keep his tone neutral or Ann would know that something was wrong. "It was long and exhausting. We landed about a half an hour ago and unfortunately, I have one of Maggie's bags. Do you have her address so I can drop it off at her place? She already took a cab home."

"Oh, no problem..." Within a minute, Jason had the address and was programming it into his GPS and was on his way.

He drove like a man possessed. He'd been torturing

himself for weeks for nothing. She had lied to him about being married. There had been nothing to feel guilty about because there was no husband. Each time he said those words in his head, Jason's heart beat a little bit faster. Maggie was free. There was nothing stopping them from exploring what had clearly begun on their trip.

Within twenty minutes, he was pulling into the parking lot of the apartment complex where Maggie lived. There were no spots near her unit and he had to park at the far end of the lot. The rain was coming down in torrents and he'd be lucky to get through this without catching pneumonia. Maggie's apartment was on the second floor and Jason took the stairs two at a time and soon found himself pounding on her door.

Maggie opened the door and was shocked to see Jason standing there, staring at her and completely out of breath. "*Jason*? What are you…?"

"There's no husband," he said sharply and watched as she paled.

"What?"

"There. Is. No. Husband. Do I have that right?"

Maggie looked up at him, eyes wide, and nodded. "No, there is no husband."

"Good," was all he said as he pushed his way into her home, turned her into his arms, and kissed her.

Chapter 8

WHAT FOLLOWED WAS MADNESS. JASON PINNED Maggie to the wall while he feasted on her mouth. The only thing that kept urging him on was the fact that she seemed to be right there feasting along with him.

When he moved from her lips to kiss her jaw and then down the column of her throat, Maggie spoke. "I'm sorry I lied to you," she said, and then let out a moan of pure pleasure as he gently bit her. "I didn't think it would ever be an issue."

Jason lifted his head and stared intently down into Maggie's eyes. Without ever breaking contact, he reached down and took her left hand in his, pulled the fake wedding ring from her finger, and threw it across the room. "Do you have any idea how I've been berating myself for the thoughts I've been having about you?" he asked before lowering his head to go back to the task of nipping and kissing her neck.

Maggie merely shook her head. "I didn't know, Jason," she rasped as his hands began to move from her waist upward. She'd dreamed about this moment, fantasized about Jason's hands on her, and yet it was nothing compared to the reality of it. "If it helps, I've been having thoughts about you, too," she admitted.

"Oh, yeah?" Jason asked, lifting his head once again before bending slightly to scoop her up and into his arms. "How about you point me in the direction of your

bedroom and we can compare notes?" His tone was serious, but his eyes were bright with mischief.

Maggie couldn't help but smile as she wrapped her arms around his neck. "Straight down that hallway, last door on the left."

In a flash, Jason had her in her bedroom and was laying her down on the bed. He stood and simply looked down at her, taking in the sight of her sprawled out on the champagne colored comforter. She was so beautiful. He couldn't believe he finally had permission to touch her and not feel guilty about it or have to stop himself before going too far.

He was going to go as far as he could; and his hands actually began to twitch with the need to touch her again. "I've thought about this for so long, Maggie. I need to know that we're on the same page here."

"I want you, Jason," she said honestly. "It almost killed me to leave the airport earlier."

It was all the encouragement he needed. He peeled his wet shirt off and let it drop to the floor before kicking his shoes off and removing his trousers and socks. Maggie leaned up onto her elbows to watch him. When Jason stood before her in nothing but dark briefs, she gave an appreciative smile.

Silently, she stood and slowly unbuttoned her own plain white blouse, adding it to the pile Jason had begun. Reaching behind her, she unzipped her skirt and let it fall to the ground, leaving her in nothing but simple white lace. "Is this the page that you're on?" she asked, "Or am I missing something?"

Her words were meant to tease, but Jason was too on edge to play along. Jason lifted his hands and cupped

Maggie's face. "I'm going to apologize right now for not taking the time to go slow. I need you, Maggie."

She gave him a sexy smile and stepped back, and lay down on the bed in invitation. "I don't care about slow, Jason," she said. "I just care about feeling you here beside me." She crooked a finger at him.

He didn't need to be asked twice.

It could have been days or it could have been hours, Jason wasn't sure. He was flat on his back with Maggie wrapped around him as he tried to catch his breath. In his wildest fantasies he'd never imagined how explosive they would be together. Once he had joined her on the bed, it was as if they had been two starving people who were finally allowed to eat.

He smiled at his own analogy because he had certainly feasted on every inch of Maggie's amazing body. She kept it pretty well hidden underneath her conservative clothing, but now that he knew what was underneath, he would never be able to look at her the same way again when they were in the office.

The room had darkened quite a bit, so Jason knew they'd been in there for hours. A quick glance around the room revealed a clock; it was nearing eight. He turned his head to the side and smiled at the sight of Maggie's head on his chest and her blonde hair in wild disarray.

"Hey," he said softly and waited for her to raise her head. When she did, he asked, "Are you hungry?"

That wicked grin he was really beginning to love appeared. "I could eat," she said simply and then gave

a little shriek when he reached out and rolled her under him, pinning her to the mattress.

"Food, woman," he playfully snarled as he kissed her soundly. "You have worn me out. I need something to eat."

Maggie pushed him off and rose from the bed to grab a robe from her closet. "Well, obviously I don't have anything here since I've been gone for three weeks, but we can order some takeout," she suggested.

Minutes later they were rummaging through her collection of takeout menus until they agreed on someplace. "Their pizza isn't the best, but they do deliver," she said of the one place Jason finally suggested. "I don't really feel like going out in this weather again."

Jason took that as a sign she wouldn't want him going out in it either; hopefully that would include for the remainder of the night. He wasn't ready to leave yet and he had a feeling it would be quite a while before he'd actually *want* to leave. Mentally shaking his head, Jason knew he'd have to wait and see what Maggie wanted. After all, they had been together nonstop for three weeks; she might want some time away from him.

True, they hadn't been sleeping together for three weeks, so maybe she wouldn't mind him being around while they explored this new aspect of their relationship.

Relationship? Normally that word had Jason breaking out in a cold sweat, but right now, it made him feel good. He already knew they were compatible at work and he genuinely enjoyed just spending time talking with Maggie. The last couple of hours had proved they were compatible in bed, too. What more could he ask for?

"I'm going to call this in," Maggie said as she stood and reached for her phone.

Jason reclined on the pillows, sheets draped over his hips, as he watched her. The last five weeks had been transforming. The woman he had met initially was uptight and prickly, and now he understood why. The thought of someone doing something so horrible to Maggie made his fists clench. If he had known who that lousy SOB was while they were at dinner last night, Jason had no doubt someone would have had to come and bail him out of jail, because he would have taken great delight in beating the man into the ground.

"They said about thirty minutes but I'm thinking closer to forty-five in this weather," she was saying as she sat back down beside him. "I hate that I don't have anything to offer you to drink other than water." Maggie blushed slightly.

Sensing her discomfort, Jason reached out and pulled her down beside him so her head was back on his shoulder. "I can wait for the food to get here," he said softly, kissing the top of her head and sighing with contentment. When she didn't say anything, he gently shrugged his shoulder to get her attention. "What's going on, Maggie? Do you want me to go?"

She sat back up. "I don't want you to go, but I'm just a little…well, compared to the places that we've stayed my place is a little…dumpy."

Jason reached out and placed a finger under her chin, forcing her to look up at him. "There is nothing wrong with your home. I don't give a damn where we are, Maggie. I just want to be with you."

That made her relax and smile. "I want to be with you, too, Jason. But I have to admit, you've spoiled me."

"Me? How?"

"I was thinking how it was going to be great to come home and sleep in my own bed, but after some of the luxurious hotels we stayed in, I realize this bed is old and not that comfortable."

He laughed and pulled her back down beside him. "I didn't even notice because I was perfectly comfortable having you wrapped around me."

"Still, you have to admit that a comfortable bed would be a nice bonus."

He made a noncommittal sound. "We may have to go back to some of those hotels and do a comparison." A slow smile crept across his face at the thought of going back to New York, being able to share a room with Maggie, and doing all the things they had missed out on because it wouldn't have been appropriate. Carriage rides through Central Park or taking in a Broadway show after dining out at some exclusive restaurant all seemed perfect to him.

"I'll tell you, I wouldn't mind going back for one of the pretzels we had in New York and maybe going to the Statue of Liberty," Maggie said as if reading his mind. Jason let out a small laugh.

"I was just sitting here thinking how I'd like to take you back to New York to see a show or maybe to eat at some fancy restaurant and you're talking about pretzels. It's funny!"

She playfully punched him in the arm. "I don't care about the fancy stuff, Jason. That doesn't impress me. I had fun running around the city and taking in the

experience; meeting people, tasting the food…it was all just so amazing! I'll never be able to thank you enough for giving me that day. It was perfect and I'll never forget it."

Her words were so sincere, and the look in her eyes told Jason more than anything how much it all had meant to her. In that moment, he vowed to himself to take her back there and give them the time to do what they wanted at their leisure; no time limits or constraints, just the chance to enjoy themselves and relax.

"You're very welcome. Someday we'll go back and play at being the ultimate tourists," he said and kissed her again. He was just settling in, enjoying the feel of Maggie relaxing against him, when they heard the doorbell ringing.

"Don't take this the wrong way," Maggie said as she jumped from the bed, nearly giddy, "but I'm so excited that dinner is here!" She bolted from the room and Jason could hear her laughing as she went to open the door.

He climbed from the bed and winced as he reached for his still damp pants. It was not at all appealing to put them back, on so he wrapped a sheet around his middle, scooped the clothes up off of the floor, and walked out to the kitchen, where he found Maggie setting their food down. "Would you mind if I tossed these in the dryer? They're still pretty wet."

Maggie took the clothes from him, making sure the pockets were empty, and tossed them in the dryer, turning to admire the sight of Jason wrapped in a sheet. Slowly she walked toward him and placed her hand over where his was holding the sheet together. "Nice outfit,"

she said saucily, and got up on tippy-toes to place tiny kisses along his chin. "You look good in my sheets."

Jason let out a low growl as her hands began to wander over his chest, his shoulders, and his arms. "You think so?"

Maggie nodded. "I do. But..." She reached back down and pulled his hand away from its makeshift fastening. "I think I like you much better out of them." In a flash, the sheet dropped to the tile floor.

"What about dinner?" he asked and groaned as she began to kiss her way down his body.

"That's what microwaves are for," she said.

~

The rain had stopped by the next morning and Jason's clothes were long-since dried. He could very easily go out to his car and grab his luggage so he had clean clothes, or he could go home and unpack and let Maggie get herself settled back in.

He didn't want to leave. The thought of going home to his big, empty house left him cold. He'd bought the big townhouse on the golf course because it suited his needs. But now? It just seemed like a place that was way too big for a man alone. Maggie stretched beside him and then snuggled closer. She was a snuggler, and Jason found that he enjoyed it.

Unfortunately, the thought of cold pizza for breakfast was not doing it for him, and he knew it would be best for him to get up and go and get them breakfast and for them to talk about how they were going to spend their day. It was funny because he thought after spending so much time together that he'd be ready for some

time alone, but he wasn't. If anything, now that he knew that there wasn't any reason for them not to be together, Jason didn't want them to be apart.

"I can hear you thinking from here," Maggie said sleepily, yawning. "What time is it?"

"Almost nine," he said. "I was thinking about breakfast. Then I was thinking about clean clothes and my luggage. And then..."

"Then you were thinking about going home," she said quietly and sat up beside him. "It's okay for you to leave, Jason. I don't expect you to move in or anything just because we slept together."

"Do you want me to leave?" he asked, sitting up beside her.

She huffed with frustration. "Please don't answer my question with a question, Jason. It's annoying. All I'm saying is I know that you have a life to get back to. Obviously you didn't go home after we landed yesterday, and just like I've got things to do around here to get settled back in before we have to go back to work on Monday, I'm sure you have things to do at your place. It's okay."

He leaned in and kissed her squarely on the mouth. Short and sweet. "I know I have stuff to do but I just wasn't ready to...leave yet."

That made Maggie smile. "I'm not kicking you out, Jason."

"That's good," he said and his smile matched hers. "But I am hungry and leftover pizza is not what I want for breakfast. How about I go and get us some bagels and coffee or something?"

Maggie shook her head. "I know you'd never know

it after all the breakfasts we've shared in the last month, but normally I am not a breakfast person. I think I gained a good five pounds just from the breakfast foods. I'm kind of anxious to shower and get laundry going and then hit the grocery store. Monday will be here before you know it."

He nodded in understanding. "Can I take you to dinner tonight?"

She blushed and her smile grew. "I would like that very much."

"That's good. I want to take you out someplace nice and not talk about business and not have to share you with anyone."

"You don't have to make a fuss, Jason. I'd be happy just going someplace casual."

He knew she would put up an argument, but he also knew that for one night, he wanted to spoil her a little. "You'll just have to wait and see," he said distractedly.

"How will I know what to wear?" Maggie asked, leaning in to trail kisses down the column of his throat to his sculpted chest.

"Whatever you wear, Maggie, will be perfect."

She raised her head and looked at him doubtfully.

Jason whipped the sheet away from them both and scooped her up into his arms. "Personally, I can't wait to see you wearing nothing but bubbles..."

Jason arrived back at Maggie's promptly at seven. "Wow," he said, stepping inside and handing her a bouquet of white tulips. "You look absolutely beautiful."

Maggie blushed. All day she had worried about what

to wear, because Jason had essentially seen most of her wardrobe over the last several weeks, but then she remembered a cocktail dress she hadn't had the opportunity to wear.

Now, dressed in the curve-hugging black dress with the tiny straps and wearing a pair of killer skinny heels, Maggie knew she had made the right choice. "Well, I wasn't sure where we were going, so I decided I couldn't go wrong with a little black dress."

He leaned in and kissed her, slowly and thoroughly, and when he lifted his head, he scanned her slumbrous and sexy eyes and smiled. "It's perfect."

Maggie turned and grabbed her purse and a wrap to take with her and then walked out the door that Jason was holding open for her. "Are you going to tell me where we're going?"

"We'll be there soon enough," was all he said as he placed a strong hand on the small of her back and led her over to his sporty BMW.

Within minutes they were in downtown Charlotte and pulling up in front of one of the best steakhouses in the state. Maggie was more than a little impressed with Jason's choice and then heard a commotion across the street. A sports bar. She sighed wistfully and jumped when Jason called her on it.

"Is there a hockey game on tonight?" he asked with a knowing smirk.

"I don't know…maybe."

Indecision marked his face. On one hand, he wanted to take her out for a romantic dinner where it was just the two of them and he could spend time getting to know her. Then he remembered how much fun Maggie had

when they had gone to see the game at Madison Square Garden. His mind made up, Jason walked around the car, took Maggie by the hand, and began leading her across the parking lot.

"Jason? The restaurant is back there."

"Yeah, but you know you'd rather be over here watching the game and eating a burger," he teased and was surprised when Maggie stopped short and stood her ground. He turned and faced her. "It's not a big deal. As long as I'm with you, I don't care where we eat."

She closed the distance between them and kissed him. "I can watch the game later on the DVR. I'd very much like to have a quiet dinner, just the two of us."

Nothing could have pleased him more. They walked back toward the restaurant and were seated immediately at a quiet corner table. Maggie was overwhelmed by the atmosphere as well as the menu, but it didn't take long for her to relax and order. When all of the preliminaries were out of the way, Jason reached across the table for one of her hands. "Thank you for coming out tonight."

"Thank you for inviting me." She took a look around and sighed at the beautiful surroundings. "So tell me," she began, "do you think we accomplished everything that you wanted on this trip?"

"Oh, no. No talk about business tonight. Tonight I want to learn more about you," he said seriously, his thumb gently stroking her knuckles. "I want to know about your family, where you grew up and... everything."

Maggie blushed as she ducked her head on a chuckle. "That's quite a list. I grew up in Virginia and went to college at the University of Richmond. My parents are

great; they're retired now and down in Florida."

"Why didn't you say anything? We could have stopped to see them," Jason said, concern marking his handsome features.

"Jason, we were working *and* on a tight schedule. Believe me, there is no such thing as a quick visit with my family. I don't see them as much as they'd like, and so whenever I do make arrangements to visit, it's for at least a week. Anything less and I get the huge guilt trip."

"Should my dad ever retire and he and Mom move away, I think we'd have to deal with the same thing. Working with Dad ensures that we see him every day, and Mom stops in enough that we see her several times a week. I think it would be strange not to see them so often."

"You get used to it," she said and reached for her water. "Luckily I have older siblings who are each married and keep my parents entertained with grandchildren. As the baby of the bunch, I do get a little more smothering than they do, but they claim it's all out of concern."

"They just want to make sure you're okay and taken care of."

"Yeah, well, it's nice not to have them living so close by. When everything happened…three years ago, I didn't tell them. I didn't want them to worry, and as your father stepped in and took care of everything, all they needed to know was that I had gotten a fabulous job offer and jumped on it."

Jason nodded and then felt his rage building just thinking about her ex-boss again. "Maggie, I hate to bring up an uncomfortable subject, but I need to know. Was this guy at any of our meetings? Was he with any of the companies that we met with?"

She shook her head. "No, no…I hadn't seen him anywhere else and the company that he ran back in Virginia was owned by his brother-in-law. I doubt he left it. It was all just a terrible coincidence that he was there."

"Can I ask his name?"

Maggie's head snapped up and she looked at Jason in horror. "Why? Why would you even want to know?"

"Maggie, if there is even the slightest chance this guy is doing business in the same circles as I am, I need to know who he is so Montgomerys doesn't do business with him. The last thing I want is to do business with someone who would treat a woman the way this creep treated you."

For a moment she felt oddly deflated. Secretly she had hoped Jason wanted to know the name so that he could track Martin down and defend her honor. It was a ridiculous thought, she knew, but still, it was easy to picture Jason in the role of knight in shining armor. "Martin Blake," she said quietly.

Jason simply nodded and quickly changed the subject. "So, two older siblings? Tell me about them."

Maggie was relieved that he wasn't going to pursue the conversation about Martin any further. Smiling, she took a sip of her water and launched into a funny story about growing up as the baby of a family of five.

Chapter 9

Being back in the office on Monday wasn't nearly as uncomfortable as Maggie had thought it would be. After debating extensively whether or not it would be wise to continue working together, ultimately neither one was ready to admit it wasn't a good idea. So it was with confidence that she walked through the executive office of Montgomerys and went about getting settled at her desk.

"Maggie!" William Montgomery's voice boomed from across the room. "You're back from your whirlwind trip. I saw from all of the reports that it was a rousing success." He walked over and gave her a hearty embrace that made her smile. "Not that I expected anything less from you and Jace. I knew you would be the perfect assistant for him. So tell me, did everything go okay?"

She couldn't help the smile growing across her face. "Everything was wonderful. We met so many people, and while not all of them were a good fit for Montgomerys, we had some interesting stories to talk about afterward. Then there were the places we stayed and the things we saw… I got to stand next to John Lennon's guitar at the Rock and Roll Hall of Fame! Then we went to see a hockey game at the Garden… Oh, it was just amazing!"

William couldn't help his own grin. He knew that

pairing the two of them together was the right thing to do! While he couldn't be sure that anything had clicked romantically yet, from the exuberance in Maggie's voice and the spring in Jason's step, William could tell it was just a matter of time.

"I am so glad it went so well," he said when she finished talking. "I know you were worried about going on the trip, but it sounds to me like you had nothing to worry about. Jason would never do or say anything to hurt anyone."

"No, I know now that he wouldn't. You've raised an amazing son and I'm so glad I've had the opportunity to work with him."

"Well now, you're going to keep working together, aren't you? I mean, Jason still needs an assistant, and I can't imagine after all the interesting things you two managed on this trip that you'd be anxious to go back to customer service."

"Actually, Jace and I talked about that and we're going to see how it goes. We still have a lot to do to wrap up all of the dealings from the trip and then we'll see if it's really necessary for me to stay up here."

"Nonsense, Jason has always had an assistant. Granted, he and Mac had Rose splitting her time between them for a while, but with all of this new growth, Jason's going to need his own assistant. Plus, I think Mac likes having an assistant of his own, too."

Maggie shrugged and gave a noncommittal "We'll see" before reaching over and getting her computer booted up. "I hope you're right, but for now I'm content to live in the moment and see where Jason needs me to be."

William smiled knowingly. "So, um...how did the whole husband thing work for you? Did you have to play the married card much?"

Maggie blushed. "Actually, it didn't come up to much while we were on the trip but I did end up telling Jason the truth. I'm not sure how to go about doing that around here."

"No worries," William said. "I'll take care of it. We'll just tell people that you've been legally separated for some time and now you're finally getting a divorce and would like everyone to respect your privacy."

"I can't ask you to do all of that for me again. I got myself into this mess, I'll get myself out."

William waved her off. "Maggie, it is worth it for me just to see you looking so happy and relaxed. I've never seen you smile so much. I hated pushing you into this trip, but I'm glad now that I did."

"Me too, sir," she said wholeheartedly. "Me too."

It was almost lunchtime when Jason finally had time to call Maggie into his office. From the moment he had gotten in earlier, he had been wrapped up in conference calls and returning messages, and then meeting with his father and brother to discuss all the contacts he'd made while he was away and where he saw all of this expansion going. His frustration level at not having a minute to himself was getting to him. Picking up his phone, he buzzed Maggie's desk and essentially barked for her to come into his office.

Less than a minute later she was standing in his doorway, notebook in hand and looking anxious. "I wasn't

sure what else you needed me to bring," she said nervously. "I left all the essential files on your desk while you were in with your father and brother."

"Come in and close the door, Maggie," he said sternly and while her back was turned, he quickly moved around his desk so he was right behind her when she turned around.

Maggie nearly jumped out of her skin at the sight of Jason so close to her. "Oh, Jason! You scared me half to death." It was the last thing she got to say for a long time. Jason's mouth came down on hers and claimed her in a slow, wet kiss that went on and on and on. When he finally released her, Maggie sagged against him. "Oh, my…"

Jason reached up and cupped her face, taking in the flushed skin and bright eyes, and smiled. "Hey," he said softly.

"Hey, yourself. How is your day going?"

"Much better now that I have you to myself for a few minutes," he said, taking Maggie by the hand and leading her to the sofa to sit down. "How about you? How has your day been so far?"

They talked business briefly, and when Jason invited Maggie to join him for lunch, she hesitated. "I don't know, Jason," she said, chewing her bottom lip. "I don't think it's a good idea for us to be socializing here at the office."

"We're not; it's just lunch, Maggie. It's not a big deal."

"Trust me, it is. None of the other assistants go out with their bosses."

"Emma used to go out with Lucas all the time!"

"They're married; it's not the same thing."

Jason sighed with frustration. "Fine, I get it. You don't want anyone speculating on the nature of our relationship. I can respect that. How about dinner? Can I take you to dinner tonight?"

She smiled. "Actually, how about I make dinner for you? You can come by when you're done here and we'll just hang out and relax. What do you say?"

He narrowed his eyes at her. "Is there a hockey game on? Is that why you don't want to go out?"

Maggie couldn't help but giggle. "Maybe. Either way, after a long day back at work I think it will be nice just to be able to relax and be casual and *maybe* catch a game on TV."

Jason leaned forward and kissed her on the nose. "Sounds good to me. I normally leave here around six so I could be at your place by six thirty. Will that work?"

"Perfectly."

When six thirty rolled around, Maggie was ready. She had the table set, a salad made, sauce simmering on the stove, and a pot of water ready to come to a boil for the pasta she had waiting to go. All she needed was Jason.

At six forty-five, she was mildly concerned, and by seven, she was on her way to being seriously pissed. She had put off calling Jason as long as she could and before she could let herself be genuinely angry, she needed to call him and make sure he wasn't hurt somewhere on the side of the road.

The fact that he answered and there were no sirens in the background confirmed he was perfectly intact.

For now.

"Oh, damn, Maggie..." he stammered distractedly. "What time is it?"

"It's seven o'clock. I was just wondering if something came up or if you were still coming over." She tried not to come off sounding annoyed but she didn't think she quite pulled it off.

"Um...yeah, I lost track of time. I got a call from the people we met with in Atlanta and it turned into a conference call and then I was going over some projections with Mac and we're trying to figure out..."

"It's okay, Jace, really." She did her best to squash her disappointment. "It's not a big deal. It was just a quick dinner and some TV; no worries. We can do it another time."

He hesitated before responding. She heard him whispering "Give me a minute" to Mac, she assumed, and then he spoke. "I really am sorry, Maggie. It's just that this project is so big and time-consuming and it didn't all come to an end when we got back."

She wanted to yell that she knew that because she had been working on the damn project with him for weeks! But she held her tongue and spoke sweetly. "Jason, I knew from the get-go that your work is very important to you. I would never expect you to blow it off for me."

"Dammit, Maggie, you're important to me, too. I honestly lost track of the time. I'm sorry," he said sincerely. "If it's not too late..."

She smiled at his effort. "Jason, you're obviously in the middle of a bunch of stuff. Go back to it so you and Mac can actually go home tonight. I'll see you in the morning."

"But I wanted to see you tonight." She could almost see the pout from the sound of his voice.

"Go back to work, boss," she said, ignoring his statement. "I'll see you in the morning. Good night."

He wished her a good night and wanted to say more but she had already hung up. Jason reclined in his chair, thinking about their conversation, when his brother came back into the office.

"Care to tell me why your assistant is calling you and what you were apologizing for?" Mac was the oldest of the Montgomerys, and far more serious than his younger siblings. If Lucas had made the statement, there would have been a hint of teasing; when Mac made it, it was an accusation. That had Jason's back up in defense.

"None of your damn business. Let me see that contract for Atlanta," he said, leaning over his desk toward the file in Mac's hand.

"Hell, no. I want to know what's going on, Jace. You've been distracted all day, walking around with a sappy grin on your face, and now Maggie's calling you after hours and… Oh, no…you didn't."

Jason merely glared at him. "Choose your next words carefully, Mac," he warned.

"After all your bitching and complaining about your previous assistants all hitting on you and you're sleeping with Maggie? What the hell's the matter with you?"

"Maggie is nothing like those other women," Jason defended. "And neither of us planned on this happening, it just…did."

"Geez, Jason, isn't she married?"

Jason hated to betray Maggie's confidence, but he felt it was best if his brother understood the whole story.

By the time he was done explaining about her former boss and the way their father had saved her, Mac had visibly relaxed.

"I think you're making a mistake, bro," he finally said. "Sleeping with your assistant never ends well."

"It did for Lucas and Emma."

Mac swiped a hand over his face. "I honestly wish the two of them had met some other way. I am tired of everything getting compared to Lucas and Emma. I mean, don't get me wrong, I am happy for them both, and Emma is terrific, but every time someone has a problem around here, it all comes back to the two of them and how everything worked out."

"This is different, Mac. I mean, I fought it, I really did but there is just something about her that I can't explain. She's smart and funny and we have great—"

"Sex?" Mac teased.

"Watch it," Jason warned again. "I was going to say great conversations. She's exciting to be with."

"So this is serious?"

"I think it could be," Jason admitted and found it wasn't such a hard thing to do.

"How does Maggie feel?"

"I'm not sure. We were supposed to have dinner tonight and I'm sort of treading carefully with her because of her past. I don't want to rush her or do anything to scare her off."

"So then what are you doing here with me working late when you had plans with her?"

Jason shrugged. "This is who I am; work has always been first and foremost in my life. Maggie knows that."

Mac laughed and shook his head. "Yeah, there's a

difference between knowing your boss is a workaholic and dating a workaholic. You'll have to pay more attention to the time, Brother; otherwise you may find that she's not as understanding as you thought."

Jason waved him off. "You don't know Maggie. She'll understand. But you're right. I will start paying more attention to the time and try to get out of here more often at a reasonable hour. How hard could it be?"

By the end of the week, Jason knew how hard it could be. Damn near impossible. He didn't realize how much of himself he gave to the business until there was something else that he wanted to do, and yet he couldn't tear himself away. Maggie had been patient all week long, always quick with a word of understanding. It was Jason who hit the breaking point.

At six o'clock on Friday evening, Mac walked into his office and smirked. "Working late on a Friday night? Nice."

"Shut up," Jason snapped as he walked around collecting paperwork and shoving it into his briefcase.

"You've been here late every night this week," Mac said lightly. "How's that working for you?"

Jason flipped him the bird and closed his case, walking toward the door.

"Big plans tonight?"

Jason stopped and hung his head down. "Is there something you wanted, Mac?" he finally asked.

Mac was the king of poker faces, and he gave Jason his best *dude, I'm really sorry to have to do this to you* face. "Well, actually, I just needed to come in here and

let you know"—he paused for dramatic effect—"that I'm glad you're finally taking your sorry ass out of here and hopefully going out with Maggie."

Jason was so relieved he practically sagged to the floor. "You're an idiot," he murmured as he turned and strode out the door.

"I do not want to see you back here until Monday!" Mac called after him.

By the time Jason got to his car, his brother was all but forgotten. He had to get to Maggie. All day he had tried to pin down plans for them for tonight, but she had been elusive, telling him just to give her a call if he had the time. He hated letting her down. All week. He had not had any time alone with her since that brief time in his office on Monday, and he was ready to explode with need for her.

Looking at his phone, Jason thought about calling her and telling her that he was on his way over, but he wanted to surprise her. After a quick detour to pick up flowers, he finally pulled in at Maggie's complex and, as he had the first time he'd come here, he sprinted up the stairs two at a time to get to her.

"Jason!" Maggie exclaimed when she opened the door to him moments later. "I thought you were going to call when you left the office."

Not quite the greeting he was hoping for, but he could work with it. "I had to see you," he admitted. "I didn't want to call and give you the chance to tell me not to come by." He handed her the bouquet of exotic flowers and waited for her to invite him in.

She didn't.

"Is…is this a bad time?" he finally asked.

"What? Oh, no…sorry. Bad manners. Come on in." She stepped aside as he walked in and then she headed for the kitchen to find a vase.

Jason watched as she arranged the flowers, fluttering around the kitchen, and he wanted to just grab her and kiss her and make love to her all night long. Fortunately, he was smart enough to know that caveman tactics would probably not be appreciated right now. "Have you had dinner yet?"

"No, I haven't. I was planning on heating up some pasta and watching a movie." She waited a moment before asking, "Would you like to join me?"

A wicked smile crossed his face as he stalked her from across the kitchen. Without asking permission, he hauled her up against him and kissed her with all of the pent up passion and frustration he'd felt all week. Luckily, Maggie was ready for his sexy assault and wrapped her arms around him to keep him close.

Jason broke the kiss long enough to pick her up and haul her over his shoulder while she shrieked with laughter.

Maybe caveman tactics weren't such a bad idea after all.

Chapter 10

Six weeks after Jason and Maggie had returned from their trip, their work was done. Not completely done, because these were new clients and they'd be working with them for a long time, but all of the initial set up and meetings and the like were finally in place. It was a late Friday night and Jason was sitting at his desk staring at his computer screen, barely able to hold his head up, when his father walked in.

"Another late night?" William asked.

Jason nodded. "Hopefully the last one."

His father arched an eyebrow at him. "Seriously?"

Looking away from the computer, Jason focused on his father. "Yeah, seriously, why?"

"I'm just surprised to hear you talk like that. You are the king of the late-night negotiations. I thought you were going to move in here at one point."

"Ha, ha, very funny," Jason said and then scrubbed a hand across his weary face.

"What's going on, Jace?"

What could he say? For weeks, Jason had felt a level of discontentment with his life. The long hours, going home alone—it was starting to wear on him. All of those feelings were compounded by the fact that he had little to no time to spend with Maggie. She was always patient and understanding, but Jason knew it was just a matter of time before she'd had enough.

When they had been on the phone the previous night, Maggie had made a small comment about how there was a new movie out that she wanted to see on opening night. Tonight. Jason had told her he would try his best to leave the office early and Maggie had just given him a sad laugh. When he pushed her for what was wrong, she'd told him she was just going to plan on going alone or with a friend.

The thought of her going out without him wasn't really an issue; the thought of her going out without him and meeting someone else did. Maggie was a beautiful woman, and since they had gotten back from Miami, she had blossomed with a new level of confidence. How long would it be before other men noticed that about her?

He'd tried feebly to explain his position and how important Montgomerys was to him. Her simple response of "But at what cost?" had hit him square in the chest. At what cost, indeed? Life was passing him by, and while everything he was doing was helping the company grow, Jason realized he'd lost friendships and missed out on weddings and parties and casual get-togethers with people who really mattered to him because he was spending his life behind a desk.

How much more was he willing to sacrifice in the name of the company?

"Jace?" his father interrupted his thoughts.

"What? Sorry, Dad. I just sort of zoned out there for a minute."

"I thought you'd be with Maggie tonight." Jason's look of shock made his father laugh. "Oh, please, you didn't think you were going to hide that from me, did you?"

"We thought we were being careful," he grimaced.

"You were. I just knew what I was looking for."

"What the hell does that mean?"

William stood and waved his son off. "Nothing, nothing at all. Go home, Jace. Or go to Maggie's. Just leave the damn building and go and enjoy yourself for the weekend for crying out loud. Montgomerys is not going to crumble and fall because you're not behind your desk."

Jason knew his father was right, and hated that he was that transparent. He stood and closed his laptop and packed up while William watched, and the two men left the office together. Placing an arm around his son's shoulder, William gave him a firm hug. "Life is meant to be enjoyed. There's nothing wrong with working hard, but you have to remember to focus on the people who mean the most to you."

"I do, Dad. I enjoy working with you and Mac and Lucas…"

"And Maggie?"

For a minute, Jason was sure he blushed. "And Maggie."

William's smile went from ear to ear. "You won't find a better woman than Maggie, Jace. Don't keep her waiting too long or some other lucky man will come in and sweep her off of her feet."

A frown marred Jason's features. Like hell some other man was going to take Maggie from him! "I have to go, Dad," Jason said, his stride quickening. He looked down at his watch and saw it was after ten. He had no idea if Maggie was home or at the movies, but no matter where she was, he would find her and maybe whisk her away for the weekend or bring her home to his place and

pamper her. It didn't matter what they did, as long as he was with her.

In the time they'd been together, neither had made any grand commitments or even talked about their feelings. Well, that was going to end tonight. When he finally found her, Jason was going to tell Maggie how he felt.

He just hoped he wasn't too late.

Tired of sitting home and waiting for the phone to ring, Maggie had taken a bold step and called an old friend to go to the movies with her. It had been a long time since she'd had a girls' night out and once she had parked her car at the theater and met up with her friend Theresa, she knew it was the right thing to do.

She had been too focused on Jason for weeks now, and found herself becoming more and more dissatisfied with the relationship. While she admired Jason's work ethic, it was becoming painfully obvious that work was Jason's first love and probably always would be. The thought made her sad because when he finally stepped away from the office, they always had an amazing time.

It wasn't all about sex, although that was fantastic. There were times they would stay up all night just talking, and Maggie loved hearing about all the places Jason had visited and what it was like growing up with his brothers. The problem was that as much as she loved spending time with him, she didn't see their relationship going anywhere, and she was tired of taking second place to Montgomerys.

After the movie, she and Theresa went out for coffee

and dessert and spent the night just getting caught up with one another. It was well after midnight when Maggie got home and while she was getting settled in, she remembered that she'd turned her cell phone off. Taking it from her purse, she turned it on and saw that she had several missed calls.

Eight of them to be exact.

Sighing, Maggie knew that each and every one of those missed calls was from Jason, and while she hadn't intentionally blown him off, she kind of felt that it served him right. See how he liked waiting all night for the phone to ring!

She was beyond tired after a long day at work and a late night out, but decided she should call him back. Maggie changed into a pair of cotton boxers and a cami, then settled on the couch and dialed Jason's number.

"Maggie? Are you all right? Where have you been?" No greeting, just an anxious demand for answers.

"I'm fine, Jace, how are you?" she said, dripping sarcasm.

She heard his frustrated sigh. "Okay," he began. "I'm sorry. I was just worried about you. Your phone was off and I didn't know where you were!"

"I told you I wanted to go to the movies tonight. So I did."

"Alone?"

She didn't like his tone. Sure they were sleeping together, but that didn't mean that she had to report to him every time she went out. "As a matter of fact, no." She knew she'd have to elaborate but enjoyed his shocked silence. "I went with someone."

Jealousy was new to Jason and he knew immediately that he didn't like it. He did his best to stay calm but his

words came out through clenched teeth. "With who?" he practically growled.

Maggie could just picture the look on his face and almost burst out laughing. She knew that would only fuel his anger but again, it served him right. "Actually, I met up with an old friend."

"Maggie," he said in his best menacing tone, letting her know she was testing his patience.

"I hadn't seen Theresa in well over a year. We met up at the theater, saw the movie, and then went out for coffee and dessert. It was a lovely night."

He let out a sigh of relief. "Oh…that's good. How was the movie?"

"We enjoyed it very much." As for this conversation? Not so much. As much as Maggie wanted to talk to Jason, she was hurt. And tired. He needed to understand that she wasn't the type of woman who would be happy just to sit around and wait until he made time for her. Maybe it was time for her to let him know.

"Look, Jace, it's late and I'm tired. I just wanted to call and let you know I was okay."

It was her tone. Jason knew Maggie well enough by now to know that something was definitely wrong. "I was worried about you," he said softly, "and I miss you."

She smiled sadly. "I miss you too. The thing is"—She paused to collect her thoughts—"I can't keep doing this, Jason." There, she'd said it.

"What do you mean?" Worry laced his voice and Jason had a feeling that he wasn't going to like the answer.

"I love being with you, but your work is your life, and I'm just starting to live mine again. I don't want to sit

home waiting for the phone to ring or have you call me after you've already missed our date."

"That happened once—" he began, but she cut him off.

"It's been more than once, Jace, and you know it. I'm not going to make you choose between Montgomerys and me. I think I need to step aside so that I'm not a distraction."

Jason desperately wanted to get in the car and see Maggie in person, to make her see how wrong she was. "You're not a distraction, dammit! You have to believe me! I know things have been crazy at work and I promise it's going to cut back some now. Things on the expansion are all in place; there won't be any more late nights, Maggie. Trust me. Please."

She wanted to believe him. Oh, how desperately she wanted to trust in him. "I think maybe we just need to take a break," she said quietly. "On Monday I'll talk to Ann about finding you another assistant and—"

"Don't do this, Maggie," he said urgently. "I'm asking you not to do anything drastic. Give me a chance to prove to you that I can put work aside and put you first!"

A lone tear rolled down her cheek and she was glad she was all alone. "I don't want you to have to prove anything to me. I want to be important enough to someone that I'm a priority just because of who I am, not because I've laid a guilt trip or given an ultimatum. Eventually, you'll resent me for it, and you'll be making excuses to me or your family, and I just don't want to be in that position. I'm sorry."

"One more chance," he begged, his voice thick with

emotion. "I'm not perfect, Maggie, I know that. All I'm asking is for you to let me make this right. I had no idea you were so unhappy. How can I possibly know if you don't tell me? And then how can I fix it if you won't let me?"

He had a point. Her mind was spinning and all she really wanted was to crawl into bed and sleep for a week. "Okay, Jason."

"Thank you, sweetheart. You won't regret it, I promise. No more missing dates, no more late nights at work. From here on out, I want you to know that you can count on me." He paused and felt himself relax for the first time in hours. "Can I see you tomorrow? Maybe we can go to lunch and then…"

"I really think I need the weekend to myself," she said hesitantly. "I need to have a little time to myself, even though you've let me have more time alone than I wanted. I need to think about all that we talked about tonight."

"I'm not going to lie and tell you I'm not disappointed, because I am," he said honestly. "I wanted to see you tonight. I stopped by your place and I waited for an hour just to see you."

"Please don't try and make me feel guilty…"

"No, I'm sorry; that was wrong of me. I just want you to know, Maggie, that when I'm not with you, I truly miss you."

More tears fell and she almost caved. "I miss you when we're not together, too, Jason. But it's really for the best for us to just take the weekend to do our own thing." She paused and wiped at her wet face. "I'll see you Monday morning, okay?"

"Okay. Sleep well, sweetheart," he said sadly.

"You, too…"

Chapter 11

By Monday, Maggie felt much more in control of her emotions. She was confident that she could work with Jason and yet hold herself back enough that she wasn't going to be tempted to jump when he was ready to spend some time with her.

Jason was the consummate professional all day. As much as it pained him, he kept his distance and treated Maggie in a professional manner, much as he had on their business trip. It wasn't until five o'clock that he finally was ready for something more.

"Maggie, can I see you in my office for a minute?" he asked as he saw her gathering her things to leave for the day.

"Sure," she said, placing her purse and jacket back down and following Jason into his office. "Was there something else you needed?" she asked once they were alone.

He smiled at her. He was a respectable foot away from her and yet his fingers itched to touch her. Holding himself in check, he replied, "I was hoping that I could take you to dinner tonight."

Without conscious thought, Maggie launched herself into his arms and initiated the kiss she had been craving for days. Jason was on board immediately and he lifted her off the ground as he reached for his office door and closed it. "I swore I wasn't going to do this," she said between kisses.

Jason's hands were finally on her, and it pained him to release her just long enough to lock the door. "This whole day has been hell for me; the weekend seemed as if it would never end." His words were clipped as he dragged his mouth along her jaw, her neck and then finally up to her lips again. His tongue dueled with hers and when he placed her back on her feet, he led her over to the large leather sofa and tugged her down with him.

Maggie kicked off her shoes and smiled as Jason lay her down and lined his muscled body down on top of hers. He stroked her cheek and gazed down into her eyes. "You are so beautiful, Maggie," he said reverently. "I don't know what I ever did to deserve someone as beautiful as you."

She blushed at his words. A sassy comeback was on the tip of her tongue but the way he was looking at her, she knew he was being deadly serious. She whispered "thank you" and reached up to touch his face. His jaw was scratchy and it felt good against the palm of her hand.

"I love to look at you," he said, "to touch you." He paused as his hand wandered over her in the gentlest of caresses. "I love being with you."

"I love that, too," she replied. And in that moment she realized something that made her heart actually lurch: she loved *him*. She was in love with Jason Montgomery. Maggie wasn't sure when it actually happened. For all her issues with him as of late, the truth of the matter was she was so hurt because she was in love with him. She wanted to say the words to him, to tell him exactly how she felt, but he was lowering his head, his lips a whisper away from her own.

"I know I said dinner," he said softly, his breath hot against her mouth. "But I think I'd like to start with dessert."

"That's the best part," she said as she threaded her hands through his dark hair and pulled him down for what promised to be the most decadent of desserts.

They did manage to make it out of the office and to dinner. Maggie was a little self-conscious of her slightly disheveled appearance, but the fact that she and Jason were finally out and away from the office made her slight discomfort worth it.

"I meant what I said, Maggie," Jason began as he reached across the table and took one of her hands in his. "I want a chance to prove to you that you're more important to me than work."

She smiled at him but it didn't quite meet her eyes. "Jason, I don't expect you to change who you are. I fell in love with the man that you are." The words came out before she could stop them and by the look of surprise on Jason's face, she knew it was too late to take them back. That didn't stop her from trying, though. "What I mean is…I respect your work ethic and—"

"I'm in love with you, too," he interrupted.

There was so much Maggie wanted to say, but their waiter appeared to take their orders. She was so flustered she could barely read the words on the menu through the tears of joy welling up in her eyes. "You order for us," she simply said to Jason and then delicately wiped at the tears threatening to fall.

When they were alone again, Jason leaned across the table and caressed her cheek. "I want a future with you, Maggie. I wasn't sure how you felt about me, especially

after our conversation Friday night. I promise you, things are going to be different from here on out."

His words thrilled her and if there was one thing she knew about Jason, he did his best to be a man of his word. Maggie knew she could trust him and that their issues with the relationship could probably just be attributed to poor timing. After all, Montgomerys was in a time of major transition, and she would be foolish to think something of that magnitude wasn't going to impact Jason's life.

"I want us to go back to New York," he began. "I want us to take a real vacation where we can relax. I was thinking maybe a long weekend at the Four Seasons. What do you think?"

Maggie remembered the amazing room and the spa bathroom and how at the time she had fantasized about sharing it all with him. "I think that sounds perfect! Let's do it!"

Jason found himself thrilled that they were on the same page, and he could finally see a future for himself beyond working late nights and going home alone. If anyone had told him six months ago that he'd fall in love with his assistant, he would have told them they were crazy. As much as he hated the comparison, knowing how Lucas and Emma had made it work, he was confident he and Maggie had just as big a future ahead of them. Nothing was going to get in his way.

A week and a half later Jason was sitting at his desk smiling. Reservations were made for his and Maggie's weekend, and Jason had planned the most romantic getaway ever. They would leave right from work on Friday,

take the private plane up to New York where a limo would take them to the Four Seasons. He had dinner reservations right in the hotel because he knew that once they got there, it would be late, and he wanted to make the most of their time in the room.

On Saturday, they would go out and explore and shop. He made plans to take that carriage ride through Central Park where he was going to ask Maggie to marry him. He thought he might be moving too fast, but now that he knew what he wanted for his future, he was anxious to put it in motion.

Mac walked in and rolled his eyes at the sappy look on Jason's face. "All right, we get it, you're in love," he said dramatically before sitting down in a chair facing his brother. "Geez, I don't know who is more sickening, you or Lucas!"

"Please, you're just jealous. And Lucas hasn't been sickening for a while," Jason replied, keeping his tone light. Nothing was going to bring him down, not when his future with Maggie was right within his reach.

"You mean he hasn't been in here yet?" Mac asked.

"I didn't even know Lucas was in the office today. What's going on?"

Mac waved him off. "I'll let him tell you."

As if on cue, Lucas walked in and Mac was right, his sappy grin was worse than Jason's. "Emma's pregnant," he said as he came to a stop in Jason's office. Jason stood and came around to hug his brother.

"That is great news! How is she feeling?"

"So far, so good. We realize that could all change at any time and morning sickness could set in, but for right now everything is great."

The brothers stood and laughed and did their best to rib Lucas on how much his life was going to change, but Jason's words were halfhearted at best. "What's going on with you?" Lucas finally asked, suspicious at his brother's lack of sarcasm at his expense.

"I'm going to ask Maggie to marry me," he said, his chest puffed out with pride.

"Oh, for crying out loud," Mac grumbled. "Already?"

Lucas punched Mac in the arm. "I cannot wait for it to be your turn, Mac. You are going to fall harder than the rest of us and you can be sure we'll be right there, sitting on the sidelines, mocking you!"

"Do it and die." Mac glared.

"Wait and see..." Lucas said before turning back to Jason. "So when are you doing it?"

Jason told them both of his plans for the upcoming weekend and Lucas wished him luck. "Listen, I'd love to stay and talk some more but we're having dinner with Mom and Dad and I have to go and pick up Emma. Good luck, bro!"

Once he was gone and it was just Jason and Mac, Mac turned and closed the door and got serious.

"What's going on?" Jason asked, concern lacing his tone.

"We were contacted by a major company who wants to do business with us," he began cautiously. "If it all goes as I can see it going, this one company has the potential to bring in more business than all of the companies you just signed on."

Jason collapsed into his seat. "Damn, that's huge! Who are they? When do they want to meet?"

Mac stared down at him and watched as realization hit Jason. "I'm not going to like this, am I?" Jason asked.

"Brother, you don't know the half of it."

Chapter 12

Maggie was giddy for their weekend. She took off early on Friday so she could go home and pack. Jason was going to pick her up at six and their flight was at seven. Ever since they had admitted their feelings to one another, Maggie had been floating on a cloud. She was afraid to let herself hope too much, but she had a feeling Jason might propose this weekend.

He hadn't done anything outright to give her that impression, but they were so in tune with one another that she just had a feeling. She wouldn't be disappointed if he didn't, but she couldn't help but wonder how he would actually do it. Would he be traditional and get down on one knee? Would it be someplace public? Would they be alone? Her heart raced at all of those scenarios because at the end of it all, she really wanted to be Mrs. Jason Montgomery.

Jason had been true to his word and had cut back on the late nights at the office. They had been spending more time together and he had actually asked Maggie to move in with him. She had planned on giving him her answer this weekend—that answer was going to be yes! As much as she loved having her own place, the hassle of going between their homes and packing stuff for overnights was just getting to be a pain. Plus, she wanted to wake up with the man she loved every morning and not have to think about where they were going to be the next night.

She was throwing the last of her cosmetics into her luggage when Maggie realized she had left her phone charger back at the office. While it would be easy to call Jason and just have him bring it, she knew he had enough on his plate today. Looking at her watch, she saw it was only two o'clock. The office was only ten minutes away and there were a few last-minute errands she needed to run; one more stop wasn't going to make a difference.

The drive over to the office was quick and when Rose saw her, she faltered in her steps. "Maggie? We didn't expect you back this afternoon."

"Just forgot my phone charger," she replied, smiling as she held it up. "What's going on?"

"Oh, nothing," Rose said, looking over her shoulder. "They've got a client in there and I need to get back. I hope you have a good weekend." And then she was gone.

"Well, that was odd," Maggie said under her breath and then looked toward Jason's office. His door was open but the lights were off, so she figured he was in with either Mac or his father. Walking toward Mac's office, she noticed his was also dark, so she stopped at his assistant's empty desk. That was odd, too. Maggie didn't remember them having any appointments on the calendar, and Diana rarely left her desk.

Looking around, Maggie took a glance at the open planner on her coworker's desk and gasped. "No," she whispered. Walking briskly, she headed toward William Montgomery's suite. When she approached Rose's desk, she stopped short. "Is Jason in there?" she asked sharply.

Rose couldn't quite meet her eyes. "Maggie, don't

worry about what's going on in there. You're supposed to be getting ready for your weekend."

Maggie arched her brows at Rose. How much did the other woman know about her relationship with Jason? They hadn't been particularly secretive these last weeks, but it still irked her a little to know that everyone was privy to their business. "I am more than ready for my weekend. Why wasn't I informed about this meeting?"

Rose sighed. "It was a last-minute thing and really, it's nothing you need to worry about."

"Why don't you let me be the judge of that?" Her voice came out louder than she had planned and suddenly Jason was stepping out of his father's office.

"Maggie? What are you doing here? I thought you left early to go home and pack?"

"Why is everyone so concerned about my packing?" she asked. "I'm already packed and I forgot my phone charger here. I had some errands to run and thought I'd swing by and get it. I didn't realize I wasn't allowed to come to my place of business. Care to tell me why that is?" She glared at him while waiting for an answer.

"No one said you weren't allowed here, Maggie, it was just that we all thought..."

"What? You thought that you could plan a business meeting with the one person who you know I would have a problem with? I cannot believe you, Jason! When is it ever going to be enough? You have more business than you can handle and you know my history with this particular client, and yet you still invited him here to do business?" Her eyes welled with tears and she cursed herself for showing weakness.

Maggie knew she shouldn't be surprised. Montgomerys

was always going to come first, but she didn't think it would hurt so much or that Jason would choose to do business with Martin Blake. Her heart actually hurt, and when Jason went to reach for her hand she jerked away from him.

"You know, there are a lot of things I can overlook. I understand your commitment to your family and to your business, but I can't work for someone—or live with someone—that I don't trust. You knew my feelings on this and rather than talk to me, you snuck behind my back to meet with him."

"Maggie," Jason began but she cut him off.

"No, I'm done, Jason. You asked me for a second chance and I gave it. You asked me to trust you and I did. But this?" She waved toward the office. "This is something I can't overlook. I don't doubt for a second that Martin made some outrageous offer to you and I can't blame you for wanting the business. It's just not something I want any part of."

"You don't understand, Maggie," Jason pleaded. "Let's go to my office and I'll—"

"Hey, Mags," Martin Blake said as he strolled into the outer office. "Fancy seeing you here." His gaze raked over her and Maggie felt violated all over again. "I had to do a little research to see who the big shot you were working for was, and after talking to Alan down in Miami, he told me all about Montgomerys. I figured, if Alan's working with them, then we should, too. It'll be like old times, right, Mags?"

She wanted to vomit. Her lunch turned in her stomach, and she couldn't believe Jason just stood there and let Martin even talk to her. She was just about to comment

on it when Martin asked Rose where the men's room was. Once he was out of earshot, she glared at Jason.

"Let's go talk," Jason said again.

"No," she said adamantly. "I'm done talking. I quit." She turned and walked away, her stride quickening to get to the elevator. Maggie expected Jason to come after her, or at least to call her name. But he didn't. When the elevator arrived in the lobby, she expected him to come out through the door to the stairway to stop her. But he didn't.

How could she have been so wrong about him? How could she have misunderstood all the plans they had been making? By the time she reached her car, Maggie could barely see through the haze of tears. She had trusted Jason; she had put her trust *in* Jason, and he had betrayed her, all in the name of business.

She felt numb and hollow and didn't know where to go or what to do. The thought of going home was unappealing because all her luggage was packed, full of promises for a romantic weekend that was never going to happen. She was now without a job and had no idea where her life was going to go from here. So she put the car in gear and drove. She had no direction, so she just hit the interstate and let the miles fill the void inside of her.

~

Jason was frantic. He wanted to run after Maggie and explain everything, but he knew her mind was made up and there was nothing he was going to be able to say to make her see things for the way they really were. He couldn't blame her; if he were in her shoes, he wouldn't believe him either.

"Why didn't you go after her?" his father said quietly behind him.

"She wasn't going to listen."

"You don't know that, Jace. She didn't know what was going on."

"I know Maggie. I've screwed up too much, and no matter what I said she wasn't going to believe me."

"I told you you should have been up front with her. No good ever comes from lying, Son."

Jason turned and looked at his father. "What was I supposed to do? Admit that this slimy piece of crap contacted us and the only way I could ensure he never, ever got near her again was to bring him here and confront him? Threaten him with financial ruin if he ever did to another woman what he did to Maggie? She wouldn't agree with it!"

"All I'm saying is…"

"And then he came out here and started talking like we were honestly going to do business together! There was no way for me to tell her the truth with him blathering on like an idiot."

"You should have gone after her and made her listen," his father said patiently.

"To what end, Dad? She's never going to trust me again and I can't blame her. She was finally moving on with her life and the only times she's had to face that bastard was because of me! The hurt in her eyes…" he said and his voice clogged with emotion. "I'll never be able to forgive myself for being the one to put that look there."

Just then, Martin walked out of the restroom and looked from William to Jason. "Ready to sign?" he

asked, walking back into William's office with a confident swagger.

Jason glared after the man and then looked at his father. "Let's finish this."

Maggie drove for hours and eventually ended up back at home. She half expected to find Jason there, but he wasn't. Sluggishly, she walked up to her door and let herself in. The silence was deafening. It was a little after eight and she sighed sadly at how they would have been landing in New York now and on their way to the hotel. She would never know what Jason had planned for the weekend; it would always be a "what if" scenario in her mind.

Her body was weak and her mind was blank as she went about unpacking her luggage and carefully putting things away. She looked at the sexy negligee she had bought at Victoria's Secret and wanted to burn it. She'd never get to wear it; even if she lived to be one hundred and had dozens of lovers, she would never allow herself to wear it because she had bought it with Jason in mind.

But Maggie was nothing if not practical, and so she kept it securely wrapped in tissue and tucked into the back of her drawer. *Out of sight, out of mind.* When the last of her stuff was put away, she decided to order in and reached for her trusty file of takeout menus. She had no appetite but knew she needed to eat. No sense in making herself sick on top of having a broken heart. With her Chinese food ordered, Maggie changed into a pair of yoga pants and an oversized T-shirt and flipped on the TV to distract her until it arrived.

Thirty minutes later there was a knock on the door, and she padded over to answer it. William Montgomery stood on the threshold with her takeout bag in his hand. "Mr. Montgomery? What are you doing here?"

"May I come in?" he asked quietly. Maggie nodded and stepped aside. "I hope you don't mind that I swooped in and shanghaied your delivery boy." He took a whiff and smiled. "Is that Szechuan I smell?"

"That's fine," she said shyly, taking the bag from his hands and walking to the kitchen to place it down. Now her appetite was completely gone. What in the world was she supposed to say to this man? Not only was he her boss…er, former boss, but he was the father of the man who had just destroyed her life. "Can I get you something to drink?" she asked, trying to keep her voice calm and steady.

"No. I'm fine. May I sit?"

Maggie inclined her head toward the living room and waited for him to take a seat on her sofa before sitting across from him on the matching love seat. "What can I do for you?" she asked carefully.

"Well, that was going to be my line," he said with a soft chuckle. "I wanted to make sure you were okay."

She smiled sadly at him. "I'm not okay but I will be. Eventually."

William leaned forward, his elbows on his knees. "Maggie, I know that things looked bad this afternoon—"

"Please don't," she interrupted. "I just need this whole ugly phase of my life to be over. Martin Blake was the reason I came to Montgomerys and I guess it's only fitting that he be the reason I'm leaving. I'll admit I was shocked by his appearance there today, but I understand

that business is business. It was stupid of me to expect you to lose a big client just because of something that happened to me years ago."

"Maggie, look at me," William said softly. "I didn't tell Jason or anyone that I was coming here. I wanted you to know there was never going to be a business deal with Martin Blake. He did approach us with a very attractive offer, and had it come from anyone else, we would have jumped at the opportunity. Knowing what we do, however, that was never going to happen."

Maggie looked confused. "Then why was he there? Why was it such a big secret?"

William sighed wearily. "Jason wanted to protect you. Martin was aggressive in his approach and wasn't willing to take no for an answer over the phone so Mac and Jason thought it best to take the meeting with him and take care of it in person."

"But when Martin came out of your office, he said we'd be working together! That he was looking forward to doing business…"

"I'll admit we strung him along a little," he replied sheepishly. "It made it just that much more fun to let him down."

Confusion was written all over Maggie's face. "I'm not following you…"

William stood and then sat beside Maggie on the love seat. "Maggie, Jason wanted to confront Martin face-to-face. He and Mac had done a little investigating and found out that you weren't the only woman Martin had harassed. So once we had him in the office, Jason confronted him with what he'd found and threatened to ruin him financially if he ever came near you or any other

woman like that again. You never have to worry about the likes of Martin Blake bothering you ever again."

"Oh my God," she whispered. "Oh, what have I done?"

William reached for her hand and gave her a comforting squeeze. "You did what anyone would do in your position. I had hoped that Jason would tell you what was going on, but he thought it was best to keep it a secret until it was over. He didn't want you worrying or being uncomfortable. Mostly he didn't want you to worry about seeing Martin. He thought he was doing what was right."

Tears streamed down her face. "And I accused him of being selfish when he was trying to protect me. What am I supposed to do now?" Maggie stood and began pacing her small living room.

"Go to him, Maggie. He's at home kicking himself for what he put you through."

Without conscious thought, Maggie grabbed her purse and keys, threw on a pair of sneakers, and was about to run out the door before she remembered that William was still standing in her living room. "Feel free to help yourself to some Chinese, but I have to go!" Slamming the door behind her, Maggie rushed down to her car and hoped that on the drive to Jason's she'd figure out just what exactly she was going to say.

It was a starless night. Jason sat out on his deck, letting the early winter weather wrap around him. He'd probably get pneumonia from it but he didn't care. Nothing mattered anymore, not without Maggie.

Why hadn't he listened to his father and just told her what was going on? Why had he been so insistent that it all be a secret? His father had never steered him wrong, and the one time he went against his father's advice it had cost him everything. He took a pull from the beer he was drinking and it tasted bitter going down. Right now he should have been drinking champagne off of Maggie's body. They would have been enjoying the sight of the New York skyline and making love and planning their future. He reached into his pocket and played with the ring meant to go on her finger but now never would. Now he was just sitting alone outside in the cold kicking himself.

Some Friday night.

A loud pounding on his front door shook him out of his reverie. He placed his beer down on the deck and walked into the house. His hair was disheveled and his shirt was open, his feet bare. Jason had no idea who could be at his door at this hour, but he didn't give a damn about how he looked. When he opened the door, he wished he had taken the time to put himself mildly back together.

"Maggie? What are you doing here?"

She didn't answer right away; she was too taken aback by Jason's appearance. Maggie had seen Jason dressed in suits and tuxedos and in jeans and T-shirts. She'd seen him first thing in the morning all mussed up from sleep, and slick with sweat after making love, but she had never seen him look so utterly devastated. Holding her tongue, she stepped around him and into the foyer and shut the door.

"You lied to me," she said by way of an opening.

He could only nod. Jason wanted to defend himself

but knew it had taken a lot of courage for Maggie to come here and confront him, so he wasn't going to interrupt her. She deserved to have her say without him trying to make her see his point of view.

"Why didn't you tell me the real reason you had Martin at Montgomerys?" she demanded softly.

"I tried to tell you, Maggie, but you wouldn't..." He stopped. "I should have told you from the beginning. I'm sorry I didn't."

She nodded. "Yes, you should have." The look of defeat on Jason's face was almost more than she could bear. "I don't appreciate having you make decisions for me and thinking that you know what's best."

"That wasn't my intention, Maggie. I honestly wanted to protect you from ever having to see him again. In Miami, you told me how it had taken you months to be able to close your eyes and not see him or hear him. I thought I was doing the right thing."

Maggie was about to walk into Jason's living room, but she stopped and turned to face him again. "That was before, Jason! I don't have to be afraid of him anymore, and do you know why?" He shook his head. "It's because of you! I know that there is nothing someone like Martin Blake can do to me and even back then, I did nothing wrong. I don't have to hide. I don't have to feel ashamed. I would have loved the opportunity to see his face when you told him you had proof of all of the hideous things he's done!"

Jason's eyes went wide. "I didn't want him anywhere near you!" He strode toward her and grabbed her by the shoulders. "I never want anyone ever to hurt you again, Maggie. Don't you understand?"

She looked up at him and saw in his eyes how much he meant what he was saying. "But you hurt me, Jace. You didn't trust me enough."

"Sweetheart, I do trust you. I honestly thought I was doing the right thing. I wanted to make it all go away and know he couldn't ever hurt you again."

"He couldn't, Jason. He doesn't hold that power over me anymore, and I have you to thank for that. You did that for me back in Miami. I'm stronger now. You make me stronger! I wanted us to be strong together."

Jason pulled her closer and was relieved when she didn't pull away. "We are stronger together. When you walked out today I thought I'd lost everything. Please tell me we're okay. Tell me that you're here because you know I love you and I need you."

No words came to mind because she was so overwhelmed with emotion. So she answered him the only way she knew how. Stepping up and aligning their bodies, Maggie reached up and threaded her fingers through his mussed hair and pulled him down for a scorching kiss. She felt his sigh of relief as Jason pulled her tight against him. When they finally broke apart, Maggie cupped his face and stared up at the man that she loved. "I'm here because I love and need you, too."

"Thank God," he said before reclaiming her mouth with his.

Epilogue

"You know people think we're crazy, right?"

Maggie shrugged. "I don't care."

"We had at least fifty other options that would have been more fitting."

Glancing over her shoulder at him, she gave him a bland stare. "Still don't care."

Jason leaned back in his seat and huffed. "I can't believe we missed going to Paris for this."

Just then, Maggie jumped to her feet. "Oh, come on!" she yelled. "He hooked him! What is wrong with that ref?" Slumping back into her seat, she reached for her beer and pouted.

"Need I remind you that we could be drinking champagne at the Eiffel Tower right now," Jason said in a teasing tone, "rather than sitting here in this cold arena watching your team get slaughtered?"

Maggie turned and punched him in the arm. "They're not getting slaughtered, and you were the one who got the tickets for the playoffs," she reminded him.

"I didn't think you'd actually choose this over Paris for our honeymoon," he pouted.

"Aw..." She leaned in and kissed him sweetly. "I didn't choose this *over* Paris. I just chose to stop here first."

"All I'm saying is I want to take you on a romantic getaway and you keep thwarting all my best attempts." He wanted to say more, but his new bride was up on her

feet again cheering as the Rangers scored and tied up the game.

"When are you going to learn that it doesn't matter to me where we are, just as long as we're together?"

He stood, wrapped her in his arms, and pulled her in for another kiss. "I'm a slow learner where you're concerned," he admitted. "But I promise to get better."

"Excellent," she purred against his lips. "Besides, this little side trip makes up for the trip we missed when you proposed."

"Yeah, sorry it took so long to reschedule."

"Well, with you wanting me to move in right away and then all the wedding planning, there just wasn't time. I'm not complaining; this is perfect timing as far as I'm concerned."

They sat back down and Maggie rested her head on Jason's shoulder, sighing with happiness.

Yes, having the man she loved sitting beside her while watching the team she loved, knowing that their future was wide open ahead of them, was definitely worth the wait.

Where to Find Samantha Chase

Facebook: www.facebook.com/SamanthaChase FanClub
Twitter: twitter.com/SamanthaChase3
Website: www.chasing-romance.com